Journey
Home

a novel

Jennie Hansen

Covenant Communications, Inc.

Covenant.

Wherefore, ye may also have hope, and be partakers of the gift, if ye will but have faith." (Ether 12:9)

This book is dedicated to my daughters—Sharon Robinson, Mary Jo Rich, Lezlie Anderson, Janice Sperry, and Esther Hansen. It is also dedicated to all those women who have faced breast cancer and carried forward with faith and courage.

I wish to thank Cathy Brasher for allowing me to use her poem, "The Support Group," and for being there when I needed her. Thanks also to Richard Andrews who checked my Alaska facts for accuracy.

Published by Covenant Communications, Inc.
American Fork, Utah

Printed in the United States of America
First Printing: August 1997

04 03 02 01 00 99 98   10 9 8 7 6 5 4 3 2

Library of Congress Cataloging-in-Publication Data

Hansen, Jennie L., 1943-
    Journey home / Jennie L. Hansen.
        P.   cm.
    Sequel to: Run away home.
    ISBN 1-57734-131-7
    I. Title.
PS3558.A51293J68   1997
813' .54--dc21   97-24068
                                                              CIP

chapter one

Holland! What kind of name is that? Allen shook his head in disbelief. Why couldn't Hank have given his daughter a name like Susan or Mary? Holland belonged to windmills and tulips, not to a young girl huddled against Alaska's cold in thick woolen pants and a heavy khaki coat.

Allen cast a regretful eye over the heavily bundled, tall, skinny kid leaning against the mesh fence. Thick mittens pressed against the wire and her fur-lined parka obscured her face. She didn't make a sound, but he knew by the way her shoulders trembled that she was crying, which wasn't surprising as they had just loaded her father's body on the plane that was now preparing to lift off. Allen hoped the saying about a person's face freezing if she bawled in this country wasn't true. More than that, he hoped he could find some way, if not to comfort, to at least distract her from her pain.

The plane taxied to the end of the runway, turned, then catapulted forward. In minutes it disappeared in the semi-light of an early fall northern night. Allen pulled his own parka closer against the sharp wind. He didn't want to rush the kid; she was hurting, probably feeling pretty alone and scared too, but that wind was cold and spoke of the snow that would soon blanket the land. They needed to get started.

"Ready?" Allen tried to cover his growing sense of urgency by lowering his voice.

The girl lifted her eyes one last time to the sky, but the plane had disappeared. Her shoulders slumped and she nodded her head.

"Here, get in the truck out of this cold." He handed her a set of keys. "Start the engine and get the heater going while I pick up the thermoses at the cook shack."

Obediently she accepted the keys and trudged slowly toward the truck parked near the end of the fence. Allen watched her walk away and wondered how he would manage the two-week trip to Salt Lake City in the girl's silent company.

It had been four days since Hank's accident and he hadn't heard the girl speak once, not even when her father finally lost his fight early this morning. She had waited silently beside his body most of the day for the plane that would carry him to Fairbanks, then on to Seattle, and finally to Salt Lake City. Grief manifested itself in different ways, but come to think of it, Allen realized that he'd never heard the girl speak. He frowned as he considered the possibility that Holland might not be able to talk, but surely Hank would have mentioned it if the kid was mute. Even so, the old man had been in a great deal of pain and communication had been difficult.

Chance had brought Allen into camp just hours before the accident. Completing his photo assignment for a major travel publisher, Allen had made one last stop at the camp to collect the gear he'd stored there before starting back to the lower forty-eight. He'd been traveling about Alaska for over a year.

He'd first met old Hank when his bush pilot set down near the construction camp and asked Hank to do some minor repairs for him. Their paths had crossed several times since as Allen had used the camp as a jumping-off point and base throughout the summer. Each time he passed through, he'd seen Holland around the camp, but she'd kept to herself; he hadn't even learned Hank's kid was female until the old man had asked to talk to him alone last night. Perhaps Allen had been foolish to agree to Hank's request—demand was more like it—but he didn't know how to say no to a man who knew he was dying.

Inside the low log building several men sat around the cook-stove relaxing in its warmth.

"You leaving tonight or waiting until morning, James?" one of them asked.

"We'll be on our way as soon as I get these thermoses loaded." He picked up the two heavy jugs.

"If ya wait a coupla days, we could all drive out together. Boss says we're breaking camp and high tailing it out of here this weekend before an early snow catches us," another burly construction worker spoke up.

"Thanks, but it'll be easier on Hank's kid if we leave now. There's a good camping spot on a little river about four hours from here. I'd like to make it that far tonight."

"Good luck. I don't envy ya the trip with that kid. He's an odd duck, never talks to no one."

Allen made no effort to correct the man's misconception about his traveling companion. Hank had told him he'd kept Holland's hair short and dressed her like a boy deliberately. He figured the rough loggers and construction workers in the various camps where he worked would be less likely to bother her if they thought she was a boy.

Swinging open the rear door of the truck, Allen set the thermoses in the slots Hank had built for them and took a careful look around. They were headed over some rough roads; it wouldn't do to have any loose objects floating around. He took a minute to make certain his cameras and photo equipment were securely stored.

The back of the truck bed was a portable tool shop at one end, and he could see at a glance that Holland had secured all of her father's tools and equipment in their places. Allen closed and locked the heavy door, then wandered forward to where Hank had outfitted the front part of the enclosed truck bed with two curtained bunks, storage cupboards, a gas stove, an ice box, and a drop leaf table. Hank had even rigged up a shower and a commode, similar to those found in fancier RVs.

From the narrow aisle between the bunks, Allen moved forward into the cab of the truck. Holland had already scooted to the passenger's side, so he settled into the driver's seat, took a minute to fasten his seat belt, then turned to her.

"Ready?"

She nodded her head, and then turned away, pressing her face against the glass window at her side. He hadn't expected anything more. His left hand gripped the wheel and with his right he reached for the gear shift. Slowly the lumbering truck began to move.

The road was more wishful thinking than road, and Allen heaved a sigh of relief forty minutes later when he pulled onto the pipeline road. As far as highways go, the deeply rutted gravel road left a lot to be desired, but he could make better time on it than on the rough cut he'd been following. There was a measure of security, too, in knowing an occasional bus or truck traveled the lonely road even in late fall.

Spectacular rain-washed scenery tempted Allen to stop the truck and grab a camera even though light conditions were less than perfect. Once he was forced to slow to a crawl when a moose cow and her nearly grown calf sauntered leisurely across the road. He shifted his eyes toward the young girl riding beside him. Her face was lost inside her fur-lined hood, but she appeared to be asleep. If she slept, so much the better. Poor kid. The past few days had been hard on her. From the time Hank's crushed, unconscious form had been fished from the storm-swollen river until he died, she'd scarcely left his side.

The foreman had tried frantically to radio for a plane to take Hank to Fairbanks, but a raging storm had interfered. This land never did anything by halves, Allen had learned. Even a rainstorm struck with all the bluster and fury of a blizzard. By the time he was finally able to get the message through, it was too late, although Allen had suspected it was too late the moment the huge saw blade snapped, thrusting the old man over the bank into the white water.

Allen shifted down as he approached a steep curve; the engine growled but moved steadily along, and he sent a silent, skyward thanks to Hank for the meticulous care he'd lavished on his truck. It was well-stocked, balanced, and carried extra fuel tanks, tires, and even a spare windshield.

Hank had been just as meticulous in planning for his daughter's future. He'd explained how he'd been on the move his entire life and been well past the age when most men think about marriage when he'd met Holland's mother. Her family had objected to the marriage, but she'd married him anyway. Two years later Holland had been born. Hank had tried to settle down—bought a house and even went to church. But when his wife died, he took six-year-old Holland and went back on the road, drifting between construction sites and logging camps. He told Allen that now he wanted Holland returned to her mother's family and given a chance at the stability and education he'd denied her. Against his better judgment, Allen had agreed to see Holland and Hank's truck safely back to Utah.

Allen remembered how tears had seeped from Hank's eyes as he'd faulted himself for Holland's upbringing and confessed to a selfish need to have her near him. He'd loved her too much to send her away to school or to let his sister-in-law raise her. Holland's aunt had wanted to care for the motherless child, and even though Hank knew a little girl needed a woman's influence, he hadn't been able to let her go. Oh, she'd attended schools where possible for a few months at a time and taken correspondence courses, so she wasn't illiterate, but she didn't know anything about people except what she'd read in books. Comforted by knowing he had enough set aside for Holland's education, Hank didn't mind dying. In fact, he looked forward to being with his beloved Nancy again, although he hated the thought of being separated from Holland, who had to get to Salt Lake somehow after he was gone.

A twinge of sadness passed through Allen's thoughts. He envied Holland in a way. Though her upbringing had been unorthodox, she'd had the security of her father's love. Allen's closest friends had that kind of closeness to their fathers and he'd always envied them. He didn't have a bad relationship with his own father, he just didn't have any kind of relationship at all. Allen James, Sr. was never cruel or abusive, just uninterested in his son. His business, social connections, and status had always consumed all of his time and attention. Father-son outings, Little League games, high school award assemblies, even Allen's college graduation had gone unattended by his father. For years Allen had wondered what he had to do to attract his father's attention and had finally concluded there was nothing a short, intellectually average, untalented boy could do to impress a wealthy former college athlete who dominated his corner of the business world.

Allen knew his dad wouldn't approve of this trip. He'd waste no time pointing out that spending two weeks alone with a kid could leave him wide open to accusations of improper behavior that could ruin his career. He would never understand why Allen couldn't refuse Hank's request and simply walk away leaving the girl in the care of the camp foreman.

As he mused, Allen considered that he had never been able to fall back on his mother's support either. Her world revolved around her husband and her social responsibilities; she almost seemed unaware that she'd given birth to two children. Allen thought wistfully of his sister. Cecelia was thirteen years older than Allen, but she'd mothered him more than his own mother had. Cecelia had married at eighteen and had four babies in quick succession, which hadn't left her with a lot of time for a little brother. At least she'd tried to be there for him, and he loved her for that. He was grateful that they'd stayed in touch through the years.

The dingy light had all but faded by the time Allen turned the truck off the road and entered the camping area. There were no hookups or amenities other than crude outhouses, but the truck was pretty self-sufficient. They only needed a place to park for the night.

Holland stirred and he knew she was awake. "We won't need to cook anything tonight. There's coffee and soup in the thermoses," he spoke as he shut off the engine. "I need to stretch my legs. If you want to walk around too, don't stray far from the truck. I'll be back in a few minutes."

He climbed out of the truck and placed both hands on the small of his back, stretched, then ambled toward the small structures at one side of the clearing that passed for restrooms. He could see a heavy-duty, four-wheel drive pickup truck with a camper shell on the back parked at one side of the clearing. All was dark and quiet, its occupants likely asleep.

When he returned to the truck he caught the aroma of hearty beef and vegetable soup the moment he opened the door. His eyes went to the small table where Holland had placed two bowls of the steaming soup and a loaf of bread. She turned from the storage cupboard and his eyes widened in surprise. She no longer wore the bulky parka. She was tall and thin, probably only an inch shorter than his own five feet nine. Her short hair was pushed back from her face, and her widely spaced brown eyes and high cheekbones highlighted a face far lovelier and more mature than he'd expected. His glance flew to the cupboard where he'd stashed his cameras. He'd never seen a face that cried out to him more to be captured on film.

When Holland placed two aluminum drink cans on the table, then seated herself on one side, he warily eased onto the seat opposite her. Little alarm bells had started going off in the back of his head.

Sure she was wearing a heavy flannel work shirt, but there was something about the way it settled against her body that told him Holland wasn't as young as he'd been led to believe. Unconsciously he reached for the can she'd set in front of him and sputtered as grapefruit juice ran down his throat.

"Hey! What happened to the coffee?" He shuddered at the tart bite of the fruit juice.

"Hank told me you're a Mormon," she said quietly. "Mormons don't drink coffee, so I dumped it out."

Allen did a double-take. He didn't know which shocked him more—that she'd dumped his coffee or that she'd spoken to him.

"What a waste," he grumbled. "It's cold out."

"The soup's hot," she countered.

"How come you're suddenly speaking to me? For four days you haven't said a word." Allen waited for an answer. The coffee wasn't important. It would have probably kept him awake anyway, and he didn't drink it often enough to have developed a deep craving for a caffeine jolt. The real question was, exactly how old was Holland and why hadn't her father made arrangements for her to fly to Salt Lake instead of insisting that Allen accompany his not-so-very-young daughter on a two-week odyssey in the close confines of the truck. Most fathers would never have considered such a thing. But then, Hank was obviously not like most fathers.

Holland blushed and fiddled with her spoon for several minutes before answering. "Hank said I shouldn't talk to anyone in the camps or they might guess I'm not really a boy. Not talking sort of got to be a habit. But he told you, and he said I could trust you, and anyway, we're away from the camp now."

"Just how old are you, Holland?" Allen enunciated the words carefully, going right to the point bothering him most. Minute by minute, he was becoming increasingly aware he was sharing this truck with a very attractive young woman, not the little girl he'd agreed to escort to her aunt.

"Twenty." She said the word as though she defied him to contradict her. But he didn't doubt her word. Something told him she spoke the truth. She was eight or ten years older than he'd assumed from her father's plea. And thirteen years younger than his own thirty-three years, a perverse little math demon computed in his head—old enough to make him uncomfortably aware of her. He'd have to rethink this entire expedition.

Holland knew she'd made a tactical error. She should have been in bed with the curtain pulled tight around her bunk before Allen returned for his supper. Hank had warned her to keep quiet and not reveal anything about herself until they were far enough away that Allen couldn't stick her on a plane and abandon the truck.

She blinked back sudden tears. She missed Hank. It had been just the two of them almost as long as she could remember. If the accident hadn't happened, she would have been making this trip with him in little more than a week. They'd planned for such a long time for the day he would retire, and they could return permanently to the lower forty-eight. He had been sending money regularly to a bank in Salt Lake. Plus, there was the gold. With that they'd buy a house and Holland could go to the University of Utah. Her father was gone now, but she still intended to carry out their plans.

Going to school was her idea; Hank wanted her to marry some nice Mormon man and give him a passel of grandbabies to tell his travel yarns to. At times she thought wistfully of getting married, but she had to be realistic. Any woman who had lived in lumber camps and on construction sites as long as she had without any man noticing she was a woman didn't have what it takes to attract a husband.

There were times she regretted that she didn't know the first thing about clothes or hair or flirting or any of the other things women in the books she read did to be pretty and appealing to a man, but mostly she didn't care about men. She'd seen a lot of them and none had interested her as much as a good book. Going to school was her big dream.

Looking up, she caught Allen watching her and quickly glanced away. She didn't want him looking at her—but she silently admitted she liked to observe him when he didn't realize she was watching him. He wasn't as big as most of the men in the various camps where she and Hank had stayed. He wasn't even as big as Hank. But he was awfully well put together and the way he moved fascinated her. There was a kind of grace in him that reminded her of the carefully controlled movements of an elk she'd once seen, which had appeared suddenly at the edge of a thicket and stepped with fluid grace to a nearby pool. Other times he reminded her of a sleek cat, all sinew and muscle, moving so silently and swiftly he didn't appear to walk at all.

She didn't know what to say to him. Conversation wasn't something she'd ever had much opportunity to practice. Besides he made her nervous. She'd always been a gangly klutz, but Allen James made her aware of herself in a way she'd never before experienced. How was she going to get through two weeks traveling with a man who made her feel gauche and stupid—that is, more gauche and stupid than usual?

"I'll get you something else to drink." She turned away from his scrutiny to search for a can of orange juice, and they ate the rest of their meal in silence. Holland kept her eyes on her bowl because every time she glanced up through her lashes she found Allen staring at her. She had to struggle to avoid squirming and revealing her discomfort.

When she finished eating she silently gathered their bowls, intent on putting them away. A hand settled around her wrist, stilling her movements. Her heart beat faster as brown eyes stared searchingly into her own. A ruddy streak highlighted his cheekbones and she felt her own face grow warm.

"We'll get an early start tomorrow and reach Fairbanks in time to get you on a flight for Seattle." His voice held a warning which ignited a sense of panic in her. She couldn't abandon the truck. Walking away from the truck would be literally walking away from her future.

"If you don't wish to continue on with me, you can do as you please, and I'll drive on to Salt Lake by myself." She thrust out her chin and tried to look confident, praying he had no idea how scared she was of being alone.

"You're flying and that's that."

"This truck is mine, and I won't leave it behind. Hank said you might change your mind, but that no matter what, I should get this truck to Salt Lake. Besides, you don't have any right to tell me what to do!" She jerked her arm free and flounced toward her bunk.

She snapped the curtain closed behind her and sank onto the bed. She couldn't believe she'd spoken to Allen like that, but what could she do? She shivered at the prospect of going on by herself, but she couldn't abandon the truck to fly to Salt Lake. She'd promised Hank she'd return to Salt Lake, but she wouldn't have any money to buy a house and go to school without the truck. Somewhere in the vehicle was her inheritance.

"Pretty good," she heard Allen drawl. "Not as effective as a slammed door, but pretty good. I made your father some promises, too, so you needn't worry about your precious truck, I'll get it to Salt Lake."

She didn't answer. She couldn't. Allen James didn't understand and she certainly couldn't tell him. Somehow she had to convince him she had to stay with the truck. Even if she didn't have the gold to worry about, she wasn't brave enough to travel alone out here. The thought occurred to her that if she were pretty and knew the right things to say, he wouldn't be so eager to put her on a plane and drive on by himself. Where did that idea come from? She'd never in her life thought about being, let alone wanting, to be pretty.

Allen stood outside the curtain waiting for a response. It soon became obvious she wasn't going to speak to him and he might as well crawl into bed and get some sleep. He was certainly tired enough. In the morning he'd try to reason with her.

He pulled off his heavy hiking boots, hesitated, then pulled on sweat pants. Under the circumstances, sleeping in his shorts probably wasn't a good idea.

Stretched out on the narrow bunk, his mind still buzzed with questions and a hodgepodge of impressions. This had been a long difficult day, but his mind wasn't ready to release him to badly needed sleep. He hadn't been prepared for the grieving little girl he'd agreed to escort safely to her family to metamorphose into the most attractive woman he'd ever encountered. He had briefly considered the inferences someone might make of his odyssey with a young girl, but had concluded that keeping his promise to Hank and ensuring the child's safety was far more important than any untoward assumptions someone might make. This grown-up Holland was an entirely different matter. She scared him as the child never could.

He didn't even know why he found her so attractive. She wasn't his type. Briefly Megan's angel face and pale blonde hair came to his mind, and he felt the familiar little ache thoughts of Megan always brought to his heart. Swiftly he clamped down on the memories and replaced her image with all the glamorous, sophisticated women he'd known from Texas to Montana. He'd had a lot of fun and admired their style, but there wasn't one who lingered in his mind.

Next, Cathy's glowing red hair appeared before him and he heard the sound of her laughing chatter. He'd been half in love with the tiny fireball since the day he'd first met her. But then, everyone loved Cathy, including his friend Brad, who had married her more than a dozen years ago. Together Brad and Cathy had produced five red-haired daughters who looked just like their mother. He smiled as he pictured Brad's family. Theirs was the kind of family he'd longed to be part of all his life, a family that thrived on love and laughter, and where everyone made time for everyone else.

Cathy was the dynamo at the core of her family's existence. Allen had dreamed of finding his own Cathy someday, and thought he had when he'd found Megan, but it wasn't to be. He grimaced at the irony—the only two women he'd ever cared deeply about were married to his two best friends.

He drifted off to sleep, not with Megan's ethereal paleness nor Cathy's vibrancy haunting his dreams. Cathy's warmth and style were replaced by a stubborn chin and a defiant stance. Megan's polish disappeared behind wool pants and logging boots.

Allen awoke to silence. Careful not to disturb Holland, he reached for his clothes, dressed hastily, and picked up his parka. He hoped he could slip outside for a quick check around the vehicle and a trip to the restroom without waking her. He'd like to let her sleep as long as possible, then pull off down the road someplace a little later to fix breakfast.

He slid back the curtain and was surprised to see Holland's curtain open and her bunk neatly made, but she was nowhere in sight. He frowned, not liking the fact that she'd left the truck and he hadn't heard her.

Climbing down from the truck, he glanced around the clearing, struck anew by the vast emptiness of the land. A sense of his own smallness and insignificance swept through him like a huge tide of loneliness, and he hastily narrowed his vision to the clearing. The pickup truck still sat where it had the night before, but there was no sign of Holland. He called her name and when she didn't answer, he hurried toward the small building that housed restrooms. He waited impatiently for several minutes, then called her name again. He stood with his head cocked, listening, but only the sough of wind high in the trees caught his ear. When Holland didn't respond, he tapped on the door. Still no response. Cautiously he opened the door to find no one there.

Perplexed, he scanned the clearing again. A trail disappeared into the trees in the direction of the river. He hurried toward it and in minutes stood on the riverbank wondering whether to proceed left or right. Still, he saw no sign of Holland. A sharp wind stung his cheeks, but he felt a sweltering heat. He couldn't avoid the guilty fact that he'd been sleeping so soundly he hadn't heard Holland leave. He had to find her and quickly. Too many things could happen to a woman alone in this wilderness. He'd worry about anyone under these circumstances, but this woman particularly aroused his protective instincts. She was his responsibility. He tried to ignore the sense that more than responsibility was involved. He tried to close his mind to thoughts of bears and other wild creatures, of Holland alone and scared, her large brown eyes shimmering with grief.

A sound caught his attention and he stopped to listen, then slowly began retracing his steps. It was an engine, a truck engine, one larger than the pickup. A sudden premonition urged him to run and his feet flew down the path.

He broke out of the trees and entered the clearing in time to see Hank's truck lurch as it hit a pothole, then pull onto the road where it rapidly picked up speed. He dashed after it even though he knew pursuit was hopeless. He followed for more than a mile, but finally stopped. A cloud of dust settled around him as he watched the truck round a corner and disappear from sight.

He knew she'd been angry last night when she'd gone to bed, but he'd never once considered she'd ditch him in the Alaskan wilderness in order to get her way. While he'd been worrying about what was best for her, she'd had no qualms about his welfare! She might think she'd seen the last of Allen James, but she was in for a big surprise. Sooner or later he'd find her and when he did . . . !

chapter two

Holland stood shock still staring at the spot where the truck had been parked. It was gone! He'd left her! A cloud of dust slowly settling on the unpaved highway told her she was too late. Terror climbed her spine and she fought an urge to throw herself on the ground to scream out her rage and fear.

How could he do this to her? She'd trusted him. Hank had trusted him. It could be days before another vehicle came this way. Even if someone gave her a ride to Fairbanks, she had no money until she reached Salt Lake and she'd have trouble claiming her father's account because all her ID was in the truck. It had been ten years since she'd seen her aunt, and she didn't know if the woman would accept a collect call even if Holland did manage to get to a telephone.

Along with her ID, the truck held her clothes, food, the few mementos Hank had left her, protection from bears, and shelter from temperatures that dipped below freezing at night, as well as Hank's gold. Allen didn't know about the gold. Hank had said he wouldn't tell Allen about that, but Allen did have all of her father's cash. Hank had given it to him for gas and "incidentals," so he could take care of old Hank's "little girl" on the long trip. Holland felt a rush of resentment. Why hadn't Hank trusted her to take care of his money? Instead he'd hired a baby-sitter to get her to Salt Lake where he was supposed to turn her over to her aunt. That thought added a layer of resentment. Maybe she didn't want to live with an aunt she didn't even know, and who had tried to separate her from her father at one time.

Well, Mr. James had taken care of Hank's little girl all right. He'd left her stranded in the wilderness at least a hundred and fifty miles north of the Yukon River with snow or bears, maybe both, due to arrive any day. If only Hank had been able to understand that she had grown up!

Her eyes lit on the pickup truck parked on the other side of the clearing. If she could wake the owner and persuade him to follow Hank's truck, perhaps she'd have a chance. Following thought with action, Holland ran toward the vehicle. Dropping her pole and trout string, she hammered on the shell and called for someone to open up. When no one responded, she dashed to the driver's side. She didn't have to knock; she could see that no one occupied the cab.

Again she made her way to the back of the truck. She raised her fist ready to knock again when a sound behind her sent a shiver down her back. Hank said if she were ever confronted by a bear, she should stay absolutely motionless even if it bit her. He'd repeatedly warned her that bears couldn't see too well, but they considered movement a threat to their territorial claim. She froze.

"Holland?" An incredulous whisper reached her ears. It sounded like . . . No, she must be imagining. Slowly she turned. Allen stood at the edge of the clearing, his parka open and the hood falling away from his dust and sweat-stained face. She hadn't imagined his voice.

"Allen? You came back," she croaked hoarsely. She took a hesitant step toward him, then her feet flew faster and faster. He met her halfway, then she was in his arms, her cheek pressed against his. Tears coursed down her cheeks. She'd been so scared.

"I thought you left me behind," she choked out the awful words, her voice revealing the extent of her fear. Allen's arms moved down her back to draw her into an island of peace and security. He whispered consoling words into her ear, and she longed to close her eyes and luxuriate in the comfort he offered her but her pride wouldn't let her. As the fear dissipated she wondered why he had found it necessary to frighten her with such a rotten trick. Surely he had an inkling of the terror she'd experience thinking herself abandoned.

Holland's back straightened as she pulled herself away from the comfort she'd savored moments ago. Allen had told her the night before not to leave the truck. Granted, she should have told him she was only going a short distance to a fishing hole Hank had shown her on their last trip to Fairbanks. She knew better than to leave the campground alone, but she hadn't wanted to wake him. He'd been sleeping soundly, following a restless night. Several times during the long night, she'd heard the thrashing movements of a person who slept uneasily or not at all. She'd been foolish, but he needn't have shown his disapproval in such a cruel fashion.

"I'll get my pole and we can be on our way," she spoke stiffly.

"Look around." Allen ran his fingers through his thick hair, then gestured broadly at the clearing. "The truck isn't here. Someone stole it."

"Stole it?" Holland's knees felt weak. "I thought . . ."

"I know what you thought; I thought the same thing about you."

"You thought I left you here alone?" Her voice rose in a squeak at the end. "I'd never do that."

"Well, I wouldn't leave you either." His mouth twisted in a mocking grin. "Now that we've settled the point that neither of us would abandon the other, we'd better get on to figuring a way out of here."

"I was trying to wake . . ." She waved vaguely toward the pickup. The gesture ended weakly as the truth hit her. The pickup was empty, broken down or out of gas. Its owner had to be the mysterious thief or thieves who had stolen Hank's truck. She was back to being stranded—only this time she wasn't alone. Somehow knowing that helped.

Allen looked at the decade-old truck and groaned. It didn't look encouraging. He wasn't mechanically inclined, but he had learned a few basics from his brother-in-law. He knew a spark plug from a distributor cap, but that was about all. He reached for a door handle and was relieved to find the vehicle wasn't locked. Candy wrappers, empty cookie boxes, aluminum cans, crushed cigarette packs, and a couple of lighters caught his eye. It was messy but at least the camper shell would provide shelter.

Using a stick, he checked to see if there was gas in the tank. Once he knew the tank wasn't empty, he walked around to the front of the truck to look under the hood.

Holland stood beside him as he stared into the tangle of wires and engine parts and shook his head. He had no idea what to look for. Every wire and gizmo appeared intact and in place. A shoulder nudged him aside as Holland reached out to touch a belt, shake a few wires, then attempt to loosen a bolt with her fingers. She took a step sideways, edging him out of her way.

"See if there's a toolbox in the back of the truck," she muttered in an abstracted voice. Allen's head jerked up, landing him a solid crack across the back of his head as he struck the truck hood. Staggering backward, he clasped the painful spot with his hand and gingerly rubbed the lump rising beneath his fingers. As he stared at Holland's back, he curled his lip in self-derision. It hadn't occurred to him that she might know more about truck engines than he did; almost everyone knew more about auto mechanics than he did. He was still grappling with the fact that she wasn't a child; he wasn't prepared for the authoritative way she took over the stalled truck.

"Hurry." She scarcely turned her head his direction before delving deeper into the intricate puzzle before her.

Did she really know what she was doing? Was it possible she could fix it? Hank was reputed to have been one of the best mechanics around, and he might have trained his daughter. Allen frowned, thinking she might make matters worse. He didn't doubt that a woman could be a mechanic, but Hank had intimated his daughter was next to helpless. Of course, he'd also hinted his daughter was about ten or twelve.

Allen turned toward the rear of the truck. He might as well let her try; he didn't have a clue what was wrong with the vehicle other than the obvious fact that there were no keys dangling from the ignition.

The back of the truck yielded an array of clutter. He dug through foam pads, various articles of clothing, empty bottles and cans, and finally turned up a small metal toolbox. As he slid off the tailgate with the box in one hand, he spotted Holland's fishing pole and her string of trout lying in the dirt. That explained her earlier disappearance, and since she'd caught them he might as well cook them. At least he knew how to do that, and it looked like it might be some time before they found anything else to eat.

He set the toolbox at Holland's feet, told her what he planned to do, and turned to the river to rinse off the fish. He decided to cook them there, too, in case he and Holland had to spend the night in the clearing. If there were any bears in the neighborhood, it would be best if any food odors were well away from where they slept.

After three or four attempts he persuaded Holland to stop to eat some breakfast. She ate one of the fish quickly, muttered a complaint about the inadequate contents of the toolbox he'd found, and hurried back to the truck.

For several hours Allen hung over the gaping mouth of the truck, but Holland didn't seem to need his help or his conversation. The more apparent it became that she knew a great deal about truck engines, the more useless and incompetent he felt. Eventually he drifted away to sit with his back against a tree. Brilliant light filtered through the trees and a panorama of mountains and trees blanketed the land as far as he could see. He loved the raw beauty and majesty of this northern state and would treasure always the places he'd seen and photographed.

The past year had been a time of healing and discovery that had endeared Alaska to him. Allen was proud of his work and felt for the first time in his life that he could measure up to anyone's professional standards. He likely would never be wealthy like his father, but he could support himself and do it well. The knowledge gave him a new sense of peace—until he remembered how quickly he'd managed to botch his promise to take care of Holland, and she was doing more than he was to get them on the road again.

Slow anger boiled to the surface. Having the truck stolen and being left stranded was bad enough, but Allen's cameras and several months' work were in that truck, too. Not only was a healthy chunk of his career at stake, but he felt like a hard-earned piece of himself had been stolen. When he caught up to the thieves, he'd make certain they had reason to regret this day. He didn't have any idea whether or not Holland could really fix the truck—he didn't even know what was wrong with it—but one way or another he would get out of here and find the people responsible for their predicament.

By late afternoon Holland had greasy engine parts spread across a shirt she'd dug out of the back of the truck and laid on the ground. She had removed the spark plugs one by one, then cleaned and replaced them. As near as he could tell she'd removed, cleaned, or tightened every belt and piece of metal in the truck, and Allen had a sinking feeling she'd never get it back together again, and even if she did, it still wouldn't run. *At least she was trying*, he reminded himself. That was more than he was doing.

His stomach growled and he decided to check the truck for something edible. After searching randomly for several minutes, he located a plastic bag and began to use it to clean up the trash littering the truck as he conducted a more methodical search for anything useful. It didn't take long to fill the bag, and he smiled in grim satisfaction when along with the trash he discovered credit card receipts for gas.

The shell looked better when he finished and they could sleep on the foam pads, but he hadn't found much to eat, just an airline packet of peanuts, a couple of stale cookies, a few unopened beer and soft drink cans, and half a bag of red licorice.

As Allen picked up the beer cans, a sudden memory came to his mind of the last time he'd been to the cabin that he and two friends owned near Park City. He had a clear picture of the disappointment on Cathy's face when she'd discovered his six-pack in the creek. He hadn't had a beer since. Staring thoughtfully at the can, he remembered a long-ago day when he'd found a beer can on the lawn of his family's home. He'd picked it up and carried it toward the trash cans in the garage. As he'd stood beside his car with the can in his hand, his father had driven up. He'd taken one look at the can, and a look of contempt crossed his face.

"Beer?" Allen could remember his father's sarcastic tone of voice. "If you're going to drink, couldn't you have the good taste to choose a decent wine?"

He'd gone right out and persuaded an older acquaintance to buy him a six-pack of beer, which he took home and blatantly stuck in his mother's refrigerator. In time he'd learned to even like the stuff, if it was cold enough.

With a sigh he dropped the can in his trash bag. Holland had dumped his coffee, he might as well beat her to the punch and get rid of the beer before she saw it. He picked up a soft drink can, popped the top, and took a deep swallow, then carried the can to Holland.

She swiped her forearm across her brow before reaching for the can he offered. She tipped it up and he watched in fascination as her throat undulated with each swallow. He found himself swallowing too as he watched her. Mentally, he slapped himself. The girl had gone through enough already, first losing her father, then finding herself stranded. She didn't need a man thirteen years her senior gawking at her like a dazzled adolescent.

"Hey, kid, you're bushed," he said. "Why don't you rest for a while. You can try again in the morning."

Her voice was determined. "No. I've got to keep at this. I have to get Hank's truck back."

Allen found he wanted to reassure her. "I want it back as badly as you do, but let's be realistic. We're not likely to get back to civilization until a patrol truck or the pipeline crews come through. Even if you find a way to repair the pickup, we don't have any way to start it."

"I can start the pickup," Holland looked up at him and thrust out her chin, daring him to contradict her assertion. "Hank taught me how to hot-wire anything."

Her stubbornness against accepting reality annoyed him. "Do you even know what's wrong with it?" he asked impatiently.

"Of course, I know what's wrong with it." She spoke as though it had never occurred to her that he didn't. That rankled. "It needs a new timing belt, but I can adjust this one. A couple of teeth are missing, making it slip out of alignment, but if I can turn it just a little, it will get us to a service station. I don't have the right tools, so it's taking a long time to turn it, and once it's fixed it might not stay fixed."

Good grief! Maybe she did know something about mechanics. He swallowed his pride and offered to help her. As she looked at him dubiously, he felt his irritation rise along with long-buried memories of a little boy who was never big enough, or smart enough, or loved enough. He was tempted to turn away, but controlled the impulse.

"I'll admit I don't know anything about truck engines, but I'm pretty good at electronics," Allen snapped. "I can repair a camera or tear apart and reassemble a computer, so I'm not exactly stupid. Tell me what you want me to do in layman terms, and I'll do it!"

"Okay," Holland responded hesitantly to his outburst. "There's a clamp I need to loosen, and I need channel locks to do it with, but there aren't any in the toolbox. I've been trying to do it with pliers, but I don't have enough strength in my hand. Do you want to give it a try?"

"Sure," he grinned. He was glad she'd agreed to a tacit truce.

After considerable struggle he loosened the clamp. Holland smiled jubilantly before returning to work, and he found himself basking in her approval. Shadows were already creeping across the clearing by the time she stepped back and reached for the greasy shirt to wipe her hands.

"Let's try it." Her voice was little more than a croak.

"Can you really do that without a key?" He struggled to keep his voice matter-of-fact and not get his hopes up too high.

"Sure, hot-wiring is no problem." She closed the hood, returned the tools to the box, and moved to the cab of the truck. "I'll have to make a mess of the steering column and the dash though," she said as she stripped away the cover on both. She reached under the console and he glimpsed a bundle of brightly colored wires. In minutes the roar of an engine filled the clearing.

She did it! She really did it! She backed slowly out of the cab, and her eyes, sparkling with triumph, met his. Nevertheless, her expression remained solemn as she asked, "You driving? Or me?"

Allen reached for her and swung her around in a circle. "Lady, you earned a rest! I'll drive." Their laughter blended together as the clearing became a blur twirling in the dusky light. Suddenly, as though they'd both received the same invisible signal, they stopped. The laughter died away and Allen found himself momentarily lost in her eyes. The deep chocolate pools held him trapped. Several seconds passed before he shook himself and returned to reality. Slowly he released her.

He tried to smile as he gestured toward the open truck door. "Hop in," he said.

Without a word Holland slid across the wide bench seat, and Allen climbed in behind her. He reached for the gearshift, settled his foot against the gas pedal, and the truck began to move. He was glad Holland didn't seem inclined to speak. He concentrated on the road in an attempt to block out the memory of how Holland had felt in his arms, wanting to erase all traces of the euphoria he had felt as they had danced together in the clearing.

They rounded a curve just in time to see a huge, shaggy brown shape disappear into the trees. A wave of relief swept over Allen. How fortunate that they hadn't had to sleep in the clearing with a bear nearby! When he turned his head to catch Holland's reaction to the beast, he saw that she'd already fallen asleep, her head resting against the window. There was just enough light to see a greasy black streak across her forehead and several dark splotches on her cheeks and chin. Unexpected tenderness welled inside him, causing his hands to tighten on the wheel.

Right now she looked as young and vulnerable as old Hank had implied that she was. Watching her made Allen feel warm and protective inside. Holland was a strange mixture of child and adult, he mused. One minute she behaved like the young boy the construction crew thought her to be; the next, the woman in her exploded into impossible-to-ignore splendor. She might look like a sleeping child at the moment, but back in the clearing there had been a moment when she'd been all woman, a woman he wanted to know a whole lot better.

The gravel road didn't permit much speed and a couple of hours had passed before Allen began watching for a place to stop. The gas gauge read less than a quarter of a tank and the auxiliary tank showed empty. Allen thought that they couldn't be far from a service stop he remembered, which boasted a small motel, a gas pump, and a handful of homes. He hoped the motel hadn't closed for the season yet.

Ten minutes later he stopped in front of the long, low building across the street from the service station. As soon as he stopped, the engine died and he felt a flicker of alarm. There were no lights to be seen anywhere. Closed signs hung on the motel office door and the service station. He eyed the few houses speculatively then turned toward his sleeping companion.

Her eyes opened and she turned her head to look around.

"Should we try the houses, see if we can rouse anyone?" she asked dubiously.

Allen yawned and rubbed his eyes. "We could try."

"Or we could crawl in the back and sleep on those foam pads for a few hours. It's not as cold tonight as it was last night, and we have our parkas." Holland struggled to hold back a yawn.

"There's a sheet of canvas and some plastic trash bags," Allen added as he smothered another yawn. He needed sleep and the sooner the better. He'd looked forward to a bed at the motel, but right now he figured he could sleep on a train track if he had to. He'd get a few hours sleep, then hunt up the guy who operated the service station, and they'd be on their way.

He was almost asleep, beneath their makeshift covers, when Holland's worried voice reached him.

"How are we going to buy gas? Everything we own is in the truck."

"Not everything," he mumbled. "My wallet is in my coat pocket. Your money is safe and I've got plenty of plastic."

"My money?" She felt a strange flutter.

"Yes. Hank gave me cash to pay for our trip and to make certain you had a little money of your own when you get to Salt Lake."

"I thought he gave the money to *you,*" she mumbled.

Allen yawned again. "He figured we'd need money for gas and other expenses, but the rest is yours. There's enough for an airline ticket for you. When we get to Fairbanks, you can fly on home."

Holland's voice was stubborn. "I'm not flying to Salt Lake. I can't go until I get my truck back."

Allen sighed. "I'll find it and send your things on to you. Now go to sleep."

"I have to find Hank's truck." Her voice took on a touch of desperation. "It's my home, and everything I own is in it. Hank's tools alone are worth a lot of money."

"You're not the only one with a big investment in that truck. You can be sure I'm going after my cameras, and there's a bag of exposed film in there I'd challenge a Kodiak for. I promise I won't leave Alaska without recovering both your things and mine."

A sniffle reached his ears and he clamped his teeth together to smother a groan. She was crying, and he had no idea what to do about it. He recognized that she'd had more than her fair share of grief in the past few days. Her father had died and she'd been uprooted to begin a trip that could last for weeks with a man she scarcely knew. She'd gone through the terror of thinking herself abandoned in the wilderness, then spent a full day repairing a truck. She had a right to cry for the mementos and trinkets of her life, Allen decided. It was probably a case of weeping over the small things to keep from letting the enormity of the big things shatter her.

Awkwardly he reached across the small space separating the foams pad to pat her shoulder. Instead of consoling her, he could feel her shoulders shake with the sobs she struggled to control. Moving closer, he wrapped his arms around her.

"Sh-h-h, it'll be okay. I'll catch up to them," he promised. Gradually her tears stopped and she lay still. The quiet seeped into the truck and Allen's weary eyes closed. He should move back over to the other mat, but Holland felt snug and comfortable in his arms. He'd move in a minute, when he was sure she was asleep. His thoughts ran together as his body relaxed and sleep gradually staked its claim.

"I don't know what to do." Her whisper reached him through a deep fog. He wasn't sure she was even speaking to him. It was more like she was thinking aloud—or praying. "I don't want to lose my mother's picture nor Hank's hand-carved totems, but most of all I don't want to lose my chance to go to school. I need Hank's gold. Please help me get it back. He hid it, but the longer someone else lives in the truck, the greater the risk that they'll find it."

Gold? His sleep-dulled brain struggled with the word. Had Holland said her father hid gold in the truck? Or was he already asleep and this was merely some fantastic dream? He tensed, ordered himself to wake up, and for several moments fought the exhaustion claiming his senses. He had to be dreaming.

Slowly he relaxed. And as sleep claimed him, he smiled to see Holland running toward him with her hood thrown back and a smile of joy on her face. She stopped to pet a huge shaggy bear and he tried to warn her it was dangerous, but she ran on with the huge beast gamboling at her heels. They ran through a meadow of flowers and butterflies, and the butterflies turned to gold. Old-fashioned doubloons and pieces of eight rained from the sky and fluttered on the wind.

chapter three

Holland shivered at the sudden loss of heat. Instinctively she burrowed deeper into the foam mat. Rough canvas brushed her cheek and she slowly came awake. The stars were beginning to fade, but there was enough light to pick out Allen's dark shape seated on the other mat. He bent forward to pull on his boots.

She didn't know how long he'd remained beside her. All night? Of course, all night couldn't have been very long. It had been after midnight when they'd arrived, and it couldn't be much past five now. The last she remembered was his arms around her as she fell asleep. She felt warm inside as she silently observed his silhouette. He was a nice man. Around him she wasn't tongue-tied and he'd cooked her fish, driven most of the night, and comforted her when she was frightened. Though she suspected he'd doubted her ability to fix the truck, he hadn't laughed at her efforts or talked down to her.

As she thought about the way he'd held her, heat suffused her face. There hadn't been anything improper in his actions, but there had been something more than a sense of comfort in the feel of his arms around her and her cheek against his chest. No man had ever touched or held her before, other than Hank. She'd never had a boyfriend or a brother and no experience to compare the feeling to, except what she'd read in books.

Hank had warned her about the dangers of letting a man get too close. They would always try for all they could get, he'd said. She felt a little tingle of happiness. Allen wasn't like that. He hadn't even tried to kiss her. If he had, would she have stopped him? She wasn't sure. Thinking about Allen kissing her wasn't at all unpleasant.

A mean little thought intruded past her hazy daydreams. She sat up abruptly and reached for her own boots. Perhaps Allen hadn't tried to kiss her because he hadn't wanted to kiss her. He might not find her attractive. After all, why should he even think of her as a woman? He'd thought of her as a boy all summer—if he'd thought about her at all. Hank had finally told him she was a girl, but she suspected her father had convinced Allen she was much younger than she really was. And then, the one day Allen had known her true age, she hadn't done anything to encourage him to think of her as a woman. Holland wasn't even sure why it was important to her that Allen see her as a woman. But she was willing to bet that catching fish, overhauling an engine, and running around in heavy wool pants and a thick parka weren't the kind of things the women Allen knew did.

Thinking of Allen with a woman like the ones she saw in magazine photos brought a sudden chill, and she shivered.

"You don't have to get up." Allen straightened as far as the camper shell would allow. "I'll go find someone to pump us some gas. You stay here and keep warm."

"No, I want to go with you." She swept her hair back with her fingers and hurried toward the tailgate, jumped to the ground, then straightened to stand beside Allen. Too late she saw his extended hand and turned away to hide her embarrassment. Men in books offered a hand to assist women out of vehicles or over obstacles, but no one had ever attempted to help her in that way before. Of course, she didn't need any help, but it brightened her mood to know Allen had offered. It reassured her that he'd noticed she was a woman, though she couldn't say why that mattered.

Together they trudged across the graveled parking strip to a small weather-beaten house behind the service station. After Allen knocked on the door, he crossed his arms and stuck his gloved fingers under his arms, rocking back and forth on his heels while he waited. Holland huddled deeper inside her parka. An arctic wind swept across the bare step, rattling the dry weeds that had blown against the side of the house. The air held a taste of snow.

Allen knocked again, harder, and was rewarded by the sound of footsteps approaching. When the door finally swung open, Holland's eyes widened. A young woman with long, straight black hair and eyes like a doe stood clutching the lapels of a red velvet robe close around her throat. A braided gold cord circled her tiny waist, and the skirt of the robe billowed to the floor. A gust of wind swirled the rich fabric around her ankles revealing dainty bare toes.

Ducking her head, Holland scuffed the toe of her heavy lumberjack boot against the board beneath her feet while Allen spoke to the woman. As if from a distance she heard him ask if he might use her telephone or radio to contact the state troopers since their truck had been stolen. "We're also in urgent need of gasoline for our present vehicle," Allen added.

"Come on in," the woman urged them inside with a smile. Closing the door behind them, she turned toward the back of the house to call, "Better get up, Bill. There's a couple of guys here who need you to pump gas."

Holland winced. She'd never minded before that everyone assumed she was a boy, but this time it bothered her. She sneaked a peek at Allen's face to see if he'd noticed the error, but he wasn't paying any attention to her. His eyes were on their hostess, and Holland wasn't too naive to see a definite gleam of appreciation in those eyes for the dark woman in red, who tossed her long hair over her shoulder and laughed in response to something Allen said. Something heavy settled in the center of Holland's chest.

Shifting her weight from one foot to the other, Holland felt ill at ease in the woman's house. It wasn't just the ruffled curtains and flowered sofa, or even the row of lavishly dressed dolls in a glass case that disturbed her. It was the stark contrast between the woman and herself. Everything about the woman shouted her femininity. Holland couldn't help comparing herself to the other woman with the knowledge that she came off the loser. Studying the woman through lowered lashes brought on a kind of despair. She'd bet no one ever mistook *her* for a boy. Awakened at five o'clock in the morning, her hair nevertheless gleamed as though freshly washed and brushed. Her robe was soft and feminine, and there was something in the way she moved that left no doubt the lady knew who she was and enjoyed being that person.

By contrast, Holland was tired of being a boy but she didn't want to give up the freedom the masquerade gave her. What did she know about being a woman anyway? Exactly nothing. She knew nothing about soft hands and pretty clothes or how to smile at a man so he'd follow her with his eyes the way Allen's eyes followed the other woman.

Holland lifted her chin at a stubborn angle. She wasn't stupid; she could learn. If she decided she wanted to.

Allen accompanied the woman who introduced herself as Sara Whitebear into another room to use the telephone. Holland hung back, uncertain what she should say or do. She heard Mrs. Whitebear's laughter, followed by Allen's deeper chuckle. Misery sliced through Holland. She was tall and awkward and knew nothing about the things that brought laughter to a man like Allen James. That she wanted to be the one to make him laugh confused her all the more.

Shortly, the two returned to the room where Holland waited. A big man with round cheeks and a booming voice followed them. He playfully slapped the woman's bottom and whispered in her ear. She giggled and left the room, stopping at the door to wink at Allen before disappearing from sight. Bill didn't seem to mind being awakened and in minutes led them outside to the gas pumps where he quickly filled both tanks.

Holland wanted to ask Bill Whitebear if he had the spare part the truck needed, but she couldn't bring herself to speak up. Old restrictions held her tongue and she found she couldn't force the words past her lips. Fortunately Allen mentioned their problem with the truck and the two men buried their heads inside the hood. She knew she should join them. After all, it was her work they were inspecting; Allen didn't know anything about the engine, and it was anyone's guess how much Whitebear knew. Instead she hung back with her hands in her back pockets. Anything she said would sound stupid anyway.

Allen turned his head toward her and smiled an inviting smile. She returned the smile hesitantly, but continued to stand awkwardly behind the men.

"Good work." Bill straightened and reached for a rag hanging from his back pocket. While he wiped his hands, he continued to speak to Allen. "The timing belt needs to be replaced. I don't have a spare or I'd sell you one. This'll probably get you into Fairbanks, but just in case you have more trouble, I'll ask the patrol to watch for you. I can give them a fairly good description of the two guys who drove this truck through here headed north a week ago."

Allen thanked the man and while he was inside the service station paying for the gas, Holland hot-wired the truck again. Letting the engine idle, she cocked her head and listened for any uneven sound. When she looked up, she saw Sara Whitebear approach Allen as he hurried back to the truck. She handed him a paper bag and smiled widely, showing a double row of even white teeth. Allen said something to her, and she laughed and punched him playfully on the arm. Some crazy emotion that was part anger, part hurt, and part jealousy swept through Holland leaving her uncertain how to deal with an unfamiliar ache.

She didn't speak when Allen opened the truck door and jumped inside. Scarcely giving him time to settle on the seat, she put the truck in gear and lurched onto the highway with the ping of flying gravel marking their progress.

"Want a biscuit?" Allen opened the paper bag and the aroma of fresh baked bread filled the cab of the truck. Holland's mouth watered even as her heart sank. One more area where she was inadequate. She couldn't look beautiful like the woman back there, she didn't have any idea how to talk and laugh with a man, and she couldn't cook. Opening cans and heating their contents was the extent of her culinary skills.

The biscuits were buttered and dripping with jelly. A perverse little demon wanted to refuse to eat them, but good sense prevailed. Holland was hungry and the biscuits tasted wonderful. They ate in silence as the miles went by. When the bag was empty Allen crumpled it up in a ball and tossed it from hand to hand. From the corner of her eye she could tell he was watching her. His eyes were half closed and there was a questioning look on his face. The scrutiny made her so nervous she hit a pothole she should have swerved around.

"Do you have a driver's license?"

"What?"

"I said—"

"I know what you said, and no, I don't," she spoke defensively. "Hank taught me to drive, but we never lived anyplace where I could apply for a license."

"You've been to Fairbanks. You could have gotten one there."

"I would have had to show them my birth certificate."

Allen shook his head and spoke with a touch of sarcasm. "I suppose Hank figured he couldn't risk having anyone find out his son was a really a daughter."

Holland picked up on his hint of censure. "Do you think Hank was ashamed of having a daughter instead of a son?" she asked.

Allen shrugged his shoulders. He didn't want to admit aloud that was exactly what he thought. Protecting his daughter was one thing, but the old man had carried it so far, Holland had been cheated out of all those things most young girls experience. Watching her with the Whitebear woman had given him an idea of how uncomfortable she was with her own gender.

"It wasn't like that," she spoke softly. "When Hank took me on the road with him, Aunt Barbara got really upset. She tried to get custody of me when we went back there for me to be baptized when I was eight. They fought over me for five years. We'd disappear for a while, then she'd find us and we'd have to go to court again. Then one summer we camped with a construction crew near a small mining town. Hank gave me a quarter to get an ice cream cone at the drugstore." Her voice dropped lower.

"I was walking along a dirt road when a couple of guys from the construction project came by in a pickup. They stopped and offered me a ride."

She stopped speaking. She hadn't talked to anyone except Hank about that day, but she wanted to explain to Allen. It was important to her that he not judge her father too harshly. He didn't say anything, and she avoided looking at his face.

"I said no, but they both got out of the truck and one of them grabbed me. I kicked him hard as I could but the other one shoved me to the ground and sat on my legs. I was only thirteen, but I knew what they wanted so I tried to get away but I couldn't. They ripped my blouse, then a car drove up. That scared the guys and they ran for their truck and took off. I didn't wait around to see if help had arrived or more trouble. I ran to find Hank."

She glanced toward Allen and was surprised by the ashen color of his face.

"What did Hank do?" Allen's mouth had a grim firmness to it.

"He took me back to our trailer and told me to stay there. He was gone almost an hour and when he got back I knew he'd been in a fight, but he didn't say anything about it. He just hooked his truck to the trailer and we left. A couple of days later he said he'd been doing a lot of thinking, and it seemed to him I would be a lot safer from goons like the ones who attacked me and it would be harder for Aunt Barbara to find me and take me away from him if I were a boy. We stopped in the next town, and I got a haircut and some boy's clothes."

Allen didn't comment and they rode for several more miles before he finally spoke. "Pull off up there by those trees and I'll drive."

"I'm okay. I'm not tired," she protested.

"I don't think you should be driving without a license," Allen spoke evenly but his words irritated her.

"I don't think it matters that much right now whether I have a license or not. We don't have any registration or insurance for this truck either. Technically we stole it."

"I still think I should drive," Allen persisted.

Holland bit back a sharp retort. Fine, if he wanted to drive, she'd let him drive. She slowed, then pulled off where he'd indicated. She brought the truck to a stop, and it sputtered, then died.

Holland's face told Allen all he needed to know. She hadn't turned the motor off; it had just quit. He might not know as much about engines as she did, but he was getting pretty adept at reading her face, and her face said they were in deep trouble again. He shouldn't have insisted on driving, but he'd known since she awoke this morning that something was troubling her. Whatever it was, it was getting worse. She hadn't said one word to the Whitebears, and every time she looked at him she looked like she was about to cry. He was starting to feel he understood her better, especially after she'd told him why Hank had put her in boys' clothes. Allen could see that being attacked, especially at a point in Holland's life when she was beginning to recognize her femininity, had caused her to reject those changes in herself that had made her vulnerable in the first place. She loved her father and it had never occurred to her to blame him for her strange upbringing or the uncertainties facing her now.

He reached across to where her fingers rested on the steering wheel and placed his hand over hers. "Do you think you can start it again?"

"Probably not, but I'll try." With her other hand, she jerked at the door handle and Allen let her go.

After a half hour of steady tugging and twisting, she held up an oddly shaped piece of metal and shook her head. "It's busted." Her disgust was apparent.

Swallowing his acute disappointment, Allen spoke aloud. "I guess this means we sit and wait."

"Afraid so," Holland concurred glumly.

A nearby trickle of water furnished the means for Holland to clean her grimy hands, but it wasn't large enough to provide fish for their dinner. Together they hiked up the road to the next curve to see if help might be nearby. Trees and mountains spread beyond a sea of tall grass as far as they could see. Other than the narrow strip of dirt and gravel loosely referred to as a highway, no sign of civilization could be seen in any direction. Allen was no stranger to loneliness and the loneliness of this great land touched his soul as nothing else ever had. He fought an overwhelming urge to clutch the girl beside him, and feed on her warmth and reality until his own humanity was confirmed once more. Her fingers brushed his as though she'd read his thoughts, and a jolt went through him. He sucked in a deep breath and forced himself not to look at her.

Their feet dragged as they returned to the truck. Allen lowered the tailgate and they both sat swinging their feet and hoping a cloud of dust might materialize along the road. He squinted, hoping for a break in the lonely emptiness of the long unpaved highway, but it remained bare, and Allen wondered how long it would take for the surrounding wilderness to reclaim that small link with the outside world.

"Maybe we ought to pray," Holland broke the silence.

"Go ahead, if it'll make you feel better." Allen didn't bother to hide his indifference.

"No, I mean together, out loud," she clarified.

"I don't do much praying." He'd stopped praying a long time ago. The last time had been at the cabin outside Park City. Brad and

Cathy had gathered them all together for prayers before sending the children to bed. Brad's prayers had always brought him comfort and a sense of belonging, but praying on his own never seemed to work out. It was funny how he and his two best friends had gone to church together since they were little kids, but only Brad had developed a firm relationship with God. He'd even gone on a mission. Allen had considered going on a mission along with Brad, but at the last minute he'd changed his mind. He couldn't teach what he lacked a conviction of himself. Doug hadn't been a member growing up, but he'd been baptized a little more than a year ago before Allen had left for Alaska.

"Will you?"

"Will I what?" He knew what she wanted, but he'd feel like a hypocrite to pray just to please her.

"Will you pray with me?" Her face was scrunched in worry lines and he almost yielded.

"You can pray if you want to, but I'm not going to," he refused.

She was quiet for a long time and he squirmed uncomfortably, assuming she was praying silently.

"Hank said you were a Mormon." She sounded hurt and defensive again.

"I was baptized and I went to church when I was a kid."

"Why did you stop going?"

"I don't know. I guess I just drifted away after I left home. I only went because my friends went. After we finished school Brad got married and Doug went to the Middle East. I was in Texas and just never got around to learning if there was a ward in San Antonio."

"We didn't get to go to church often, but when he could Hank took me. Most Sundays we just read the Book of Mormon together, but we had prayers every night."

An old memory surfaced and Allen saw himself as a young boy spending the night at Brad's house. He remembered the sense of awe he'd felt when Brad's father had called Brad's whole family together, and they'd knelt in front of the sofa and chairs in the Williams' family room. The warmth and happiness that always permeated Brad's home was as thick and delicious as rich chocolate cake. Suddenly he'd understood why that feeling was missing in his home. Nobody prayed. He could hardly wait to get back home and tell his parents what he'd discovered.

His mother had looked at him and blinked before saying, "That's nice, dear. Do you have your homework done?" Dad had laughed and said, "Don't take that stuff too seriously. If you want to get ahead in this state, you have to be a Mormon—even show up at church now and then—but don't be stupid enough to get so involved you let them monopolize all your time and money."

"If I pray out loud, will you hold my hand and let it be from you, too?" Holland hadn't given up. Allen didn't want to hurt her feelings, but all this talk about praying made him uncomfortable. But he had a hunch she wouldn't drop the subject anytime soon, so the best way to end it might be to just go along.

"All right," he mumbled.

The smile that lit her face left Allen stunned. How he wished he had just one of his cameras! She reached for his hand and bowed her head. Her hand felt warm and strong in his, and he was aware of small calluses at the base of her fingers. A sense of comfort and peace stole over him. Listening to her pray wasn't as difficult as he'd expected.

He listened to her softly spoken words and was amazed to discover this backwoods girl's faith ran as deep as that he'd seen in his friend Brad. A nostalgic longing encompassed him, and for just a moment something touched his heart and he wished he could talk to God the way they did. Perhaps if he . . .

The growl of an engine punctuated by the rattle of gravel brought up his head. The light bar across the cab of the truck, slowing as it closed the distance between them, told him the Alaska State Patrol had arrived. Behind him he heard Holland's softly whispered amen.

chapter four

Allen returned his wallet with his ID to an inside pocket and zipped the pocket closed. The sergeant looked pointedly at Holland.

"I-I don't have any ID," she stammered. "It-it's in the t-truck."

The uniformed officer behind the desk raised his eyebrows, glanced briefly at the papers he'd kept them filling out for the past two hours and made no effort to conceal his skepticism as he spoke. "You don't have any identification. You can't provide a home address. You don't have a driver's license. Yet you claim you own a truck, which doesn't happen to be registered to you. Is that right?"

Holland nodded dumbly and twisted her fingers together in obvious nervous agitation. She jumped when the telephone at the sergeant's elbow rang.

"Just a minute," the officer snapped as he reached for the instrument. He barked a few terse words and banged the receiver back down. Instead of turning back to the two people standing beside his desk, he began a search of the desk drawers. Holland shifted her weight from one foot to the other several times, then asked in a hesitant voice, "C-could you tell me where the r-restrooms are?"

"There," the man pointed indifferently.

Allen knew Holland was hurt and humiliated. The two officers who brought them into Fairbanks had been helpful and courteous, but the desk sergeant implied she was lying each time she stammered an answer to his brusque questions. Now when she'd finally worked up the courage to ask directions to the restroom, he'd directed her to a door clearly marked *Men*.

Allen barely hung onto his temper. It would feel good to tell the oaf where to go, but he couldn't afford to antagonize the pompous jerk or their complaint would most likely disappear in a mountain of paperwork and they'd get no help at all in recovering the truck.

"Come on, Holly. Let's go." He put an arm around Holland's shoulder in a protective gesture. He hoped the sergeant caught the diminutive he'd deliberately used. He couldn't believe any man could be so obtuse he couldn't recognize Holland was a beautiful woman no matter how many layers of rough masculine clothing she wore. One glance at the man's face told him he'd failed. The sergeant's red-faced look of disgust told him the man saw his gesture in an entirely different context. Defiantly he tightened his grip on Holland and together they left the police station.

On the sidewalk they faced each other. Holland's chin went up and she stood as though braced for a fight. He didn't want to fight with her. He'd like to tell her he understood how difficult it was for her to talk to strangers and sympathize with her strange position, caught somewhere between a lonely backwoods boy and suddenly finding herself thrust into adulthood as a young woman.

"What now?" Holland raked her hair back with fingers that appeared to Allen's sharp eyes to tremble.

"There's not much we can do tonight. Let's find a store where we can pick up a change of clothing and a toothbrush, then check into a hotel for the night. We'll get your airline ticket in the morning."

"I'm not leaving until I get my truck back." Her chin came up higher and her eyes took on that stubborn streak he was learning to recognize.

"Okay, let's go shopping, then get some sleep. We can talk about it in the morning." He sensed arguing would be a waste of time. He had a hunch this was an argument he was going to lose anyway.

Holland slipped a pair of socks and a package of boys briefs on the counter and turned away, her cheeks flaming with embarrassment.

"Is that all you're getting?" Allen stared at her meager selections as he set a stack of shirts, pants, socks, and underwear for himself beside them.

"It's all I need," she mumbled.

"Are you worried about money?" he asked bluntly. "Well, don't be. I have enough to get whatever you need. Ma'am?" he turned to speak to the clerk. "My friend needs a couple pairs of ladies' pants—" he emphasized *ladies* "—one lined wool and one denim. She'll need blouses and sweaters to go with them." He glanced down at the package of boys' briefs and his jaw tightened. "Add to that some *ladies'* underthings, a thermal suit, and socks."

"Allen!" Holland gasped.

"We'll need a few measurements." The gray-haired clerk didn't bat an eye as she looked Holland up and down, then stalked toward her. Before she knew what had happened, Holland's parka was off and the woman was stretching a tape measure around her hips. As the tape moved higher, heat flooded Holland's face and Allen's grin grew broader. No doubt she'd like to get the tape around his neck!

She refused to try on any of the clothes the clerk piled on the counter. She'd never stripped to the buff in a store in her life and she wasn't about to do it behind a flimsy curtain with that old dragon lady checking to see how things fit and Allen leaning against the wall whistling a few feet away. No way! She let them pick out which clothes to buy, too. She just wanted to get out of there.

Allen handed the clerk a piece of plastic and Holland felt worse. It was bad enough having Allen buy underwear for her, but seeing him pay for it with his credit card instead of the money her father had given him bothered her more.

When they reached a drug store, he didn't even ask about her preferences, but simply grabbed the toiletries he thought they needed. While he stacked his purchases beside the cash register, her eyes drifted to a display of candy bars and her stomach growled. She realized with a start she was hungry. She hadn't had anything to eat since Mrs. Whitebear's biscuits.

"Allen," she asked hesitantly. "Could I have a candy bar?" It embarrassed her to ask, but she really was hungry.

"Buy whatever you want," he answered in a distracted tone.

"I-I don't have any money," she mumbled.

"Just add it to this stack." He indicated the items on the counter. "Get me one too, will you?"

Ten minutes later they stepped out into the late afternoon dusk and hurried toward a hotel recommended by one of the patrolmen who found them. Holland took a bite of chocolate and nuts before shoving the rest of her candy into her pocket. The wind had picked up and she needed both hands to hang onto the parcel she carried.

It only took a few minutes for Allen to secure two rooms. Ushering her ahead of him up the stairs, he indicated the first room was hers, then followed her inside to sort through the packages they dropped on the bed.

"Is an hour enough time?" he asked as he straightened with two bulging bags in his hands.

"For what?"

He looked exasperated before spelling it out. "To get ready to go out to dinner."

"It won't take me that long." She couldn't imagine needing a whole hour to get ready to go anywhere. The prospect of going to dinner with Allen both excited and scared her. Going to dinner sounded almost like a date, something she'd never experienced.

"Hungry, are you? Okay, forty-five minutes. I'll knock on your door. Enjoy a nice soak." He started for the door, then stopped to set down his packages. He reached for his wallet and counted out five twenties. "Here," he held them out to her. "It's your money. You certainly shouldn't have to ask me for it."

"I didn't mean . . ." she stammered.

"I know you didn't," he grinned at her. "I've been a blockhead. I just never thought about you not having any money, even though I knew your ID and everything you own was in the truck when it was taken."

He pressed the money into her hand and left with a warning for her to lock the door behind him. She stared at the bills. She'd never had any money of her own. Hank had handled their money, giving her only what she needed for specific items like candy bars and sanitary supplies.

She put the chain on the door before wandering around the simple room. She'd never stayed in a hotel room before. As long as she could remember the truck had been her home and before that a trailer. Since their home went wherever they did, there had been no need for hotel accommodations. There were curtains at the window, a long, low bureau with a mirror, a couple of chairs, and a little round table with a lamp on it. She eyed the bed. It looked huge but inviting.

Her stomach growled and her hand went to her pocket for her candy bar. Munching on the chocolate bar, she took a couple of steps and found herself in a white tile bathroom. The tub drew her attention first. The truck was outfitted with a shower and she'd taken plenty of showers at rest stops, but there before her sat a great, big, deep tub, something she'd dreamed about for years. She couldn't remember sitting in a bathtub since she was a little girl. Suddenly she grinned, tossed her candy wrapper in the trash, and started peeling off her clothes.

Wrapping a towel around herself, she ran back to the bed to see if Allen had bought shampoo. She found not only shampoo but bubble bath as well. Back in the bathroom she watched in fascination as the hot water burst into foam. With a giggle of delight she settled herself beneath a cloud of bubbles.

As the warmth seeped into her tired body, lethargy took over. The hot water and fragrant bubbles lured her aching muscles to slowly relax. She felt her eyelids droop as she idly played with the bar of soap she'd found wrapped in paper. She'd rest just a minute. She closed her eyes and leaned back until her head touched the tile. Behind her closed eyes she saw the annoyance on Allen's face when the police sergeant directed her to the men's room. A faint smile parted her lips as she remembered his arm around her shoulder and remembered he'd called her Holly. No one had ever shortened her name to Holly before and she wasn't sure she liked it. But it had sounded all right when Allen said it.

With a jerk she came awake. The water had cooled and the bubbles had dissolved. Afraid Allen would arrive to find her still in the tub, she frantically rinsed her hair under the showerhead before toweling herself dry.

Glancing at the greasy, soiled clothes on the floor, she was glad she had something clean to put on. Silently she forgave Allen for embarrassing her with his insistence on buying her new clothes. She looked through all her new things, laying them out across the bedspread. Allen had said there was a restaurant in the hotel, so she wouldn't need the wool pants. She reached for the denim. Her eyes lit on the little pile of underthings and she found herself blushing. Softly she stroked the silky fabric before dressing quickly in her first ever pair of ladies' jeans and a soft pink, fitted tee shirt. Fingering the tiny blue hearts embroidered around the rounded neckline, she turned and caught a glimpse of herself in the mirror above the dresser. She swallowed an exclamation of surprise. Could that really be her? A smile of delight crossed her face as she smoothed the slippery fabric against her skin. Maybe she wasn't hopeless as a female after all.

A tap sounded on the door, bringing her back to reality in a hurry.

"Are you ready?" Allen called through the door, "or do you need more time?"

"N-No!" she stammered. "I'm almost ready." Socks were next. She picked up a brush lying on the bed, ripped off the cardboard backing and made a few quick swipes to slick back her hair.

She snatched up her boots and ran for the door.

Allen lifted one eyebrow and stared at the stranger who flung open Holland's door. He'd noticed her superb bone structure before and had appreciated her beautiful face at once, but now he could see all her bones were covered with just the right amount of skin and muscle. Holland Jesperson was drop-dead gorgeous.

"Are you going to wear your shoes or carry them?" he drawled. She glanced at him and turned away, flustered. He watched her lace the heavy boots and wished he'd bought her some decent shoes. On the other hand, he wished he hadn't bought her any new clothes at all. Now he knew what he'd only suspected before. Spending the next couple of weeks alone with Holland in the truck, if they managed to recover it, wasn't going to be easy and it would be impossible now to forget for even a minute that his roommate was neither a boy nor a little girl.

A coffee shop and bar were located on the first floor of the hotel, and Allen opted to go there since there was no waiting to be seated. He placed one hand at Holland's back as they followed the hostess to a table near the window. She held herself stiffly and he wondered if he'd made her uncomfortable by touching her. When he seated himself across the table, he recognized her tense expression. Poor kid. The simplest social situation overwhelmed her. It was hard to believe anyone growing up in the past couple of decades could have lived such an isolated existence. He admired her though. She might be frightened, but she didn't lack courage.

Music spilled over from the bar and he tapped his foot to the western beat while he looked at the menu. A waitress, wearing western garb, big hair, and too much makeup appeared at their table and hovered at his elbow. Her short, full skirt brushed against his jeans and her neckline dipped much too low when she bent forward to retrieve their menus.

"Ready to order, sugar?" She batted her eyes and directed her question to Allen, pointedly ignoring Holland.

He smiled in amusement and ordered a salmon steak. Holland quickly ordered the same. He watched the waitress stroll back to the kitchen with an exaggerated sway to her hips. He'd met her kind before and she didn't interest him.

He turned his attention to Holland. Unfortunately she did interest him. Too much. He had to remember she was emotionally off-balance with the recent loss of her father and going through a difficult adjustment to being seen as a woman. She was also young and naive—and his responsibility.

The waitress made a production of bringing their dinner, making a spectacle of herself by leaning toward Allen each time she set something on the table. He made teasing remarks in response to her wisecracks and obvious flirting, but he wished she'd leave them alone so he could try again to persuade Holland to fly to Salt Lake. He could call Brad and Cathy and ask them to meet her plane and look after her. He wouldn't just abandon her to find her way to some relative she hadn't seen for ten years.

"Do you think the police are going to look for my truck?" Holland asked in a worried voice.

"They'll look. I'm just not sure how hard they'll look." He had his own doubts about depending on the police to locate the truck.

"Shouldn't we be searching for it ourselves? The thieves might be here in Fairbanks."

"Tomorrow is soon enough. You need a good night's sleep tonight." He'd already made up his mind that once Holland was settled in for the night he'd do a scan of the bars and parking lots in town himself.

"Tomorrow is Sunday." She spoke hesitantly and seemed to expect some response from him.

"I know it's Sunday, but we can still rent a car to get around."

"I want to go to church." She made the announcement almost defiantly.

"Church? Is there a Mormon church in Fairbanks?" He wasn't certain how their conversation had turned this direction.

"Of course. Hank and I always go when we're here. Will you go with me?" Her question made him squirm. He didn't want to go to church. Even if he did, there wasn't time. He had to get Holland on a flight to Salt Lake and go after the truck before he lost all chance of recovering his cameras and exposed film.

"You can't go to church. You don't even own a dress." It was a stupid remark, but all he could think of at the moment.

"I wore pants before." Holland looked hurt.

"That was when everyone thought you were a boy," he argued.

"How about dessert?" The waitress appeared again and casually draped a hand across his shoulder in a familiar gesture, offering more than the usual cake or pie.

Holland stood, rocking the table with the sudden movement.

"Holland?" He shrugged off the hand resting on his shoulder.

"I'm going to bed. I'll see you in the morning." Except for the defiant tilt of her chin she looked like she might be about to cry. "Enjoy your dessert," she added with a hint of sarcasm before bolting from the room.

He watched her clumsy retreat from the room. She had to be the touchiest female he knew. He might as well give up trying to persuade her to fly to Utah. Finding her truck was clearly her first and only priority.

"I get off in twenty minutes, sugar." The waitress winked as she deftly cleared away all traces of Holland's dinner.

"That's nice," Allen responded absently, his mind still on Holland. Something about that young lady got under his skin. She annoyed him, but he liked her. She was funny and courageous, smart, too. She was tough and brash one minute, then insecure and tongue-tied the next. The waitress clattered dishes together, drawing his attention back to her. She looked at him expectantly and he muttered an order for apple pie.

Five minutes later a movement beyond the restaurant caught his eye and he watched in astonishment as Holland, bundled in her parka and gloves, scurried across the foyer and headed for the front door of the hotel.

"Wait!" he yelled as he scrambled to his feet. Halfway across the room the waitress intercepted him.

"What about—?"

"Oh, yeah!" Hastily withdrawing his wallet he shoved a bill in her hand and continued his sprint from the room. By the time he reached the door Holland was gone. He glanced up and down the street, straining to see through the gathering storm, but saw no sign of her.

"Now what?" he asked aloud of no one. He didn't doubt she'd gone hunting for her truck. He shivered and it wasn't just the cold causing the tremors. He didn't like the picture that filled his mind of Holland tramping around in the cold from bar to bar and scouring the parking lots alone. He liked even less the prospect of Holland coming up against the thieves or some other disreputable types. He'd have to go back to his room for his coat and go after her.

A blast of cold wind carrying tiny chips of ice struck Holland as she hurried down the street. It was beginning to snow and she assured herself the stinging in her eyes was due to the cold, not because Allen still sat in the restaurant talking and laughing with that waitress. She wasn't going to cry. Hank had taught her to tackle problems head-on and go after what she wanted. Right now she wanted Allen to notice her—and she wanted a dress so he wouldn't be ashamed to take her to church.

After leaving the restaurant, she'd stumbled upstairs and caught a glimpse of herself in the mirror as she entered the room. She felt the tears rush down her cheeks as, closing the door, she decided to face facts. She made a couple of decisions. No more letting Allen take Hank's role in her life. She didn't need a surrogate father. She was an adult and she was going to start acting like one. She was also a woman and she was going to start looking like one. And she was going to go to church tomorrow!

The department store where she'd shopped earlier with Allen was closed as were the shops that catered to tourists, but there was a big discount store a few blocks away. She could buy what she needed there.

The store appeared nearly abandoned as she entered. One lone clerk occupied a checkout stand. She smacked her gum and pointed to a sign that indicated the store would close in fifteen minutes. Holland would have to hurry.

The women's apparel section was clearly marked, but the array of women's clothing was daunting. Buying a dress was a whole lot more complicated than buying a pair of jeans, and she wasn't certain what size to look for. She'd naively assumed that they came in small, medium, large, and extra large like men's shirts.

Taking a deep breath she pulled a dress off the rack. It was the same color as pretty Mrs. Whitebear's robe. That was a good color. She held the dress up against herself, then when she noticed the skirt barely covered her thighs, she hastily returned it to the rack. She'd need a larger size.

She scanned the row of dresses until she found the longest one there. Quickly she grabbed it, then raced for the shoe department. Her fingers fumbled with the laces on her boots and she glanced around nervously to see if someone might tell her she had to leave before she could find a pair on the self-help shelf that would fit. The pair she selected felt awkward, but she could practice walking in them when she got back to her room.

A nearby display of pantyhose caught her eye and she groaned. She'd forgotten ladies wore filmy stockings that went all the way up in all the books she'd read. Obviously she couldn't try them on, so she gathered up several different packages in an assortment of sizes.

Her last stop was the cosmetic aisle. There were too many colors and none of them were any shade she recognized. Persimmon Magic, Midnight Glow, Rose Dawn. Those were colors? She closed her eyes and grasped the first package her hand encountered.

The clerk pointedly glared at her as she scurried to the counter, but she didn't care. She'd accomplished what she'd set out to do. Tomorrow Allen would have no excuse for not taking her to church. She stifled a happy little giggle as she anticipated the surprise she planned for Allen in the morning. She'd get dressed early, then knock on his door. She could hardly wait to see his face when he saw her in a dress.

"Will that be all?" The clerk routinely asked, obviously hoping it was, so she could close and go home.

"I'll take one of those, too." She pointed to a display of curling irons and while the clerk reached for it, Holland added a couple of chocolate bars to her purchases. She felt like celebrating.

Allen had passed worried and angry a long time ago. Now he was just plain scared. He'd checked every alley, motel, and parking lot around. There was no sign of Holland or of the missing truck. Guilt took a swing at him, too. He'd failed all around. First he'd lost the truck, now he'd lost Hank's kid. Only Holland wasn't a kid and losing her touched him on a tender spot way beyond the promise he'd made to a dying man.

Jamming his hands inside his deep coat pockets, he hurried toward the massive log hotel. He'd check her room, see if she might have returned, then call the police. Anything could have happened to her. In some respects she was as innocent and naive as the child old Hank had implied she was.

Half a block from the hotel he spotted a figure crossing the street. His heart accelerated and he lengthened his stride. The other person paused in front of the hotel and the overhead light clearly revealed Holland shifting a bag from one hand to the other before opening the heavy door. He couldn't believe his eyes. He'd been worried sick and she'd been shopping! Wait til he got his hands on her!

"Holland!" he roared, but she didn't pause. He began to run. The door crashed back against the wall as he charged into the reception area, causing the desk clerk to raise his brows and look at him askance.

Allen rushed across the room, but as his foot touched the first step his temper began to cool. Tearing after Holland like a madman wasn't his style. Instead of confronting her now, he'd go to his room, calm down, and in the morning he'd sit her down and calmly explain to her that like it or not she was flying back to Salt Lake on the first flight he could get her a seat.

chapter five

Allen rinsed his razor under the hot water tap before patting his face dry. Grimly he stared into the mirror. Convincing Holland to return to Salt Lake without him wouldn't be easy, but after last night he was more certain than ever she couldn't be part of the search for her father's truck. He'd half expected to see gray hair when he'd faced the mirror this morning. He couldn't remember a time when he'd been more frightened—or more angry.

He was a man who took responsibility seriously, but it was more than that. He was beginning to care too much for the young woman left in his care. Telling himself she was too young for him and totally lacking in the graces he enjoyed in his women friends did nothing to suppress his feelings each time they were together. He'd tried comparing her to Megan, but Megan was an ethereal dream while it was impossible to forget for two seconds that Holland was very much a flesh and blood woman. Holland had no trace of Megan's exquisite perfection, not a glimmer of cool sophistication, no hint of mystery. No, Holland had none of those things. Instead she had a hint of vulnerability in her beautiful eyes and a smile that invited him to be a boy again. No, even if they recovered the truck, he couldn't risk all those days—and nights—alone with her.

A call to the airport told him he had two options. A direct flight to Seattle would leave at three and a flight to Anchorage, connecting with a Seattle flight, was scheduled to depart at noon. He booked Holland on the three o'clock flight. Brushing aside a twinge of guilt, he set down the phone and prepared to face Holland. She'd be angry, but it was for the best. He just hoped she'd eventually believe that.

He'd take her to breakfast and make certain she ate before he told her.

There was no response when he tapped on her door. He waited a few minutes and knocked again. This time he heard a muffled sound on the other side of the door.

"Holland?" he whispered as loud as he dared. He didn't want to disturb everyone in the hotel. "Holland!" He spoke a little louder.

"Go away!" came a strangled cry from behind the wood panel.

"Holland, is something wrong?" Allen felt alarm shoot through his body.

"No, just go away." Her voice ended with a tremor. She sounded suspiciously like she might be crying.

"Open this door!" Allen forgot to lower his voice. Something was wrong. He knew it.

"I-I don't want to."

"Holland, open this door or I'll go get a key from the manager." Silence followed. He was beginning to think he'd have to make good on his threat when he heard the security bolt rattle.

Holland opened the door a crack and he pushed it open wide. "Holland, what . . . ?" His voice trailed off and he stared.

She lifted her chin and stared back defiantly. A slight tremble at the corner of her mouth gave away her agitation. She looked a fright and obviously knew it. Slowly his eyes traveled from her kinked and singed hair, across her garishly red mouth, dropped to a fire-engine red dress at least four sizes too large for her slender figure, and settled on what was obviously her first pair of high-heeled shoes. He didn't know where she'd gotten the ill-fitting costume, but he suspected it had something to do with her mysterious shopping trip the night before. Something inside him began to soften. She looked absurd but at the same time utterly appealing.

Suddenly her shoulders sagged and she sat down on the edge of the bed. Tears trickled down her cheeks and he fought an urge to take her in his arms. He sensed that one wrong word or one misplaced sympathetic touch would only make matters worse. He didn't know what had prompted Holland to buy a dress, but he hoped this first disastrous attempt to don feminine apparel wouldn't prove so traumatic she'd withdraw once more into her silent boy persona.

"Holland, why?" He crouched in front of her, balancing on the balls of his feet.

She sniffed and swallowed before raising her eyes to meet his.

"I-I want to go to church. You said I couldn't because I didn't have a dress." She turned away, staring with unfocused eyes over his shoulder. Even with her hair poking out at strange angles and the red smear across her mouth, she touched his heart. He wanted to comfort and make everything right for her. With a sinking sense of inevitability he knew what he had to do. He had to take her to church.

"We can fix it." He reached out to touch her chin, turning her face back to his. "Go wash your hair and face. I'll be right back."

"Where are you going?" He wasn't certain, but it seemed to him he heard a slight wobble in her voice.

"There's a dress shop here in the hotel."

"How do you know what size I wear? This dress seemed the right length in the store." She held her hand to the front of her dress where it appeared ready to drop off her shoulders any minute. The dress really was pathetic; the waistline sagged below her hips, the would-be mini skirt hung raggedly around her knees, and the wide, floppy sleeves fluttered to her elbows.

"Honey, you haven't been watching women's fashions the past few years. I have." He grinned and sauntered toward the door.

"Allen!" She stopped him. "You can't buy clothing today."

"Sure I can," he attempted to reassure her. "The shop is open and they welcome credit cards."

"But today is Sunday." He cocked his head to one side and watched her face for several long seconds. Finally he flashed her a cocky grin and reached for the doorknob.

"I think you'll have to consider this a case of the ox being in the mire." His laughter followed him out the door.

Holland stared at her reflection in the mirror and nearly burst into tears again. Allen had gotten the ox part right and she certainly was in the mire. This wasn't the way she wanted Allen to see her. She'd dreamed of showing him she could be as pretty as Mrs. Whitebear and that waitress; instead she'd made a fool of herself. She attempted to stand and staggered as she took a step in her high-heeled shoes. The shoes had to go. She didn't need to be any taller or any clumsier. She'd break her neck if she tried to walk down the street in them.

She stepped out of the shoes and made her way to the bathroom. She might as well follow Allen's instructions. She knelt down and stuck her head under the bathtub tap. Her hair slicked back like a boy's looked better than the tortured mess on her head now.

When Allen returned she eyed the packages he carried with a good deal of skepticism as he dropped them unceremoniously on the bed. Why should a man know more about women's clothing than she did? After all, down deep she was supposed to be a woman, though she certainly didn't feel like much of one at the moment.

"Put these on," he ordered, pulling a pale blue denim skirt and vest from one bag. He thrust them into her arms and reached for the other bag. From it he extracted a soft yellow sweater and added it to her armful. "And these." He stacked matching calf-length boots and a leather belt on top of the skirt and sweater. "I'll be right back. If the boots don't fit, we'll stop and exchange them on our way out." He turned and walked out the door leaving her with her mouth open.

To her amazement the clothes fit perfectly, even the boots. The swirl of the skirt against the backs of her legs felt strange and though a glimpse of herself in the mirror didn't hint at sudden glamour, she liked the look. Perhaps she wasn't exactly pretty, but no one would direct her to the men's room.

When Allen returned he let out a soft whistle. "That's more like it." His smile showed his admiration and lifted her spirits. "Okay, sit down." He waved toward the chair in front of the mirror and she noticed for the first time he held a hair blower in one hand, the cord trailing on the floor behind him. She'd never used one before and after her disastrous attempt to unlock the styling mystery of the curling iron, she eyed the blow dryer warily.

"It won't bite and I've used one for years on my own hair." He plugged it in and with one hand on her shoulder nudged her into the chair.

The warm air and a stiff brush lifting and turning her hair had a soothing effect. Slowly she relaxed and watched in amazement as Allen coaxed her hair into soft waves. She was lucky to be with Allen. What he was doing to her hair bordered on being a miracle. Another man would probably have laughed at her, but not Allen. And she suspected there weren't many men who could have chosen an outfit she truly felt comfortable in, especially for her first attempt at dressing like a woman.

"Okay, what do you think?" He turned off the blower and watched her reflection in the mirror. A look of awe appeared in her eyes and she smiled back at his reflected image. She could scarcely believe the woman in the mirror was herself. She liked what she saw and wished she knew a way to let him know how much she appreciated both the transformation he'd wrought and the gentle accepting way he'd allowed her to salvage her pride.

Carefully she stood, keeping her eyes on the mirror. "Thank you." She wanted to say more, but the lump in her throat made speech impossible.

"Just one more thing." Allen grinned and pulled a small tube from his pocket. He held her chin in the palm of one hand and gently stroked a shiny lip balm on her lips. His fingers were warm and his face hovered inches from her own.

The tube stilled against her mouth and his eyes met hers. The sparkling laughter, there only seconds ago, disappeared to be replaced by something profoundly silent, deep, and compelling. She felt drawn to him as though connected by an invisible string. He was going to kiss her. She wanted him to kiss her. Her eyes drifted shut of their own volition.

Allen's hand dropped away from her face and she heard him clear his throat. Her eyes flew open to see him beat a hasty retreat across the room.

"Ah, what time does church start?"

Stunned, his words didn't register for just a moment. Disappointment warred with excitement as she mentally switched gears.

"You'll take me to church?" She almost stammered the words.

"Well, you're all dressed up. I'd hate to see all that effort go to waste." Laughter was back in his voice, but he didn't meet her eyes again until some time later.

Allen felt like a rat as he escorted Holland from the Fairbanks stake center several hours later. The distant sun beamed through a few lingering clouds, belying the previous night's brief storm, and turned the dusting of snow to muddy puddles. He looked at Holland's face and noted the glow of happiness he was about to shatter. He still hadn't gotten up the courage to tell her he was taking her to the airport, but he would. He'd do the right thing if it killed him. And it just might kill him at that. He'd never been more tempted to toss aside all considerations of her youth and innocence, her grief, and his responsibility. It would be so easy to return to the hotel, not saying a word about her airplane reservation, instead of taking her to the airport as he had planned.

Attending church meant a lot to her, and he had to admit it hadn't been too bad. There had been a few bad moments when one of the speakers spoke about the redemption of the dead and he'd become concerned she'd start grieving for Hank again, but in a way she'd seemed to take comfort from the words. He realized with a start that he'd not only enjoyed church, but he'd enjoyed Holland's company. He hated to spoil what had turned out to be a pleasant day.

If he were perfectly honest he'd have to admit that for him personally there had been a pleasant sense of returning to a simpler, more peaceful time as he sat on the padded bench listening to the hymns of his youth. He'd been surprised to discover the Fairbanks church wasn't much different from the ward houses he'd attended in Salt Lake.

His thoughts had drifted to Brad and Doug and a sense of peace had enveloped him as he thought of their friendship, a friendship that had endured since their shared childhood when the two bigger boys had rescued him from a playground bully. They'd hiked, skied, studied, played ball, dated, and gone to church together. Not until Megan entered their lives had their friendship temporarily faltered.

Thoughts of Megan brought a twinge of sadness, but the pain was gone now and he experienced a quiet confirmation that his facilitating Megan's return to her husband had not only been right, but had brought Megan far more happiness than he could have given her.

"Thank you for taking me to church," Holland whispered, breaking into his thoughts. "I know you didn't want to go but I'm glad you changed your mind."

"I enjoyed it." To his surprise he meant it. He'd enjoyed seeing Holland turn into a butterfly, maybe a little too much. He'd almost kissed her back in her hotel room before good sense had intruded. And he had enjoyed sitting beside her through sacrament meeting and Sunday School. He didn't know if it was Holland's presence or the service itself, but he'd felt a peace in that chapel that had eluded him for a long time.

"Where are we going now?" Holland asked as she snapped her seat belt into place in the car Allen had rented before leaving the hotel.

Allen tightened his fingers on the steering wheel. The time had come. He'd ignored her questions when he'd handed her a bag and told her to pack her things before leaving for church. He couldn't ignore her now. Her plane would leave in an hour. He started the engine and pulled onto the street before answering.

"I'm taking you to the airport." He kept his voice calm and even. When she made no response, he glanced quickly sideways at her face. He'd expected anger, but he found hurt and sadness. Finally she spoke.

"I won't go, you know."

"Holland, be reasonable. You'll be safer in Salt Lake and I can search faster by myself."

"No, you can't. You need me. Besides it isn't safe for one person to travel alone."

"Just say the word," he spoke impatiently. "And I'll pack up both your stuff and mine, sell the truck and tools, and catch the first flight to Salt Lake where I'll place the money from the sale in your anxious little hand and you won't have to worry about me traveling alone."

"I can't sell the truck," Holland gasped.

"Surely you don't plan to continue your father's business!" He hadn't considered that possibility before. Did she plan to support herself as a mechanic?

"I could if I wanted to." There went her stubborn chin. He hadn't meant to offend her and he'd be the first to admit she probably could succeed as a mechanic. Something inside him balked at picturing her in men's clothing and continuing her father's vagabond life.

"I thought you wanted to go to school." He grasped at the first argument that entered his head and slowed for the airport entrance.

"I do. That's why I have to find the truck." She touched his arm, and he didn't miss the plea in her voice.

"You're not making sense. What does the truck have to do with going to school?"

"That's where Hank hid . . . Stop! Allen, stop!" Her grip tightened on his arm and her voice turned shrill as she screamed. Startled he swerved to the edge of the road and slammed on the brakes.

"Are you trying to get us killed?" he roared. "I don't care what kind of tantrum you throw, you're getting on that plane and that's that!"

"Look!" She ignored his outburst and pointed toward the fence in front of them. He followed her pointing finger and stared in astonishment. The truck, Hank's truck, sat dead ahead in the airport long-term parking lot.

"We found it!" Laughter and excitement tinged Holland's words. She squeezed his arm tighter and leaned her forehead against his shoulder. He felt like whooping with his own laughter and cheers. He wrapped his other arm around her in a fierce hug and suddenly her arms slipped around his waist and he turned to hold her in both arms. Soft and comfortable, she fit perfectly. It was the most natural thing in the world to bend his head toward hers.

He was losing his mind. Roughly he set Holland away from him. What was the matter with him? He couldn't kiss Holland. She was Hank's kid, he reminded himself. No, she wasn't exactly a kid, but she was thirteen years younger than him and naive and vulnerable. She had dreams of going to college and no doubt those dreams included school dances, dorm parties, and boyfriends. Living the way she had, she'd had no experience with dating, no first kiss. He couldn't take advantage of her newly discovered femininity. He had no right to regret that he wouldn't be the boy who would bring her flowers, hold her in the moonlight, and give her her first kiss.

"Allen?" He hated seeing the happiness leave her eyes to be replaced by a cloud of uncertainty.

"We better call the police and claim your truck before the thieves return." He shifted gears and pulled back onto the road.

Light had gone out of the day by the time the police finally released the truck to them. They also verified that a man with the same name as the one on the gasoline charge slip Allen had found in the pickup truck and a companion had boarded a plane for Vancouver the previous morning. The officers insisted he and Holland check the truck thoroughly for any missing items and promised the department would follow up on the gasoline charge receipts he'd found, but Allen suspected that now the truck was back in its rightful owner's hands, no one would expend a lot of effort searching for the thieves.

When the only things missing appeared to be food, Allen signed the clipboard produced by one officer and watched them walk away.

Holland continued to move around the truck, counting soda pop cans, peering in toolboxes, and running her fingers across cushions with a dazed, half-scared expression on her face.

"What's the matter?" Allen asked. "Do you think we missed something? I could still call the officers back."

"No! I don't know. Hank never told me where he hid it and everything is such a mess." Her eyes traveled around the small space in dismay. The thieves had helped themselves to cans and packages, then left the wrappers where they fell. The beds were unmade and dirty dishes cluttered the table and small sink. Doors and drawers hung open with their contents spilling out.

"Hid what?" Allen asked as he reached for the dirty plates on the table. Carefully stacking them, he carried them to the sink before turning back to Holland, catching a strange expression on her face.

"Nothing." She hesitated. "Nothing important. Just some papers." She appeared agitated as she fumbled with a broom and began sweeping a bit too vigorously.

Allen watched her for several minutes. She was hiding something from him. Was it something important enough to insist she tell him or was she simply excited and confused over the sudden recovery of the truck? He knew that people who came home to find their homes trashed by burglars often felt insecure for a long time, and frequently suffered from a sense of violation. Holland might be experiencing much the same feelings. He wouldn't hassle her for answers. What she needed was to see the truck cleaned and returned to its former orderly condition.

The roar of an engine overhead reminded him Holland had missed her flight. Frowning, he squirted detergent into the sink and chapter six

Allen set down the bucket and flexed his fingers before opening the door. A hose ran into the truck's water reservoir, but neither he nor Holland had wanted to wait for the tank to fill and heat before getting on with cleaning. He'd volunteered to haul hot water from the campground services building while Holland took advantage of the laundry room to wash and dry bedding and towels. He hoisted the bucket inside and headed for the sink.

While he washed dishes and scrubbed woodwork, he found himself making frequent trips to the door to look for Holland. She wasn't late; he just didn't like the idea of her being alone in the laundry room. He wanted to be certain that if anyone dropped in on her, he'd know it and be able to get to her quickly.

What was the matter with him? He chastised himself when he poked his head out for the tenth time. Holland wasn't exactly helpless, so why did she stir such strong protective instincts in him?

A dark shape materialized in the doorway of the small building. His pulse accelerated and he couldn't blame the dishwater for his damp palms. He recognized Holland's silhouette and knew with blinding clarity that he was in for another sleepless night. Of all the women he'd known, dated, and flirted with, why did this one invoke such strong feelings in him?

And why should it matter so much? He was thirty-three years old, for crying out loud, and celibacy wasn't exactly the rage these days. Several women had nearly enticed him to cross that line, but something had always held him back. He knew what that something was. A promise—a silly childish promise he and Doug and Brad had made to each other seventeen years ago that they would wait for marriage. Both of his friends had married young, but Allen had never found a woman he wanted to settle down with—except Megan, and she'd always been out of reach. Now he probably never would marry.

Holland's shoulders stooped as she struggled with the load she carried. He started toward her to lend a hand. No, it wasn't because of an old promise that he had to keep his relationship with Holland platonic. She deserved better. She had a right to find that good Mormon man her father wanted her to marry and marry him in the temple. He wouldn't be responsible for shattering her dreams. If it killed him, he'd get her to Salt Lake and into her aunt's keeping safely. He hurried to meet her, relieving her of part of the load she carried.

"Thanks," she said. "I'm bushed. Let's just make the beds and get some sleep. We can finish up in the morning before we start out."

"I'm taking you back to the airport as soon as it's light," he blurted out and watched her recoil. But day after day of sharing the cab of the truck, followed by night after night of sleeping less than three feet from her, was just asking for trouble. And he wasn't looking for trouble.

Holland fell into an immediate deep sleep as soon as she lay down, but awoke a couple of hours later to stare sightlessly into the dark above her bunk. She couldn't let Allen send her on to Salt Lake without first discovering where Hank had hidden his small cache of gold and coins. As long as she could remember he'd sent a small portion of his checks to the bank in Salt Lake, but had kept the larger part for their living expenses. Every payday he'd emptied his pockets of the bills and coins he had left from the last check and stuffed them into bottles and cans. She remembered a long, lonely time in Nevada when she'd played with a shoe box full of silver dollars.

They'd been in Alaska for more than six years and during all that time Hank had spent his spare time panning in the icy streams near where they camped. Sometimes he'd found gold. On several occasions he'd shown her a particularly fine nugget. She had no idea how much gold her father had accumulated, but she suspected it was a considerable amount.

Where were the dollars and the gold now? Hank had been secretive about his hiding place, and had continuously reminded her that while the few thousand in the bank wouldn't last long, his hidden store would buy them a house and pay her way through college, if that was what she wanted.

She had to find Hank's hiding place. As soon as daylight came she'd begin her search in earnest, but she couldn't just start tapping on walls and pulling up floorboards. Allen would demand to know what she was hunting for. She frowned remembering his adamant insistence that she fly to Salt Lake. She'd have to tell him. She'd almost told him just before they found the truck, but could she trust him? She mulled the question over in her mind and finally concluded she had no choice but to trust him.

Honesty compelled her to admit that her reluctance to go to Salt Lake by herself was as much reluctance to leave him as need to find the gold. Over the past week she'd come to depend on him. She hadn't meant to become dependent on him and she certainly didn't want him to assume a fatherly role in her life; she just wanted to be with him. A wave of sadness swept over her. He didn't share her desire to be together. He obviously couldn't wait to be rid of her.

Sometimes she felt a bond between them and believed they were truly becoming friends. Other times he made it clear her presence irritated him and he had no desire to be her friend. She'd never had a real friend before. When she'd been small, Hank had always found a woman to watch her while he worked, sometimes another construction worker's wife, sometimes a woman from a nearby town, and sometimes there had been other children to play with. But they'd never been real friends and when she'd become a boy, there had been no more playmates either. Her friends became books and she hadn't minded the loss of other young people in her life for a long time.

Only during the past year or two had she begun to wish for another woman to talk with, and she'd started having dreams of a boyfriend as well. She'd fantasized about meeting a young man on a campus somewhere who would hold her hand, walk her to class, and at the end of the day kiss her good night at her door. She blushed recalling how the nebulous face of a stranger had disappeared during the past few days, and it was Allen's face she now saw in her dreams.

Her spirits lifted as she recalled those few crazy moments when he'd swung her around in the clearing after she'd gotten the truck started. He'd been angry for her when the police sergeant assumed she was a boy and he'd been helpful and supportive when she wanted to go to church. A happy warmth crept close to her heart when she remembered her appearance in the skirt and blouse he'd bought for her. He liked her; she was sure of that, but liking wasn't enough. She wanted more from him. How much more, she wasn't sure.

She wished he hadn't seen her first as a boy and she wished Hank hadn't told him she was a child. She had the distinct impression he was concerned about the difference in their ages. He was older; how much older she was unsure, but surely there wasn't enough difference in their ages for him to consider her a child now that he knew she was really twenty. Perhaps if she tried harder to look and act like a woman, he'd like her better.

She wondered where he'd learned about things like women's clothing sizes and how to fix hair. She sighed. He knew about clothes and hair and he'd pitched right in cleaning the truck and washing dishes, but he didn't know beans about truck engines. Before she could search for Hank's gold, she'd have to put her old clothes on and check out the engine. It would be hours, maybe days before she could think about being a woman again.

Allen climbed out of bed and pulled on a pair of sweats, then searched around until he found his running shoes and a ski cap. Holland was awake, he knew, but he didn't call out to her. She'd been restless for several hours and he wondered why she couldn't sleep. After all, she was back in her own bed. He'd be willing to bet her restlessness didn't stem from the same cause his did. A five-mile hike followed by a trip to the airport should cure his problem. At least he hoped it would.

Before leaving the truck, he wrote Holland a note letting her know his plans. His brisk walk in the sharp morning air became a run before he cleared the campground. A momentary doubt plagued him, making him wonder if Holland might leave without him to thwart his plans to fly her to her aunt. He dismissed the thought. Holland was too honest and straightforward for that kind of tactic in spite of her determination to stay with the truck. She was being extremely stubborn on that score. He wasn't sure why, but he suspected it was fear of the unknown that prompted her to stick to Hank's plan.

He ran beside the road to avoid the gravel and mentally regretted his promise to Hank. He'd like to sell the truck for Holland right here in Fairbanks, then fly with her back to Salt Lake City. He wanted to get on with his life. He smiled with a measure of relief, realizing that the reluctance he'd felt only a week ago to return to Salt Lake was gone. He'd seriously considered returning to Missoula where he'd worked for three years as a television cameraman, but television photography wasn't what he really wanted to do. Missoula was a beautiful city and the nearby Bitterroots were a photographer's dream, but he had no one there to return to. And that was the crux of the problem. He no longer wanted to be alone.

Startled by his own thoughts, he stopped running. Carefully he examined his feelings. Warm memories, a gentle fondness, were all that was left of his feelings for Megan. He looked forward to seeing her again. She would always be a cherished friend, but it no longer pained him to know she loved Doug. For the first time his heart told him what his head had figured out a long time ago. Megan belonged with Doug. He'd finally stopped imagining Megan and her son, Jason, beside him in the years ahead, but now there was an empty space in his heart that could only be filled by a wife and child of his own. He smiled wryly. He'd heard of women having a nesting instinct, but it seemed men were subject to the same malady if his sudden desire to settle in one place and have a family of his own were anything to go by.

Whistling between his teeth, he began to run again. It felt good to use his long muscles. As he ran, his thoughts raced ahead, tumbling over each other in their eagerness to get on with the future. He would open his own studio in the Salt Lake valley. He'd had his own studio once before in San Antonio, but this studio would be different. In Texas he'd done mostly fashion and cosmetic ads for a number of slick magazines. This time he wanted to concentrate on nature, and the work he'd done this past year would place him solidly in the field he wanted. A quick glance upward and a hasty "thank you" didn't come close to expressing the joy he felt over the return of his camera equipment and film.

Of course, he'd still do people shots. He'd hire assistants to do the standard studio portraits, while he chose for himself those opportunities to capture life's mileposts—the christenings, bar mitzvahs, weddings, and golden anniversaries. The old people holding to cherished traditions and the very young chasing new dreams. And he'd photograph Holland when she was happy and when she was sad. He'd photograph her with grease on her nose and with a baby in her ar . . . Now wait a minute, he told himself. His imagination was working overtime. Once he put Holland on a plane for Seattle, he didn't intend to ever see her again. Well, he'd have to check up on her once he got to Salt Lake, make sure she was okay, but no more.

Holland debated fixing breakfast or starting her search. According to the note Allen had left, he'd be gone at least an hour. She'd better start searching. But where to start?

Her eyes slowly traversed the snug living quarters. The padded benches on either side of the table opened into two deep storage chests. The gold couldn't be there. She was familiar with every item in them. The deep drawers under her bunk and the kitchen cupboards didn't need to be searched either. She'd already cleaned out the drawers under Hank's bunk for Allen to use, so they could be eliminated as well.

Hank's hiding place had to be easily accessible, since he'd been adding to his cache for years. If it was in a wall or behind the bunk drawers or even in the floor, there had to be a door or panel Hank had been able to open and close at frequent intervals. She began moving around the room, tapping lightly on each panel. They all sounded the same to her.

She stared around the room thoughtfully until her eyes lit on Allen's parka draped over a bench. He'd left it behind. She'd peeked through the curtain and seen him bundled in sweats and running shoes before he left the truck. He must have decided the parka would be too much. She picked up the coat, and almost of its own volition, her hand gently stroked the fleece pile of the lining. Lifting it to her face, she breathed in Allen's unique scent, stirring new and exciting feelings deep within her.

She was being foolish, she chided herself. She'd hang up the coat instead of mooning over it, and get back to her search. Opening the tiny closet, she fumbled for a wire hanger, and wrestled the bulky parka onto it. As she slid the hanger onto the rod, Allen's wallet fell from his coat pocket. She stooped to retrieve it and that's when she saw a picture and a driver's license lying on the floor. They must have fallen out of the wallet. A sudden premonition warned her not to look at the picture. In an attempt to ignore it, she studied Allen's license and learned he was thirty-three years old. Thirteen years older than herself. She had a strange feeling that thirteen years was both a vast difference and nothing at all. He had just turned thirty-three and she would soon be twenty-one, so the difference was more like twelve than thirteen, she reasoned as she continued to study the small document, but the photo wouldn't be ignored. Slowly her eyes shifted.

The face staring back at her from the closet floor belonged to the most beautiful woman Holland had ever seen. Her heart-shaped face with its perfect nose and silver-blue eyes was framed by white-blond curls. The young woman looked sad and pensive, making Holland suspect the picture had been taken while its subject was totally unaware of the photographer. The photo was haunting and magic, and with a sinking sensation, Holland knew the photographer loved the woman. This was a picture of the woman Allen loved.

Slowly Holland lowered herself to sit on the floor. She cradled the wallet in one hand, but she couldn't bring herself to pick up the picture. Who was she? Was she waiting for him to return to her? Was she his wife? Or sweetheart? Sweetheart was an old-fashioned word no one used anymore. Was the lovely, fragile woman Allen's lover? All the word implied brought an ache to her heart, and a silent tear slid down her cheek.

Allen found her like that. She was oblivious to his return until he crouched beside her and she found herself longing to throw herself in his arms. He was the cause of her ache, yet instinctively she knew only he could take away the hurt.

"What's going on?" He spoke quietly. And just as silently she handed him his wallet. He turned it over several times in his hands, then his eyes met hers and she read the question there.

"I was hanging up your parka and it fell onto the floor."

"Is there something about my wallet that upset you?" He sounded concerned. "Did you think I would accuse you of stealing it?"

"N-no," she stammered and her eyes wandered to the picture on the floor. His gaze followed hers and his features seemed to freeze.

"I didn't snoop. It fell out."

"It's okay." He reached for the picture and slipped it back into his wallet.

"Allen?" She hated herself for asking, but she had to know. "Who is she?"

He took so long answering, she thought he was going to ignore her question. Finally he spoke, simply and quietly, " A friend."

"Do you love her?"

Again he took his time answering. "Yes, I love her, but I'm not *in* love with her."

She wasn't certain she believed him or what the distinction meant. How could he not be in love with a woman that beautiful? Hesitantly she asked one more question, "Is she your lover?" She wished she hadn't asked. Allen's relationship with the mysterious woman was none of her business, but something compelled her to ask.

"Lover?" Allen arched an eyebrow and grinned at her. "You're getting kind of personal, aren't you?"

"I'm sorry," she mumbled, her cheeks aflame.

"It's okay," he laughed. "No, we were never lovers and if it will satisfy that curious mind of yours, I'll go so far as to tell you I've never slept with any woman."

"Is that true?"

"You doubt my word?" He seemed to enjoy her discomfort, and she wished she'd never started this conversation or could at least control her wayward mouth. "Or do you think I'm that irresistible?" He quirked an eyebrow and twirled an imaginary mustache. Suddenly she was laughing, too. She wanted to believe him, and believing unexpectedly brightened her day. Playfully she punched his chest and he tumbled backward whacking his head against a cupboard door.

"Are you okay?" She scrambled after him.

"Fine." He rubbed the back of his head. "But I could use something to drink if you're all through interrogating me about my love life—or absence thereof."

"There's juice, but it isn't cold. I didn't restock the cooler last night," she apologized.

"All I care about is wet."

"Do you want a cold cloth for your head, too?" She reached out to smooth her fingers across the back of his head, searching for a lump. Her hand encountered silky hair and she fought an urge to run her fingers through its rich, dark thickness.

"No, just the juice." His voice sounded unusually deep in her ear and she felt an urge to pull his head closer. Instead her fingers stilled and he eased away from her and rose to his feet. He turned his back to her, leaving her feeling suddenly bereft.

"The juice? Just tell me where it is and I'll get it myself."

"No, no, I'll get it." She pulled open a cupboard door and reached inside, blindly groping for a can. The thieves had obviously helped themselves. The shelf was nearly empty. Her fingers closed around a can that she passed awkwardly to Allen's waiting hand.

"What the . . . ?" He muttered something else under his breath, but Holland wasn't listening. A thought too black and ugly to be true kept nudging all other thoughts aside. It wouldn't be denied. Allen said he'd never slept with a woman, he was thirty-three years old, he carefully avoided any physical contact with her, he didn't want to travel with her, and he knew all kinds of woman things. Was Allen gay? No! No! No! Her mind screamed its denial. That would be too cruel.

Just then something small and sharp struck her head. A cloud of dust settled in her hair, on her shirt, and fluttered to the floor. She lifted her head to see Allen shaking the inverted juice can. No cascade of juice spilled to the floor. Instead small specks of gold glittered in the early morning light.

With one arm extended in the suspended act of shaking the can, Allen struggled to assimilate what his eyes were telling him. Holland's hair and skin glittered with a fine dusting of gold. Gold! It had to be gold. Nothing else held the same glitter. Tiny flecks glistened even on her eyelashes. A sudden memory of the dream he'd had of Holland playing in a shower of gold replayed in his mind. She looked like some ancient goddess covered with gold, sitting there on the floor with her back to the cupboard and her arms wrapped around her drawn-up knees, but even as the thought ricocheted through his brain his body reminded him she was a real, flesh and blood woman.

"You found it," she faintly breathed the words.

"I found it? I didn't find anything; I didn't even know anything was lost! It was in this can you handed me." He lowered his hand and examined the can more closely. "Darndest grapefruit juice I ever saw!" He grinned roguishly at her. "I just might change my opinion of the stuff."

Holland grinned back. "Hank has been panning gold for six years. He told me he'd hidden it in the truck and if I didn't find it before we got to Salt Lake, I'd find instructions for locating it in his safe deposit box at his bank."

"Why did he put it in a grapefruit juice can? Wouldn't you have found it sooner or later?"

"I can't stand grapefruit juice. He knew I'd never open a can for myself."

"This is the second time you tried to foist it off on me." His attempt to sound aggrieved failed miserably as a silly grin split his face.

"This time was an accident. I just handed you the first can I came to. The first time, I was thinking of Hank and handed you what he always chose." He didn't miss the flicker of sadness in her eyes when she spoke of her father or the small sigh she gave as she traced a finger across the gold dust that littered the floor.

"I guess we better clean this up."

She started to rise, but he placed one hand on her shoulder and told her to stay put. "We have to reclaim as much of this dust as we can," he reminded her. "Got any idea how we go about getting it off us and the floor and back in the can?"

She was silent for a moment. "Why don't you pull the plastic tablecloth off the table and we can take turns shaking ourselves off on it," she suggested.

Allen went first. After brushing as much of the gold dust off as he could, he removed his shirt and gently shook it over the cloth, then turned to help Holland. Methodically he brushed her clothes, then her hair. She shivered when he pulled her head back against his chest, and he felt an answering response. It was a good thing they'd found the gold because now she wouldn't need to stay with the truck. She would no longer fight his decision to fly her back to Salt Lake. They could sell the truck and go their separate ways. The thought didn't cheer him as much as it should have.

chapter seven

"How could you think that can held juice? Didn't you notice how heavy it was?" Allen queried Holland as she pulled another can from the lower shelf for him to set on the table. That made six. He shook his head in disbelief. "What are you going to do with it? It's not like you can run around Salt Lake City with a can full of gold dust to do your shopping!"

"There's an assay office here in Fairbanks. I could convert the gold to cash right here or wait until we get to Dawson." She dusted her hands together and rose to her feet. "I think that's all of the gold, the rest of the cans hold juice or soda pop."

"I wonder how much it's worth." Allen weighed a can thoughtfully in one hand, testing its weight. "I think you'd better convert it here and have the money wired to your account in Salt Lake. It's not a good idea to keep anything this valuable lying around. I get cold chills when I think of our truck thieves driving around with all this gold right beneath their noses and how lucky you are that they didn't like grapefruit juice either."

"Well, they certainly seemed to like everything else just fine! If we ever run into them we should be able to recognize them by their size. The pigs went through two weeks' worth of groceries and snacks in three days!" She paused. "You don't think they found any of the gold, do you?"

She looked so concerned it required all of his willpower to refrain from hugging her while he assured her that if the thieves had found one can of gold, they would have torn the truck apart looking for more. The six cans now resting on the table would have been long gone.

"Okay, give me a few minutes to shower and shave, then we can hunt up that assayer's office. Once that's taken care of, I'd suggest we find a buyer for the truck and purchase a couple of airline tickets." Allen grinned happily at her. As soon as they got to Utah, he'd put as much distance as possible between them. Maybe then he could get a full night's sleep and get his mind back on his work.

"I can't." Holland looked nervous and apologetic, but he recognized the tilt of her chin. She wouldn't give in easily.

"But Holland," he argued. "You've got the gold. Isn't that the reason you didn't want to leave the truck?"

"Yes." She dragged the word out as though reluctant to admit as much. "But this isn't all of it."

"You mean there's more gold?" He stared at her incredulously.

"I don't know. There might be more gold, but I think it's mostly coins and paper money." She twirled a juice can between her palms and her eyes didn't meet his. "Hank has been hiding money for a long time." In a small voice she told him about the cache her father had been adding to for years. "He said it was 'dream insurance' so some day I could have a home high on a hill where I could look out and see the world, like a carpet of stars spread out before me."

He stared at her for long minutes. Why hadn't Hank kept his money in a bank? But then, hadn't he already figured out that Hank had never done the conventional thing? Take Holland's name, for example.

"Why did Hank name you Holland?" Allen continued his thoughts out loud.

Holland looked startled at the abrupt change of subject, but she laughed and told him. "You can't blame my name on Hank. My mother named me. Hank said my mother's father didn't want her to marry Hank, and he never would call him by name. Grandpa always referred to Hank as 'that hardheaded Dutchman' because Hank was the most stubborn man he'd ever met. My parents couldn't agree on a name for me so I went home from the hospital without one. Two weeks later Mamma told Hank she'd named me and there was nothing he could do about it. Since I was just as stubborn as my father, she thought I should be named after him. Besides, she'd always dreamed of visiting Holland where she imagined the tulip fields must be the most beautiful sight on earth."

"I see," Allen spoke thoughtfully. "But after you were born, you became her most beautiful sight on earth, her Holland."

She ducked her head in silent acknowledgment.

Allen knew that he and Holland would have to stay with the truck to search it thoroughly and that could take days. Every panel, cushion, and toolbox would have to be checked. He'd be with Holland night and day until the money was found and her finances put in order. He should be disappointed. Strangely, he was not. Spending so much time alone with Holland might not be a good idea, but he recognized a sense of relief that he wouldn't have to tell her good-bye for a little bit longer.

"I think we'd better find a more private camping spot," he spoke at last. "I don't think we want to risk anyone watching us dismantle this truck."

"You're right. There's a good place not far from here where we can park the truck. There aren't any hookups, so we'll have to use the generator, but it's far enough off the road we won't be seen or heard."

"No water?"

"Not for drinking, but there's a stream we can use for everything else."

Allen grimaced at her naive trust to blithely make plans to camp in an isolated spot with a man she'd known less than a week. He suspected she suffered from a mild case of hero worship, and though the thought was flattering, it placed an extra burden on him to avoid disillusioning her before she reached Salt Lake and had an opportunity to meet other men, men far more deserving of being her hero.

Allen stepped off the trail and made his way slowly to the stream. Thin streamers of pale morning light shone through the trees, dappling the water with rainbow-hued circles. He'd run close to ten miles, but his thoughts were still firmly centered on Holland. They'd been here two days now and nothing had gotten any easier. Long runs and cold dips in the creek weren't helping.

While they removed panels, unpicked cushions, and shook books and cans, Holland bombarded him with questions about Salt Lake City and the university. She had an insatiable thirst for knowledge and an intense curiosity about everything, including him. They joked and laughed, or discussed books and theories more seriously, but sometimes when Holland didn't know he was watching her, he caught a look of longing in her eyes, a kind of melancholy sadness, and he wondered if more than the loss of her father troubled her.

Last night she'd put on the skirt he'd bought for her and asked him to teach her how to blow dry her hair. For two days he'd taken meticulous care to avoid touching her, even accidentally. He should have claimed he was too tired, but he hadn't.

She was trying so hard to prepare herself for her new life and that included learning all she could about dressing and acting like a female. Unfortunately, the lifestyle Hank had chosen for her had prevented the usual adjustments a young woman makes in becoming secure with her own sexual identity. She had no idea how appealing he found her innocent struggle toward womanhood. Nor how much he feared his own reaction to her.

He'd sensed she was asking for more than a lesson in hairstyling and that were he to refuse she would feel personally rejected in some way. He'd had enough rejection in his life himself. He couldn't bear to hurt Holland.

He had shown her the settings, how to hold the blower, and how to twist the brush just right. Her hair felt like silk between his fingers and he found his hands lingering on her shoulders and against the back of her neck. He ached to shut off the blower, pull her close against him, and kiss her. Instead he'd cut the lesson short. The feelings Holland aroused in him might be inevitable and perfectly normal, but what he did with those feelings was up to him. He could and would control his response to her.

A sleepless night and a ten-mile run had brought him to this point. He sank down by a broken tree stump and let his head sink against the rotting bark. He needed help. Brad would tell him to pray. Even Holland would tell him to pray. But did he even remember how? And did he have sufficient faith?

Bright sunlight filtered through the trees making the recent snow flurry seem a distant memory. A hush settled around him and slowly the peaceful glen soaked into his soul, reviving the quiet truths of his childhood. Yes, the faith was there under all those layers of cynicism. A flash of brutal honesty forced him to admit his sporadic violations of the

Word of Wisdom were nothing more than a pathetic attempt to make his parents notice him. The lack of sexual encounters in his life went beyond an old promise; deep down he believed in premarital chastity. His attempt to live a sophisticated lifestyle was bravado, a means of forestalling the pity his friends would feel if they knew he was jealous of them; of the parents, wives, and children who loved them. What he really wanted, what he'd always wanted was to be part of a family, a close-knit family that worked, played, and yes, prayed together.

An idea began to form in his head. He could have that, too. He could begin a family with Holland. He was attracted to her, and he didn't think she was completely indifferent to him. Anyway, he'd begun to suspect Hank's real intention in making him responsible for his daughter and his insistence on their making the long journey to Salt Lake together in the truck was an attempt to manipulate them into marriage. If Allen encouraged the attraction between them and capitalized on Holland's insecurity, he could make her increasingly dependent on him. He could marry her before she met other men, before she discovered she was a beautiful woman, before she discovered he wasn't hero material.

But he wouldn't. She had a right to her dreams and she wouldn't fulfill those dreams if he denied her the opportunity to spread her wings and discover her own world. She was too young for him anyway; perhaps not so much in years, but in experience. The world was fresh and new to her while he'd seen humanity at its worst, knew how far askew justice could go, and knew firsthand that dreams didn't come true.

"Father," he began tentatively, then glanced around the small clearing to ascertain that he was alone. "Father, I seem to have a talent for wanting what I can't have. Please help me to keep Holland's needs above my desires. Help me to quickly find Hank's treasure and get her safely to Salt Lake, and I'd appreciate it if you'd let her have a good life and the chance to learn all those things she's so anxious to study. And when she's ready for marriage," he stumbled on the words, "help her to find a man with faith as great as hers."

As he imagined Holland dressed in white entering the Salt Lake Temple beside a tall stranger, Allen felt an agonizing pain in the vicinity of his heart.

Holland eyed the shop portion of the truck with a critical eye. There weren't many places left to search. She'd already gone through all the tools and checked each chest for a false bottom. Other than an old salmon can nailed to the workbench to hold bolts, washers, and paper clips, which ran over with pennies, there was no sign of Hank's stash. Was it possible he had spent the silver dollars?

No. He'd told her only hours before he died that the money was in the truck.

She wasn't getting anywhere looking for the money, and the truck engine still needed a thorough going-over before they started the long drive south. She might as well start on it now and cross her fingers that she could convince Allen to resume their trip and they could hunt for the money as they traveled. Besides, searching the truck was more enjoyable with Allen's help. By the time she finished looking at the engine, he should be back from his run.

Frowning, she picked up the tools she would need. Allen spent too much time running. He was losing weight and his face had a strained look. Instinctively she knew he wasn't running strictly for exercise. She had an uneasy feeling he was running from her. He didn't have to. If he didn't like women, there was nothing she could do about it. She certainly couldn't force herself on him. She wouldn't, even if she knew how. Look where her attempt to get him to notice her last night had led! Nowhere! He couldn't wait to end any contact with her. Knowing he couldn't bear her slightest touch twisted her heart. What kind of cruel fate had let her fall in love with a man who preferred his own kind?

She'd met several gay men since she'd assumed her boy impersonation and knew they ran the gamut from hard-working, pleasant people to overbearing bullies, no better and no worse than other men. At first their overtures had frightened and disgusted her. Gradually she had learned that most were lonely and insecure men. Some were belligerently defensive of their lifestyle while some were frightened and secretive. Hank had helped her understand that morality wasn't a question of orientation. God forbade intimate physical relationships between any parties except husband and wife.

Holland didn't like thinking of Allen as immoral. Something about him seemed too fine. Besides it was none of her business and here she was wasting time. The best thing she could do would be to quickly check the engine, make certain the spare tires had the correct air pressure, then organize Hank's tools. The sooner she and Allen were on their way, the sooner she could end their painful relationship, but it would take a long time, perhaps her whole life, to forget him.

The engine didn't require much attention. She added a can of oil and refilled the windshield washer reservoir. Tires were next on her agenda, and she worked her way with a tire gauge down the rack of tires Hank kept in the truck. The first six were identical, but the seventh made her pause.

It wouldn't fit the truck, nor any piece of equipment she was familiar with around their previous construction site. It might be a farm tractor wheel, or it might . . . A premonition crawled up the back of her neck. She knew what she would find when she applied the tire iron to where the rubber fit against the metal rim. She pressed down and coins slithered across the floor. She'd found Hank's secret stash!

She laughed out loud. Wait 'til she showed Allen! Scooping up the coins lying on the floor, she shoved two handfuls into her pockets, before heading for the door. She knew where Allen would be.

A bend in the stream and a thick grove of trees hid a small pool of water from the clearing where they'd parked the truck. Allen would end his run there with a dip in the icy water. She shivered thinking about the pool. It was so cold it made her bones ache. It would be a miracle if he didn't catch pneumonia from jumping into the pool after running for an hour or more every morning!

Holland skidded to a stop with Allen's name frozen on her lips as she entered the clearing. Standing waist-high in the water, Allen quickly submerged his head and shoulders below the surface. In seconds his head bobbed back up and with both hands he sluiced the water off his face and slicked back his hair. The droplets of water flew from him, shimmering in the air like diamonds.

Holland wanted to cry. What kind of cruel trick was nature playing on her to show her a man who was good and kind and hand-some, then make him incapable of returning her feelings?

Regret turned to anger. She'd found the money. There was nothing to prevent them leaving now. She could go to school, attend parties and dances, do all the things she'd dreamed of during her long, lonely years growing up, but none of it mattered now. She didn't want to do those things without Allen. He'd ruined it all.

"Allen!" His name tore from her throat.

His back straightened and he turned to look at her. He lifted one hand to shade his eyes. "Are you all right?" He sounded concerned, but she could only stare at him. She hated herself for wanting more of him than he could give. She hated him! No, she loved him and that made her hate him more.

"I found the money." Her voice sounded flat and toneless to her own ears. She should be jumping and shouting with happiness, not entertaining a dull ache in her chest.

"Great!" He grinned broadly and began wading toward her, only to stop, and look hesitantly at his clothes lying scattered across a rock beside the stream. "Run back to the truck, and I'll be there in a minute."

"You can get out. It doesn't matter."

"All right, turn your back." She could see his teeth chattering. A perverse streak of meanness had her suddenly wanting him to suffer. She wanted him to hurt as badly as she hurt.

"And if I don't?" she taunted.

"You're playing with fire." He took another step closer.

"Fire?" She laughed, but there was no humor in her laughter. "I think we're talking about ice."

"What's the matter with you?" He looked perplexed. "This water is cold. If I don't get out of here pretty quick, hypothermia will start to set in."

"I'm not stopping you." She gestured grandly toward his clothes.

"All right, if you have no sense of modesty, why should I?" He began walking steadily toward the shore.

"Modesty!" She tried to laugh, but the sound strangled in her throat and she turned her head partially away so he wouldn't see the tears glittering in her eyes. "Modesty is entirely unnecessary between us, since it's only a social euphemism for politely refraining from arousing physical desire where it's inappropriate or unwanted. And since I already know you don't want me, why should I allow a little nudity to bother me?"

"You're crazy!" From the corner of her eye she saw him pause, nearly at the shore, and in spite of her bold words, she turned her head away in sudden shame. Yes, she probably was crazy. She'd been wrong to force Allen to choose between propriety and freezing to death. He'd respected her privacy when she didn't want to try on clothes in the department store, she should have extended the same courtesy to him. Taunting him only hurt herself.

"All right. What's this all about?" She hadn't heard his approach until his hand came down on her shoulder. His voice, coupled with his steel grip, told her he was angry. The tingle that went through her arm at his touch refueled her own anger in spite of the voice of reason reminding her he had a right to be angry.

"Don't touch me!" She struggled to escape his hold. His touch made a mockery of her romantic dreams. Between Hank and the many books she'd read, those dreams had been tempered with a recognition that love between a man and a woman, if it were to last, must consist of more than physical intimacy, but instinctively she knew nothing strong and enduring could come of a relationship where physical desire was absent—or one-sided.

Allen released her abruptly. "Don't worry," he snarled. "I may be angry, but I've never forced myself on a woman and I don't intend to start now."

"I-I know. I didn't mean . . ." Her anger crumbled. Shame and despair took its place. "I-I'm sorry." She couldn't meet his eyes. Instead she lowered hers and realized she'd made a mistake.

Allen didn't say anything for several minutes. When he did speak, tightly controlled anger was barely suppressed behind his words. "Go back to the truck. I'll be there in a minute."

She took a few steps, then stopped. She had to say something, make him understand, but how could she embarrass them both by admitting she loved him? She couldn't humiliate herself by telling a man who wasn't interested in women that she was attracted to him.

Her gaze followed Allen across the clearing to where he clumsily attempted to gather up his clothing. She saw a deep shudder go through him and she remembered his tightly clenched mouth as he spoke to her and the goose bumps on his skin. He was freezing. The slight breeze on his already wet and chilled skin was lowering his temperature further.

"Allen!" She ran to him, jerking her coat off as she ran. "I'm sorry, so sorry," she practically sobbed as she drew it around his shoulders. "Let me carry that." She relieved him of the awkward bundle he carried. Mindful of his bare feet, she urged him to hurry toward the truck. His steps were slow and awkward and with each step her guilt and fear grew.

Once inside the vehicle she helped him to his bunk and piled quilts on top of him.

"I'll make hot chocolate. No, you should shower and let the water get gradually warmer. Soup! I'll make some nice warm soup." She paced the floor beside his bunk.

"I'm all right. Stop fussing." A shiver belied his words.

"It's all my fault." She put a pan of already warm water on the burner. While it heated further, she cast worried glances toward the sleeping alcove. Allen lay still with his eyes closed. Hypothermia victims shouldn't be allowed to sleep. Hank had drilled that fact into her. Did he have hypothermia? The best thing to do might be to drive him back to the hospital in Fairbanks.

In minutes the water was hot enough to add chocolate powder and canned milk. She gave the mixture a quick stir before carrying it to Allen's bedside.

"Allen?" She whispered. When he didn't respond, she shook his blanket-draped shoulder and called louder, "Allen, wake up and drink this."

He mumbled and she thrust the cup against his mouth, sloshing some of the dark liquid onto the quilt and down his chin.

"What the . . . ?" he struggled to sit up, pushing the cup away as he did.

"You need to drink something hot." She held the cup out to him once more. He eyed her suspiciously, but accepted the cup. He tasted the chocolate and grimaced.

"First you try to freeze me to death, and now you're determined to scald me. What did I ever do to you?"

She felt chagrined. She hadn't tested the chocolate. The steam twisting above the cup should have warned her it was too hot. She didn't seem to be able to get anything right where Allen was concerned.

"I'll get more milk," she said in a subdued voice and turned her back to him. Blindly she reached for the milk can and it was a miracle that she didn't spill any as she added it to his drink, then she sat quietly on her own bunk while Allen drained his cup, never once taking his eyes from her.

"Well?" He made the word a question when she reached for his empty cup. "What's going on? Didn't you want to find Hank's money? And what did I do to make you mad enough to want me turned into a block of ice?" The scowl on his face told her she'd better come up with a reason fast.

"Yes, I wanted to find the money and I did. Hank hid it in one of the spare tires. I'd have never thought to look there, but I was getting the truck ready to go, and I decided I should check the air pressure in the spares and there it was. Now we can sell the truck and tools and leave if you want to." She knew she was babbling, answering only part of his question, and knew also that Allen was growing impatient with her stalling.

"And why do you suddenly hate me?" He wasn't going to let her off the hook.

"I don't hate you." She ducked her head.

"As I was standing chest-deep in glacier water, it certainly looked that way to me."

"I don't hate you. I don't think I could ever hate you," she mumbled.

"Then do you mind telling me what that was all about?"

Heat moved up the side of her neck and she couldn't look at him. "You were standing in the water and I-I . . ."

"Go on."

She could feel his gaze on her but she couldn't raise her head to meet his eyes.

"Why did that make you angry?" His voice dropped to a husky whisper.

"You know why."

"No, I don't. I think you'd better explain." Was he extracting some kind of revenge by making her say it straight out?

"Well, men like you don't . . . I mean . . . Maybe you can't help being the way you are, but I can't help . . . And I just thought it was all a waste and why did God . . ." She couldn't explain. If one of those secret doors she'd imagined in the floor suddenly opened up, she wouldn't mind a bit. She kept her eyes on the floor, just in case.

"What do you mean, men like me don't . . .? You know, you're not making a whole lot of sense." His voice took on a hard edge. A shaft of fire swept through her rekindling her anger.

"At first I thought you didn't like me because I'm not pretty and I dress like a boy. I was amazed you knew so much about women's clothes and how to fix hair. I didn't catch on when you told me you'd never slept with a woman." By this time she was shouting and tears were running down her cheeks.

"You better not be thinking what it sounds like you're saying." Allen's eyes narrowed and he spoke through clenched teeth.

"I'm sorry I acted so badly. I'm not really angry at you. I'm trying to understand, but I don't understand how you can. . . I thought you didn't like me because I don't know how to be a woman, and I was jealous of the waitress that first night in Fairbanks. I didn't know then you weren't interested in her—or any other woman."

"You think I'm gay?" Allen exploded to a sitting position and the quilt dropped to his lap. "Don't say one more word." One of Allen's hands grasped the back of her neck, drawing her face to within inches of his own.

"Being gay isn't the only reason some men abstain from sleeping with women." He enunciated each word carefully. "Believe it or not, some men have moral scruples."

"You told me you aren't religious, and you're past thirty. I never heard of any man waiting that long unless . . ."

"I should let you believe anything you want. It would be a lot safer that way, I'm sure. Maybe it's just my male ego speaking, or maybe I'm just tired of fighting." The harshly spoken words sent tiny puffs of air against her lips and shivers down her spine. She tried to pull back and he tugged her closer. His lips brushed hers and she opened her mouth to protest. For him to kiss her was a taunting cruelty.

Holland forgot everything but the pressure of his mouth against hers as he slowly drew her more firmly into his embrace. Little frissons of electricity sang through her veins and it didn't seem odd at all to feel wrapped in peace and shattering into a million fragments, all at the same time.

chapter eight

Far below, faint pinpricks of light appeared and disappeared. Pressing her nose against the glass, Holland watched the scattered points appear more frequently, merge into clusters, become towns, and then spread a carpet of lights as far as she could see. Their journey was coming to an end.

Taking her eyes from the window, she turned her attention to her sleeping companion. A rush of happiness swept through her as she viewed unobserved this man she loved. He slept with his head tipped back and his arms folded across his chest. His breath was deep and rhythmic. A shadow lay across his jaw, hinting he'd been away from his razor too long, and she felt an inexplicable longing to caress that stubble with her hand. She resisted the temptation. Allen obviously didn't approve of public demonstrations of affection. A wave of uncertainty assailed her. Perhaps it was her he didn't approve of.

Her thoughts returned to the morning he'd kissed her. The whole world had gone out of focus and she'd given no thought to right or wrong or even where their passion might lead them when he kissed her. She blushed now recalling that it had been Allen who had put on the brakes and gradually eased a space between them. Pushing her away gently, he lay back, then folded his arms across his chest, and shut his eyes, much as he was doing now. His breath had sounded harsh and he didn't speak for a long time. She'd felt a flicker of fear that she might have somehow hurt him.

"Lock everything down," he said deliberately. "We're heading back to Fairbanks." It was definitely an order, but it never occurred to her to contradict him. Her heart filled with gratitude at the sound of his voice. Everything was all right. She smiled now thinking everything was more than all right if that kiss was anything to go by.

He hadn't talked much on the trip back to Fairbanks, but he'd been solicitous of her welfare in the quiet way he'd handled converting her gold and coins to her bank account. He'd even understood her need to keep a few of the nuggets and silver dollars as keepsakes. He'd insisted she move to a hotel room while he found a buyer for the truck and Hank's tools. Unfortunately, that had meant there was no time for the two of them to be alone or to talk about what had happened between them. There had been no more kisses, no hugs, and the only time they'd touched in any way was the few minutes she'd grasped his hand when the plane had taken off from Fairbanks and again as they left Seattle.

It would be different when they reached Salt Lake. He hadn't referred to that kiss, or even to the events leading up to it, but she knew he had been as affected as she. She'd tried to apologize for her muddled assumption, but he didn't want to talk about it. He seemed intent on maintaining a careful distance between them, which was all right with her because she didn't want to risk too much intimacy before they married either. Once again uncertainty troubled her pleasant dream. Allen had never mentioned marriage and she might be placing too much importance on one kiss.

The "fasten your seat belts" signal came on, and she watched Allen groggily straighten his seat and snap the two ends of his belt together.

"Nervous?" he asked as her hands tightened against the armrests.

"A little," she admitted. Actually she felt extremely nervous and it wasn't just the landing that worried her. She remembered Allen saying his sister and a friend would meet them at the airport. His sister had promised to contact her aunt.

"Nothing to worry about," he smiled encouragingly and she wished he'd hold her for just a minute. "Soon you'll put all this behind you, start college, and begin an exciting new chapter of your life." His eyes held a hint of sadness and she wondered if she only imagined that look or if he too felt a twinge of regret that their time alone was coming to an end.

A shrill sound reached her ears and a solid thump alerted her when the plane touched down. Lights flew by at a dizzying speed, then gradually slowed as they taxied toward the terminal.

Carrying the small bag Allen had purchased for her in Fairbanks with one hand, she reached with the other for his arm as they entered the exit tunnel. A crowd waited at the end of the tunnel and she felt the old nervous hysteria rising in her throat. She didn't like crowds. This crowd particularly frightened her because she would be meeting Allen's family, at least his sister. She wanted them to like her, but knowing how tongue-tied and clumsy she became around most people, she feared she'd make a terrible impression.

She'd be meeting the aunt she hadn't seen for more than ten years, too, an aunt who might be angry because of the way she and Hank had refused her help and disappeared from her life. She took a long breath. She'd be okay as long as she and Allen were together.

A flashbulb exploded as they stepped through the door and someone behind her brushed against her shoulder. Cheers erupted and a crowd surged toward them. In the confusion Holland's hand slipped from Allen's and she found herself standing alone against a wall as two big men closed in on Allen. They pumped his hand and slapped his back, then gave way to an avalanche of little girls who inundated him with hugs and kisses until a tiny woman with a riot of red curls tumbling down her back elbowed them aside and launched herself into Allen's arms. Holland suspected the woman wasn't Allen's sister.

Jealousy tugged at Holland's heart. The redhead was pretty and Allen didn't seem to mind a public demonstration now. Taking her eyes off the pair, Holland looked around the waiting room, trying to control her emotions. She wondered if she would recognize her aunt. A young boy with a camera dangling from a wide strap around his neck snapped another shot, then released a loud whoop that had everyone turning to stare as he catapulted toward Allen. Allen met him halfway, and Holland swallowed a sudden lump in her throat when she saw the moisture shining in the eyes of both the man and the boy as they hugged each other.

"I'm so glad you're back, A.J." The boy's voice broke, and Allen backed up a step and looked him up and down with a silly grin growing wider each second.

"It's good to be back, tiger." He lightly slugged the boy's shoulder, then someone beyond the boy caught Allen's attention. Holland saw him grow still and his smile disappear. He took two quick steps, then stopped. Holland followed his gaze to see a beautiful woman step away from the crowd. She had platinum hair like the angel Hank always put at the top of their Christmas tree. Holland barely noted her white silk suit and delicate high-heeled sandals. Some powerful emotion arced between the two and she held her breath, knowing if she so much as blinked she would shatter into a million fragments. This woman definitely wasn't Allen's sister either.

Allen stood still and slowly held out his arms to the angel. The woman grasped his hands in her fingers and for endless seconds her silver-blue eyes held his, then gradually like an old-fashioned, slow-motion movie, she raised up on her toes and brushed his cheek with her lips.

"Happy?" He whispered the word, but Holland heard.

"Happier than I ever thought possible," the woman murmured back. Her joy shone from her face like a brilliant light and Holland remembered the picture that had fallen on the floor, a lifetime ago, back in Alaska. She'd known then that the woman wasn't just a casual friend, and though Allen had told her he wasn't in love with her, Holland had had her doubts. Some instinct told her only a woman in love, and who knows her love is returned, could radiate an aura of joy comparable to that surrounding the woman.

Pain left her sagging against the wall. She loved Allen, but there was no way she could compete against the woman in white. She'd never seen anyone so perfect. Hair, skin, expensive, stylish clothes—everything was perfect. Even the petite redhead paled in comparison to this exquisite creature. The denim skirt and yellow sweater Holland had been so proud of suddenly appeared drab, a lifeless schoolgirl uniform.

She wanted to hide her stubby fingernails, she wanted to hide her whole self, but where could a woman her size hide? She'd been a fool to think Allen shared her feelings. In comparison to the woman who held his hands and absorbed his attention, Holland was nothing. Worse than nothing. She was a clumsy caricature of a woman, someone who had so angered Allen with her assumptions, he had simply retaliated to prove her wrong. Her heart ached as she recalled how thoroughly he'd changed her mind.

"Holland?" She blinked to clear her thoughts when Allen's voice penetrated her misery. She struggled to paste on a smile as she lifted her eyes to his. There was no mistaking the sympathy behind his gentle warm eyes. She didn't want his pity. Pride straightened her spine and broadened her smile. She'd pretend she didn't care and walk away from here with her pride intact. She scanned the rapidly dwindling crowd for her aunt, hoping there would be no obstacles to their leaving as soon as introductions were made.

"Holland," Allen repeated. "My sister asked Brad to contact your aunt, but he wasn't able to reach her. He says she's out of town and won't be back for almost a week."

"She doesn't know I'm here?" Her voice was a frightened squeak to her own ears. What would she do? Where should she go?

"Don't worry." The small red-haired woman ducked beneath Allen's arm and held out a hand to Holland. "We have plenty of room. You can stay with us. We already planned to invite Allen. His sister's kids have the flu and his parents have closed up their house and gone to Europe. We didn't figure he would want to catch the flu or open his parents' house. Brad?" she said, turning to the larger of the two men standing behind Allen. "Bring the van up closer while Allen and Doug collect the luggage. Maybe you should help them, Jason. Megan and I can take care of the girls and help Holland with her hand luggage."

Holland watched in amazement as everyone scattered. One small girl started after the gangling boy, but was intercepted by the woman she assumed was Megan.

"Come with me, Heidi," Megan's voice held a hint of laughter as she took the little girl's hand. "You can't go with Jason this time."

Meanwhile, the petite redhead continued passing out assignments. "Bobbi, you have Allen's flight bag. Let's see, Michelle, you take Holland's and Ashley can carry my purse so my arms will be free to carry Kelly." She swung a toddler who had been clinging to her leg into her arms and started walking toward the moving sidewalk.

Watching in bewilderment, Holland jumped when one of the little girls reached for her bag. Reluctantly she relinquished it, wishing desperately that Allen hadn't left her alone.

"You might as well come along," Megan whispered. "Cathy has everything and everyone organized, and it's a lot easier to just go along than try to think up an alternative plan. Really, you'll like her when you get to know her."

Suddenly Cathy stopped and her entourage stopped with her, teetering on the brink of the motorized walkway. "Men!" She stomped her foot and both her curls and those of the child in her arms shook. "Allen didn't introduce us and those other two numbskulls never thought of such a thing. Of course, we know who you are, but you probably have no idea who we are. For all you know we could be a gang of kidnappers, though no kidnappers in their right minds would take along half a dozen children, but then if they were in their right minds they wouldn't be kidnappers. I'm Cathy Williams and my husband is Brad, the one fetching the van." She waved toward the other woman. "This is Megan Beckwith, only on TV they call her Megan Nordfeldt. Her husband, Doug, went with Allen and Jason. Jason is their son. The girls—Bobbi, Michelle, Ashley, Heidi, and Kelly," she pointed to one after the other, "belong to Brad and me." With that she turned back around and stepped onto the walkway.

"You'll get used to Cathy," Megan said encouragingly as she urged Holland forward. "At first she leaves you feeling like you've been run over by a diesel truck, then you discover she's the best organizer and the best friend you'll ever have this side of heaven."

Holland stumbled along the walkway, struggling to keep up with the two much smaller women and five little girls. She felt like an elephant beside them and her mind was in a turmoil. If she understood what she'd heard, both Cathy and the cool blonde were married to Allen's best friends. Knowing that Megan was married, she felt her spirits lift slightly. Maybe she still had a chance with Allen after all.

But she hadn't missed the warmth and admiration in Allen's eyes when he'd spotted Megan. Uneasily she mulled over whether or not Allen might be in love with his friend's wife. She suspected he might be. Her first instinct was to hate Megan, but it was hard to resent someone who was being so nice to her. Besides she'd made the wrong assumption about Allen before and didn't want to make the same mistake by doubting his honor now.

She stole a glance at the other woman and acknowledged she could never be as beautiful as Megan, but she could learn from her. Yes, that was just what Holland would do. She'd learn to dress like Megan and speak in a refined voice. She'd buy pale rose enamel for her fingernails like Megan's and she'd walk around with a book on her head until she could move as gracefully as Megan. She'd show Allen. Then maybe he would love her, just a little.

He was being a coward, Allen berated himself as he swung his bags into Doug's Bronco. He hadn't missed the hurt and bewilderment on Holland's face when he told her she'd be going with the Williams and that he would be spending the night at Doug and Megan's home. He knew how much strangers frightened Holland and how insecure she felt around other women, but there was no way he could spend one more night under the same roof with her. He didn't want to hurt her either, but allowing her to depend on him to run interference between other people and her fear of strangers could cause lasting damage. If he coddled and protected her, she'd become increasingly dependent on him and never reach her potential or see her dreams fulfilled. If he didn't brutally cut the ties between them now, he feared they would drift into a marriage like his parents where there was desire and pride on his side because of her physical beauty and dependence and insecurity on hers.

Allen felt like a rat, seeing how Holland's eyes frantically searched for him as Cathy urged her to climb into the van. But he didn't trust himself to go to her. If he took one step, said one word to comfort her, he'd lose the fragile control he'd maintained for the past three days. He ached to hold her, to assure her he'd be beside her every step of the way, but if he so much as touched her he'd wind up kissing her again and he couldn't allow that to happen. He doubted he could stop a second time. He'd never before experienced such excruciating pain as that which had assailed him on that morning. Realizing how close he had been to breaking every vow he'd made to protect her innocence, he had somehow forced himself to release her. Within hours of recognizing his own faith and renewing his commitment to the faith of his childhood, he'd nearly blown it.

He should have let her go on thinking he wasn't interested in women, but oh no, his masculine ego wouldn't allow that. He'd reacted like a caveman. He owed her an apology—which she wouldn't get. She'd know he was lying if he said he was sorry.

"Allen!" He jumped when Cathy took his arm and led him a few steps aside. "I know you're both tired, but I'm worried about your friend. She hasn't said one word since your plane landed and you haven't done much better."

"Don't worry about it. Holland's just a little shy and she's still grieving for her father. Besides, why should we talk when we've got you around to do enough talking for both of us?" He put his arm around her shoulder and gave her a quick hug. His eyes went over her head to see Holland's face pressed against the glass of the van window. She looked lost and alone, and his heart twisted.

"Take care of her," he whispered in Cathy's ear. He coughed in a vain attempt to cover the lump in his throat. She glanced toward the van, then back to Allen. A slow smile spread across her face and Allen groaned at his stupidity.

"Oh, I'll take very good care of her," Cathy whispered back before turning quickly toward the van. Allen watched her walk away and knew he'd made a monumental error. One careless slip of the tongue and he'd stirred up Cathy's matchmaking instincts. Fighting himself was hard enough, but taking on Cathy would be the fight of the century.

Holland stirred. Something wasn't right. She could hear heavy breathing right next to her ear and something heavy lay across her legs. Cautiously she opened her eyes a narrow crack. A ball of soft pink flannel topped by a mop of red curls snuggled against her shoulder. She opened her eyes further and smiled. Another little girl, this one in pale lavender, sprawled across her feet.

Bright light streamed through the window telling her morning had arrived and she had slept in spite of her certainty that she never would. She'd lain in the dark for what had seemed like hours last night missing Hank and longing for Allen. The whole Williams family had been kind to her, but they hadn't been able to dispel the lost, lonely ache she felt inside. Why was Allen being so distant? Was it because of Megan? Perhaps he'd been in love with her forever and ever and then she'd married his friend and broke his heart and he'd vowed to never fall in love again. She gave a forlorn sigh and a tear slid down her cheek.

This would never do. She wasn't the sit-around-and-mope kind of woman. Actually she didn't know what kind of woman she was; she was new at this woman business, but she did recognize she needed some kind of plan of action. Using great caution not to awaken her sleeping visitors, she pulled herself to a sitting position with her back against the headboard.

First, she needed to locate her aunt, then find out how soon she could start school. Allen said she should go to the bank, sign a signature card, and get a checkbook. She ticked off each item on her fingers. Overriding every task she set herself came a picture of Allen holding out his arms to Megan and of Megan with her silvery hair and white silk suit rushing toward him.

In blinding clarity she saw herself beside Megan and Cathy. She remembered Mrs. Whitebear and all the waitresses and stewardesses Allen had talked and laughed with since their strange journey began, and she understood with a touch of sadness why Allen never touched her in public and avoided being alone with her. She'd been stupid to assume he was gay. Even if he was attracted to her, and that kiss told her he was, he was ashamed of her. A twisting pain rode low in Holland's stomach, but she refused to yield to it. Megan and Cathy were both beautiful women. They knew things about clothing and hair she obviously didn't, but more important they knew how to communicate in both words and actions a gentle, feminine kind of caring. Even the two little girls lying beside her on the bed in their pretty flannel and lace nightgowns knew more about being female than she did. Another tear made its way down her cheek as she recognized how she must appear to others dressed in her clumsy male work clothes, with shaggy hair, her nails chipped and black, and so tongue-tied with fear that others assumed she was either stupid or uncaring. She folded her arms and lifted her chin. She wasn't stupid! Even if she couldn't be beautiful, she could learn to dress and act like a beautiful woman!

"Are you mad at us?" a small voice near her feet asked.

"Oh no!" Holland answered, aghast. She felt nothing but gratitude for every member of this family who had taken her in, and she was especially entranced by these little girls who had so readily accepted her. She'd had no experience with children and found herself fascinated and drawn to these tiny exuberant creatures.

"You're frowning," the smaller child observed.

"If you're not mad at us, are you mad at Uncle Allen? Mama is. She says she'd like to shake some sense into that man. I think Daddy and Uncle Doug will have to do it, 'cause Mama isn't big enough. Daddy told her not to worry. He said Uncle Allen just has a dragon-slaying complex and that even the rustiest knight eventually gets rescued by the right maiden. I think he's mixed up 'cause in my books knights don't get rescued. They rescue princesses."

Michelle—at least, she thought that was the girl's name—obviously took after her mother.

"We have to get ready for school now." Ashley slid off the bed. Her sister joined her and together the two little girls dashed for the adjoining bathroom door with a great deal of giggling and waving.

When their chatter no longer reached her ears, Holland got up from the bed, too. She peeked in the bathroom to discover a door she'd been too tired to notice the night before. Through it she could see a bedroom with twin beds piled high with ruffled pillows, dolls, and stuffed animals. A clutter of ribbons and barrettes covered a low dresser, and a lavender nightgown trailed from a not-quite-closed drawer. A small table in one corner was set for tea with an open book lying face down on one chair. She felt strange standing in the doorway. It was as though a favorite childhood story had emerged from its paper frame, not to delight, but to spread a wave of melancholy for what had never been. She imagined herself stepping into that room, seating herself on a tiny chair, and reaching for the little china teapot to share a thimble-sized cup with the large teddy bear seated across the table.

Shaking off her whimsical mood, she hurried to dress in jeans and a sweater before finding her tentative way down the stairs. She followed the sound of voices to the kitchen where Cathy passed out instructions, buttered toast, reminded Bobbi not to dribble her basketball in the house, and quizzed Michelle on her multiplication tables. Sound and color and movement assaulted the shell of her solitary existence from every side. It was too much; it wasn't enough. She wanted to laugh and sing, to clap her hands, even cry. She stood dumbly watching, aching to cease being an observer and become part of the melee.

Suddenly the three older girls bolted for the door and Cathy was there, passing out sweaters, checking to see if they'd remembered their homework, and kissing them good-bye. With their departure, time slowed and Cathy urged Holland to take a seat at the table.

"Mornings are always chaotic around here." Cathy smiled as she dropped into a chair across from Holland. Holland wanted to tell her she thought it was wonderful but she didn't know how. It would be nice if she could express herself as easily as her hostess, but talking didn't come easily except with Allen. She hurt inside thinking of him. She should be angry with him for the cavalier way he'd deserted her, but she couldn't be angry, only sad.

"How did you meet Allen?" Cathy interrupted her thoughts.

"Hank—uh, my father fixed his plane," Holland struggled to answer.

"I'm sorry about your father." Cathy touched her hand. "But I'm glad Allen was there to help you."

Holland winced and acknowledged to herself that the only reason Allen had helped her was because Hank had coerced him into helping. "I don't think he wanted to." She was aghast to hear herself say the words aloud.

Cathy cocked her head to one side and studied Holland's face for several long minutes. Holland squirmed under her appraisal.

"You like him, don't you?" It was more statement than question.

Holland ducked her head. Finally she muttered. "He's a nice man, and he's been kind to me."

A pleased smile crossed Cathy's face. "What are your plans now?" Cathy's question was a little too innocent, arousing Holland's suspicion there was more to the words than appeared at face value.

"I have to find my aunt and register for school."

"I suppose Allen knows about your plans to go to school? Of course he does," she answered her own question. "And knowing Allen, he thinks he knows what is best for you. Men always think they know what is best for women, but Allen is worse than most. The trouble is he always sees everyone's needs but his own. Sometimes there's such a thing as too much nobility!"

Holland eyed Cathy warily. She talked and moved with startling vibrancy, but until that last speech, she'd seemed perfectly rational.

"Are you planning to see Allen today?"

"I-I don't know," she stammered.

"Well, you should. It won't do for you to lose ground. I suppose he was too noble to kiss you while you were traveling across Alaska, just the two of you."

Holland knew a fiery blush answered Cathy's question. The other woman's eyes narrowed appraisingly. She silently tapped two fingernails against the table top, then a broad grin spread across her freckled face.

"I'll ask Mom to watch Heidi and Kelly. We can be at the mall by the time it opens."

"The mall?" Holland asked in bewilderment. She'd obviously missed something along the way.

"We're going shopping!" Cathy stood and pushed her chair back in one smooth motion. "I can probably get you a hair appointment if I call right now. Let's see, deep winter green, I think. No, with your coloring you can get away with something brighter. Do you like pink? No, you're not a pink person. Perhaps topaz. Hurry now, girls," she turned her attention to her daughters.

"Did Allen tell you to take me shopping?" The fear that he found her appearance embarrassing surfaced once more.

"Of course not." Cathy sounded genuinely puzzled. "Men seldom encourage women to shop."

"Then why are we going?"

"Don't you want a new dress to wear tonight when Allen comes to dinner?"

"I didn't know he was coming." She spoke hesitantly. She'd been afraid she might not see him again. "He didn't say anything about dinner."

Cathy hummed a refrain from a Shania Twain song as she washed Kelly's face. "How could he? He doesn't know yet."

chapter nine

"I don't think so." Holland shook her head dubiously at the blouse Cathy held up for her inspection. She couldn't picture herself in the ruffles and lace her new friend favored and Cathy vetoed everything plain or boyish. They finally settled on tailored slacks and a couple of brightly colored thigh-length sweaters. Holland had no idea there were so many styles and fabrics, and she'd never before considered whether an item could be washed or not.

"Aren't these jeans cute?" Cathy exclaimed over plaid pockets and eyelet lace trim.

"The lace would get torn and greasy the first time I wore them," Holland protested. Cathy laughed and led her to a selection of plain jeans in a variety of colors and styles.

"Now for just the right dress." Cathy hustled Holland to the next department. She hummed as she thumbed her way through a rack of dresses, pausing briefly to examine one more closely.

"How about this?" Cathy held a gray jumper with a large embroidered rose on one shoulder in one hand and a frilly pink blouse in the other. Holland's heart sank. The outfit was cute, but she didn't want cute. She wanted mature and sophisticated. She wanted to look like Megan. Desperately she searched for something to say. She didn't want to offend Cathy, but she didn't want Allen to see her looking like one of Cathy's daughters either.

Her eyes settled on two girls giggling together over a display of cotton knit shirts stamped with rock star faces. A short distance away a mannequin sported a mini skirt and layered tee shirts. Everything around her appeared to be designed for teenagers.

"It's kind of short," she hedged.

Cathy looked at the jumper, then back at Holland. A look of dismay crossed her face. "I'm sorry," she apologized. "I'm so accustomed to shopping for Bobbi and myself in pre-teen and junior departments, I automatically came here." She shoved the hangers back on the rack and led Holland across the floor to another department, chattering profusely all the way. They passed a display of evening dresses and Holland's footsteps slowed.

"They're lovely," Cathy commented, "but terribly impractical. They have to be dry-cleaned and unless you're going to a prom or ball, there aren't many occasions for wearing a dress like that." She hurried on, but Holland's eyes lingered a moment longer on ice blue satin before she reluctantly followed. In the romance books she'd read, the women always seemed to be going places that required wearing evening gowns. It seemed that in the real world, at least Cathy's version, there weren't a lot of occasions for anything so glamorous. As she turned away she experienced an unsettling vision of Megan in the ice blue satin with diamond teardrops swaying gently from her perfect ear lobes while Holland stood back, tongue-tied in jeans and a Garfield sweatshirt. She closed her eyes for a moment to shut out the horrible picture, then blinked them back open, squared her chin, and plunged after Cathy with renewed determination.

Half an hour later Holland stepped into a dressing room with six outfits over her arm. One by one she tried them on. She immediately eliminated two, which were too fussy for her. Slipping a red dress over her head, she smiled remembering the red dress she'd bought in Fairbanks. This dress was nothing like that one, and she was nothing like the ignorant girl who had grabbed the longest dress she could find and assumed it would fit.

The clothing Allen had purchased for her had started her thinking about women's clothing and in Seattle she'd purchased a couple of fashion magazines that she'd studied on the flight to Salt Lake. The past couple of hours with Cathy had gone a long way toward educating her to style and personal taste, though she was still hopelessly confused about the qualities of the various fabrics.

She liked the short pleated skirt and oversize sweater Cathy suggested she buy, but her heart nearly stopped when she caught sight of herself in the mirror in a deep green silky dress with wide white lace dripping like fringe from the yoke. Her waist looked tiny and her other measurements more generous, while her skin picked up a golden tan. Turning slowly in front of the mirror, she enjoyed the swish of fabric against her legs. No question, this dress was the one. She could hardly wait for Allen to see her in it.

Next on the agenda was a stop at a beautician's shop where Cathy insisted Holland have her hair styled to take advantage of its deep natural wave. Holland memorized every brush stroke and sweep of the blower, determined to learn to fix her hair herself.

"What about cosmetics?" Holland asked hesitantly as she fingered the aerosol pump on a display bottle of perfume. Cathy paused as though considering the question thoughtfully.

"You'll probably need a moisturizer since the climate is much drier here than you're used to. Lipstick or some kind of lip balm is a good idea, too. You might want to try an eyebrow pencil and mascara just a shade darker than your own lashes, but you have wonderful skin. It would be a shame to cover it up."

"I read an article in a magazine about acrylic nails. Wouldn't they make my hands look better?" She hated drawing Cathy's attention to her stubby, chipped, and broken fingernails, but she couldn't close her eyes without seeing Megan's flawless hands and long, shining nails.

As though reading her mind, Cathy sighed before speaking. "I guess you noticed, too. You have no idea how many times I've looked at Megan's hands and vowed to let my nails grow and have them professionally manicured so they'll look like that, but I spend too much time washing dishes and digging in the garden to ever be successful. Maybe it takes special genes to grow long fingernails. I don't know about that, but I know it takes a different lifestyle than mine to keep colored polish on them. Clean, neat, and clear polish is all I have time for. Of course, looking gorgeous is part of Megan's job. Perhaps if I had to spend as much time in front of a television camera as she does, I'd learn to protect my nails."

"Television camera? Is she an actress?"

"No," Cathy laughed. "She's a reporter and she co-anchors a news program. I take it, Allen didn't bother to tell you much about us."

"He didn't tell me anything, though I saw a picture of Mrs. Beckwith once." Something about her words or perhaps the look on her face drew Cathy's attention and she appeared lost in thought while they carried their packages to Cathy's car. A quiet Cathy made Holland nervous. Had she hurt her feelings and spoiled their beginning friendship with her jealousy of Megan? She didn't know how to make amends; she only knew she'd be terribly disappointed if their friendship ended before she had a chance to savor and explore her first friendship with another woman.

Once their bags were all stowed and the two women were seated in the car, Cathy didn't immediately start the engine. Instead she turned to Holland, "I might be reading this wrong, but I sense you resent Megan because of her closeness to Allen. She and Allen are close, but there's no reason to be jealous of her. She and Doug were separated for nearly ten years and during that time Allen became her friend. Megan's perfect looks are enough to make most women want to hate her, but she's truly a kind and generous friend who's had more than her fair share of rough times. And believe me, she's totally one hundred percent in love with her husband. As for Allen, I think he cares a lot for her, but he was the one who got her and Doug back together."

"Are my feelings for Allen so obvious?" Holland buried her face in her hands.

"Not to everyone," Cathy assured her. "I've wanted to see Allen happily married for a long time, so I pay more attention than most to the women around him. Does he know how you feel?"

"I'm not sure. I tried to tell him, but I don't think he wanted to hear. My father told him I was a little girl and got him to promise to look after me and get me safely to my aunt. I don't think he's willing to see me as other than the little girl he expected me to be." No way was she going to tell Cathy about the way Allen kissed her or that she was so attracted to him she made a fool of herself every time she got near him.

"Knowing Allen, he's probably found some excuse to convince himself he's not good enough for you or he's so wrapped up in fulfilling his word to your father he thinks showing personal interest in you would betray a deathbed promise! We'll have to make him see his responsibility has ended, and now it's time to see you a whole new way." With an unmistakable glint in her eyes, she reached for the ignition and started the car. "A certain green dress just might do the trick. When Allen comes tonight it won't be a tomboy in jeans he'll find waiting." She grinned and gunned the engine.

When they reached the house Cathy sent Holland upstairs to bathe and dress while she started dinner. Once the roast and potatoes were in the oven, she joined Holland in the guest bedroom. They giggled and chattered, though mostly Cathy chattered and Holland listened as they applied makeup and a dab of Cathy's perfume.

Brad came home and took over last-minute preparations in the kitchen with a lot of help from Bobbi. The other little girls raced excitedly between the kitchen and Holland's bedroom.

"There! You look fantastic!" Cathy stepped back and beamed.

"You're pretty," Ashley echoed her mother's sentiment.

Holland examined herself critically in the mirror. The woman she saw was a stranger, not a bad-looking one, but she could hardly believe the woman looking back was indeed herself. She noted the tense expression on her face and the excited sparkle in her eyes. Anxiously she studied her hair and the light makeup Cathy had helped her apply. As her eyes roved over the emerald green dress, her spirits lifted. Allen couldn't help noticing her changed appearance and see her as more than the clumsy kid he'd escorted across Alaska.

The doorbell chimed and Holland's hands tightened on the brush she held until her knuckles turned white. He was here! She felt her heartbeat accelerate and her throat turn dry.

"Let's go for the grand entrance." Cathy giggled. "I'll go answer the door. Wait until you hear the door open, then walk down the stairs. I guarantee he's going to notice you!"

Holland watched Cathy disappear. Nervously she wiped her damp palms on a towel Cathy had left draped over a chair and slowly made her way to the top of the stairs. She heard the door open and the deep tones of a male voice. She swallowed hard and started down the stairs. Her heart fluttered. She'd be seeing Allen in a couple of seconds. Midway she stopped. A crowd of people stood at the bottom watching her descent. Brad and his daughters stood in the doorway to the dining room, smiling warmly up at her. Jason stood with Doug and Megan who chorused a cheery greeting as Cathy turned, her face full of compassion.

Frantically Holland peered past the faces turned toward her. Her eyes sought vainly for a familiar figure lounging in the doorway. He must be parking the car. Perhaps he'd decided to come by himself, so he wouldn't be obligated to leave when his friends did.

"Holland." Cathy took her hand. Holland hadn't even been aware of Cathy climbing the stairs to meet her. "I'm sorry." She spoke softly so her voice wouldn't carry to those below. "Allen won't be coming. His editor is in town and wanted Allen to meet him for dinner."

Allen wasn't coming. He wouldn't see her in her green dress. She wouldn't see him, or touch him, or hear his voice. He didn't care. This night meant nothing to him. All they'd shared since her father's death meant nothing to him. And she'd been a dim-witted fool not to recognize the truth sooner.

Her fingers curled around the oak stair rail and she bit her lip to hold back her disappointment. She suspected his dinner engagement was a ruse to avoid her. She'd been shying away from the truth long enough. Allen didn't care about her. To him she was an obligation. He'd made her father a promise and once he got her to Salt Lake he felt no further interest in her. Only a fool could believe Allen cared about the gawky, unfeminine girl he'd been saddled with for the past two weeks. No doubt, she was an embarrassment to him. Her lungs tightened and her stomach ached, the backs of her eyes felt hot and swollen, and she longed to race back to her bedroom to hide from the pity she sensed all around her. How could she go on? She'd lost everyone who really mattered to her—her mother, long ago, then Hank, and now Allen.

Slowly she straightened. Hank always said life goes on. No matter how deep the hurt or how wide the pain, life goes on, and those with an ounce of faith in God get up and meet it halfway. She was Hank's daughter and she knew about meeting life head-on. Up came her chin and her lips thinned into an aching smile. She'd get through this dinner. Tomorrow she'd find her aunt and remove herself from any possibility of bumping into Allen and embarrassing them both further. She'd go on—somehow—alone.

"Want to play one-on-one?" Bobbi stood behind her dribbling a basketball.

Holland gave a determined smile. It seemed like a long time since she'd played basketball, though it had actually been only a few weeks ago she and her father had shot baskets together at the camp. Hank had an old hoop he'd attach to a tree wherever they set up camp and together they'd spent hours dunking balls through it.

"Bobbi! It's time for you to get ready for school," Cathy called.

"There's time for one quick game," the girl pleaded.

"Not everyone is as crazy about playing ball as you are." Cathy stood with her hands on her hips and shook her head at her daughter. "Honestly," she turned to Holland, "I don't know where she gets it. She'd rather play ball than eat or shop or do anything with her girl-friends. She and Jason thump basketballs around the driveway for hours on end and every guest that enters this house gets challenged to a game. You don't have to play."

"It's okay," Holland shoved her chair back. "I'd like to play. That is, if there is time before school starts." She glanced hesitantly back toward Cathy. She would welcome the familiar activity as well as an excuse to get outside for a little while. She sensed physical exercise would help ease the pain she'd struggled through dinner the previous evening to hide and through a long, sleepless night to endure.

"Great!" Bobby flashed a triumphant grin and headed for the door. Holland followed more slowly, but just as eagerly.

"Time or points?" Holland queried as Bobbi tossed her the ball.

"Points. Eleven." Bobbi's grin widened.

"Okay." Holland began a slow, deliberate dribble. Just as Bobbi reached for the ball, Holland whirled and shot.

"Wow! Nothing, but net," Bobbi voiced her approval as she grabbed for the rebound. Holland executed a quick steal and once more sank the ball through the hoop. Bobbi looked startled for only a moment then settled down to serious play. The girl was good, Holland conceded, but she had her beat in both height and experience. It never occurred to her to let the younger girl win. She remembered how insulted she'd felt when she'd caught Hank throwing a game when she'd been about Bobbi's age.

"You're good, really good." Bobbi smiled as she claimed the final rebound. "Almost as good as my dad," she added loyally. "Want to play another game?"

"Your mom says it's time for you to leave for school."

Holland didn't turn at the sound of Allen's voice, though she felt her pulse accelerate. Reining in the impulse to throw herself into his arms, she reminded herself that he didn't care for her the way she cared about him. Slowly she willed her features to a calmness she didn't feel. She reached for every speck of self-control and poise she could muster before facing him.

He watched her silently for several minutes, minutes in which she didn't trust herself to speak.

"Hello, Holland."

"Hello," she responded quietly.

He looked away as though reluctant to meet her eyes.

"I came by to make certain you're all right."

"I'm fine."

"Uh . . . is there anything you need? Would you like me to take you to the bank to sign your signature cards?"

"No, thank you." She willed her voice not to tremble. "Cathy took me yesterday."

"Look, Holland." He fidgeted uncomfortably. "I'm sorry about . . . It's better this . . . Anyway, your aunt will be back Friday. I'll come get you and drive you to her house."

"That won't be necessary. She called me this morning to tell me she's cutting her trip short. She'll be here to pick me up tonight."

"Well, then, I guess this is good-bye." He awkwardly extended a hand toward her.

Pretending she didn't see his gesture, she smiled brightly and added her own farewell. "Thank you for all your help." She turned her head away so he wouldn't see her blink away the tears that were threatening to fall.

He stood awkwardly for a short time, then turned and walked away. He stopped once and she thought she heard him whisper, "Be happy." If she hadn't been so near tears, she would have laughed. Happiness wouldn't play a large part in her future. She only hoped for survival and the chance to fulfill Hank's expectations.

"Holland?" She jumped at the sound of Cathy's voice.

"Are you all right? I thought I heard Allen's voice, but when I looked out here I didn't see him, and you. . . well, you look like you could use a friend."

"I've never had a friend." Her shoulders shook and she swallowed hard to keep her fragile emotions in check. "There was always just Hank and me."

"You miss him." Cathy stated the fact in gentle tones as she led Holland to a couple of nearby patio chairs. "It might help to talk about him."

"I'm sorry," Holland sniffled. "I don't usually cry."

"Your father's death has totally uprooted your life, leaving you to deal the best you can not only with his absence, but with strange people in a strange place. Anyone would feel a little weepy in your place," Cathy consoled.

"It just seems so unfair for him to die just when I need him the most." Holland swiped the back of her hand across her cheek and sniffed loudly. "Deep down I know he didn't leave me on purpose, but sometimes I find myself really angry that he left me just when we were ready to start doing the things I've wanted to do for years. Then I feel guilty because I'm thinking about me instead of him and I worry about him feeling dark and lonely, too."

"Anger is a normal reaction to the death of someone close. In time you'll be able to think of all the good experiences you shared and you'll discover he never really left you at all. A part of him will always be right there in your heart. I promise you he isn't in a dark and lonely place, but is surrounded by loved ones."

"Deep inside I know that, but I have trouble getting past the black, angry skies that swallowed up his plane and left me alone and incomplete."

"You haven't had a chance to visit the cemetery yet. We could do that this afternoon. Even though his spirit isn't really there, it might help you reach a sense of closure."

"Sometimes I feel he isn't very far away and I try to imagine what he's doing. I can almost see him with Mama in a beautiful garden, both of them dressed in white and he's talking and waving his arms, catching her up on all she's missed the past fifteen years, and I hope I'm not just being fanciful."

"Do you think he's happy?" Cathy asked softly.

"I hope so," Holland responded reluctantly. "I suppose he probably is, except for the wearing white clothes part. He didn't even own a white shirt for church because he said fancy white duds on a mechanic was just asking for trouble." She paused before adding, "I think he missed Mama a lot."

"It sounds to me like your father was a good man," Cathy spoke thoughtfully. "He obviously loved you and your mother a great deal. I'm sure he's pleased that you cherish the time you had together and has high expectations that you'll build on that love by going forward with your own life. As a loving father he probably wants for you to make the most of your opportunities to develop your mind and your talents, and he most likely hopes you'll establish a new family unit with you as the link between him and his grandchildren. Those are the things your Heavenly Father desires for you, too."

"I do believe that, but sometimes it's so hard to be alone. I think Hank hoped Allen would come to care for me so when he was gone I wouldn't have to be alone."

Cathy pressed her lips together and stared off in the distance for several minutes before speaking. "Is that why you want Allen to notice you? Because you think your father chose him for you?"

"No." Holland blushed. "I wanted to be with Allen, wanted him to like me before I figured out Hank was hoping we'd fall in love. When the thought came to me, I didn't feel like he'd set us up; I was just glad my father approved of him. Hank and I had so many dreams, but they're not as important now as I once thought they were. I'd give them all up if Allen wanted me to."

"I don't think Allen would want you to give up your dreams."

"I know." She traced the toe of her shoe along the edge of a patio stone. "Allen doesn't care enough about me to care whether or not I give up anything for him."

"That's not what I meant." Cathy reached out to touch her arm. "Your father and your Heavenly Father both want you to grow, to go after those experiences and challenges that interest you and that will help you become the best person you are capable of being. Let your dreams become goals. No man worthy of being called a son of God would expect you to sacrifice your own development to pursue his dreams. You'll never be happy if your life is spent following someone else's dream, whether that someone else is your father or your husband. I believe shared dreams are the most meaningful and the most fun, but you have to be sure the dream is truly shared."

Holland's face was thoughtful. "Hank dreamed of freedom and loved traveling. I was happy just being with him, but when I was younger I wished we could buy a little house and not have to go anywhere but to church and school. When I got older I dreamed of going to a university and having a permanent home I could always return to. Hank promised me I'd have my dream when he retired. That's part of why I think it's unfair. Hank got his dream, but I never got mine."

"Sometimes parents and children have different dreams," Cathy spoke slowly. "But responsible parents prepare their children to pursue their own dreams as soon as they are mature enough to do so. It's different when you're choosing a mate. Of course you wouldn't want to be carbon copies of each other, but it's important that you share the same dreams or that your dreams compliment each other's. Brad always wanted to be a doctor and I dreamed of mothering a large family and serving a mission. I don't have to share his detailed interest in medicine, but I can appreciate that his income enables me to stay home with our children now and that we'll have sufficient savings to serve a mission after he retires. Many of our goals are the same and some just fit together well. In happy marriages one person doesn't dream all the dreams and the other serve as some kind of appendage to follow along and accommodate in fulfilling that dream. If you see your relationship with Allen as one where you change yourself so you can live his life, it won't work."

"It doesn't really matter, does it?" Holland sighed and lifted her chin. "He isn't interested in me anyway."

Allen leaned back against the deep cushions of the sofa with his arms clasped behind his neck and his stocking feet resting on the coffee table. He closed his eyes. His business was off to a good start. The generous check he'd received for the Alaska photos had been enough to obtain a lease on the studio he'd found and to obtain the equipment to outfit it properly. Luck had been on his side when Gwen Roberts answered his ad for an office manager, too.

He'd also found an apartment nearby, so he should be one happy man, but he wasn't. Actually he wasn't unhappy, he stressed that point to himself, just restless and empty. Okay, he missed

Holland, but that was only because they'd spent such an intense period of time together.

Starting his own business entailed a lot of work and left him too tired to think at the end of his days, but that was the way he wanted it. He wanted to be too tired to see hurt brown eyes, too tired to see a glitter of gold raining down on an upturned face, and especially too tired to remember the way Holland felt in his arms. And he succeeded, most of the time.

The contract he'd signed this afternoon promised a professional challenge and a promising start for his new business. Now that his professional goals were being met, it was time to start on the other half of the promise he'd made himself two months ago beside an icy Alaska stream.

Going back to church had proved easier than he'd expected. He'd gone along with Megan and Doug that first Sunday, and it had been easy to drift into long serious talks with the two of them about the gospel.

It hadn't surprised him when Doug joined the Church shortly before he and Megan were reunited. Cathy once said Doug had always been a Mormon and just hadn't known it, and he agreed with her analysis. Gaining a testimony hadn't come easy for Megan, she'd admitted, but she'd applied her investigative reporting background to her study and amassed a vast knowledge of the church. It impressed him when she told him the knowledge she'd gained hadn't been the reason for her baptism; it had only prepared the way. Brad's unshakable conviction as he stood and humbly bore testimony of the divinity of Jesus Christ the day he was sustained bishop of his ward was the one thing that finally touched her heart.

He wondered if he could do that. Stand and bear witness of his own faith. There were times when he still wavered and he frequently questioned whether his testimony was growing or whether it just was a desire for a life like Brad's and Doug's that was growing. Doubts concerning his worthiness for the life he wanted still troubled him at times, but in his heart he knew he'd not be happy any other way.

Each night as he studied the scriptures, he discovered he wasn't learning anything new. Instead he felt a quiet confirmation of what he'd always known deep in his heart.

Did he have a right to seek a place in the Church? Right at the core of Mormon belief and values was the love of family. Very little, if any, love existed between him and his parents. He'd never lacked for food or clothing. Just the opposite. He'd had his own account at ZCMI and Nordstrom since junior high, he'd received a flashy sports car for his sixteenth birthday, and his father had paid for his education and a great deal of expensive photo equipment.

What he had lacked were family meals and celebrations, vacations together, and family home evenings. His mother had never been a room mother and his father had never cheered a Little League game. Neither one had taken time from their busy schedules to watch a school performance, attend parent/teacher conferences, or attend one of his photo exhibits.

As a small child, he and his sister had unwrapped expensive gifts in solitary splendor, and after Cecelia married, the perfectly wrapped presents disappeared and a check took their place. For a long time the realization that his parents were indifferent to him had hurt like a wound that wouldn't heal. Allen had agonized over his faults, wondering what made him so unlovable that even his parents couldn't love him. Gradually he'd ceased trying to win either their love or attention.

Had the shell of indifference he'd grown against his family become so thick he was incapable of love? He wanted a family, but could he be the kind of husband and father both of his close friends had become? They'd had the advantage of loving, caring parents. They'd become the kinds of fathers their own fathers had been. And what if he became the kind of father his had been? He shuddered at the thought.

What made him think a woman like Cathy or Megan could love him? Perhaps the kind of love his friends knew wasn't for him. If the truth be known, intense emotion frightened him. How could he risk the pain of rejection by someone he cared for that deeply?

No, he wasn't in the market for a consuming love. A glimpse of Holland's expressive eyes caused him to hesitate. No, she wasn't for him. Everything about Holland was too bright, too intense. Loving her would make him vulnerable. Besides she should be allowed to find her own wings. Someday she'd meet a man who could give her a whole heart. Kindness, a generosity of heart, consideration, respect, and a shared commitment to the Church were all he wanted.

One woman came to mind, an attractive widow about his own age, raising two children alone. She was well-educated and taught Spiritual Living in her ward Relief Society. They worked together well. Yes, tomorrow he would take his office manager to lunch and if lunch went well, he'd see if he could get tickets for *Les Miserables* at the Capitol Theatre.

chapter ten

"I hope you don't mind that I'm a little early," Holland apologized as she stepped into the Williams' front room. "Class let out early and I didn't want to drive all the way to Bountiful, then right back here again."

"I'm glad you're early. That will give us a few minutes to visit before I have to leave." Cathy straightened a lace table cover as she led the way to two wingback chairs. "It's been two weeks since I last saw you. How are your classes going? Are you going to continue living with your aunt or move into a dorm?"

"My classes are going great and yesterday I finally got brave enough to raise my hand to answer a question in my Shakespeare class." Holland sat in the chair Cathy indicated. When both women were seated, Cathy reached for a basket beside her chair, withdrew her latest cross-stitch project, and picked up her needle.

"I knew you could do it." Cathy smiled. "Now what about your aunt?" She looked down at her needlework, but instead of beginning, she set it aside and rose to her feet.

"We don't argue or anything like that, and since I told her I wouldn't stay if she said one more bad word about Hank, she's really been trying. But she can't seem to remember I'm not ten years old anymore."

"Oh dear," Cathy laughed. To Holland's ears her laughter sounded a little strained. Puzzled Holland turned to watch her friend move a small figurine from one end of the fireplace mantel to the other. Several minutes passed in silence and Holland felt a growing sense of alarm. It wasn't normal for Cathy to move restlessly about the room, straightening pictures and fussing with knickknacks. And it certainly wasn't normal for Cathy to be so quiet.

"Cathy, what is it? Are you worried about something?"

"Oh, it's nothing really." She brushed off Holland's concern. "I just don't like doctor appointments." She waved her hand in an airy gesture and laughed slightly. "I know, I'm married to a doctor and I should have a more positive attitude. Now, tell me all about the good-looking guy in your institute class who keeps asking you out. Have you said yes yet?"

"No." Holland thought about Todd Chandler. She wasn't sure why she didn't want to accept his invitations. He seemed nice enough and she knew he was well liked by the other students in the class. He was tall and attractive, and a returned missionary, too. But he wasn't Allen. She sighed.

Cathy knelt beside her and patted her hand.

"Give him a chance," she advised. "Perhaps if you're seeing someone else Allen will wake up. And even if he doesn't, you should be dating and having fun, anyway." She rose to her feet, then moved aimlessly around the room again, twitching curtains and straightening magazines.

Holland attempted to make light of the other woman's nervousness. "You've given birth to five babies. You should be used to a doctor poking and examining you by now."

Cathy shuddered. "I don't think any woman ever gets blasé over a pelvic exam and pap smear."

Holland wrinkled her nose. "I've read about them and they sound awful. If you're not sick, why put yourself through that?"

"Brad says I've put it off long enough. According to him, every woman should have a checkup along with her birthday every year unless she's pregnant and having regular prenatal checkups." Cathy sat back down, picked up her cross-stitch, took a couple of stitches, then set it down again.

"I'm sure it's not an experience to look forward to, but it's not your first, so why is this one making you nervous?" Holland didn't think Cathy was the type to allow a few minutes' unpleasantness to make her so jittery.

"I'm not exactly nervous, it's just that . . ." She sat up straighter and clasped her hands together in her lap, interlocking her fingers.

"It's just what?" Holland prompted.

"It's probably nothing, but I'm afraid I might—"

"Mom, we're home!" three voices chorused to the accompaniment of a slamming door. Ashley and Michelle dashed into the room trailing books and papers, while Bobbi followed more slowly dribbling her ever-present basketball.

"Bobbi, you know the rules about bouncing balls in the house," Cathy admonished as she returned the girls' hugs. Quickly she scanned the papers the girls handed her, commented on their achievements, and promised to hang one of each on the refrigerator. "I made a fresh batch of granola today. You can have some as soon as you get your clothes changed. I have to leave now or I'll be late." She turned to Holland. "Heidi and Kelly will probably wake up when the older girls go upstairs. Kelly won't eat granola, so give her a couple of crackers. Just play with the girls and don't worry about dinner. Brad said he'd bring home a bucket of chicken." Cathy blew kisses to the girls on the stairs, opened the door, and left to a chorus of giggles.

Holland stared after her bemused. After two months Cathy still amazed her and the level of activity in the Williams' house made her head reel. Still, she'd come to love the excitement and warmth she always found here, and she and the tiny redhead had become fast friends. She wished she and Cathy had been able to talk a little longer. Instinct told her something serious was troubling the other woman. She wished instinct would also tell her what to do to help her friend.

"Holland," Bobbi said as she moved beside her, "Jason's coming over to play basketball. That's okay, isn't it?"

Holland smiled. "Sure."

Ten minutes later she sat in the kitchen with Kelly on her lap while the other four girls and Jason helped themselves to a large bowl of granola.

"Where are the chocolate chips?" Jason asked as he popped a handful of the fruit and nut mixture into his mouth.

Bobbi turned to explain to Holland. "Mom thinks we should eat healthy stuff so she makes granola for us all the time, but Dad likes chocolate, so when Mom isn't looking he adds chocolate chips or M&M's to her granola."

"I like chocolate best," Heidi added wistfully.

"Here, short stuff." Jason pulled a chocolate bar from his pocket and broke off a chunk for Heidi, who gazed back at him with an obvious case of hero worship. Breaking up the rest of the candy, he shared it with the other girls.

"Aunt Megan caught a fish with granola because she doesn't like to touch worms," Ashley volunteered importantly. "Do you like worms?"

"I've never thought about whether or not I like worms," Holland laughed. "I use them for bait sometimes, but I prefer fly fishing."

"A.J. said he'd teach me to fly fish this summer," Jason spoke around a mouthful of granola.

"Let's play ball." Bobbi tossed her ball to Jason and he lobbed it back as they headed for the door. Heidi scrambled down from her chair to follow them.

"No, Heidi, you always get in the way," the older girl scolded.

"I want to play with Jason." Heidi pouted and stuck her thumb in her mouth.

Jason good-naturedly indulged the smaller child. "Okay, I'll play one game with you. Then you have to sit on the step and stay out of our way while I play with Bobbi."

"She won't stay there," Bobbi groaned. "She follows you everywhere. Can't you make her stay in the house?" She appealed to Holland.

"We'll all sit on the step and watch. I won't let Heidi wander into your game," Holland promised.

"Thanks!" Bobbi grinned and turned to Jason. "What time is your mom picking you up?"

"She isn't. Gwen is coming for me. She and A.J. are eating dinner at our house tonight, so she said she'd pick me up because it's right on her way." The door slammed shut as he ran down the steps.

His words penetrated Holland's mind slowly. Jason always called Allen "A.J." Allen and someone named Gwen were eating dinner tonight at Jason's house. Who is Gwen? Is she a relative, a friend of Megan's, or a woman Allen had invited to spend the evening with him? She wished she could question the boy, but her pride warned her to pretend it didn't matter. Unfortunately it mattered very much.

For two hours Holland worked at blocking out thoughts of Allen. The children kept her busy and she was grateful for that. Michelle and Ashley soon tired of watching Jason and Bobbi play basketball. They wanted to play dolls and Kelly needed to go potty, so Holland dragged a reluctant Heidi back inside the house and set her in a window seat overlooking the driveway. She wasn't sure who had the most fun, she or Kelly, being guests at Ashley and Michelle's tea party.

Holland looked up from her place on the floor beside the small table as Bobbi, followed by Heidi, entered their sisters' bedroom.

"Has Jason gone?" She glanced at her watch as she scrambled to her feet. It was later than she'd realized. Brad should have been here by now.

"Yes, he had to leave. Uncle Allen's girlfriend picked him up." Holland winced at Heidi's words, so casually spoken. "Should I help you fix dinner?"

Holland shook her head. "Your mom said your dad would bring a bucket of chicken." She had to go on speaking and acting normally. The children mustn't guess how much she hurt inside.

"He's late, so he's probably delivering a baby. We better fix something ourselves." Bobbi tucked the ball under one arm and headed toward the stairs.

Holland could only surmise that the Williams family had long since learned to adjust to the impromptu demands of Brad's practice.

"Okay, let's all go to the kitchen," she agreed, urging the younger girls ahead of her.

Just as she was adding a final flourish to the spaghetti sauce that Aunt Barbara had taught her to make, the phone rang.

"Hello, Williams' residence," she answered with one hand as she set the bowl down and turned to check that Kelly's safety harness was buckled.

"Holland." Brad's voice came across the line sounding far more serious than she'd ever heard it before. "Can you fix the girls something to eat and stay with them until I can reach Cathy's mother?"

"I can stay as long as you need me. You don't need to send Cathy's mother over. I know how reluctant she is to leave her husband alone since his second heart attack. We're already sitting down to eat and everything is fine. Bobbi warned me you might have to deliver a baby."

Brad didn't speak for a minute. When he did, he seemed to choke on the words. "It's not that. I'm at the hospital with Cathy. Her doctor found something that concerned him, so he called me and sent her over here for more tests. We might be quite late. If you can stay the night, it would really help."

"Of course, I'll stay. Is-is she going to be okay?"

"God willing," he whispered hoarsely before ending the call.

Time dragged as Holland read stories to the children and helped them get ready for bed. While Ashley, Michelle, and Heidi snuggled in their beds, Holland sat in Cathy's rocker and cuddled Kelly. Across the hall Bobbi frowned over her homework. Only the baby, two-year-old Kelly, refused to accept her explanation that their mom was with their daddy and they'd be home later. Kelly wanted her mommy right now. More than any of the other children, Kelly seemed to cling to her mother, and Holland wondered if that was typical for the youngest child or if the little girl sensed something the others didn't.

Since Holland had no previous experience with children, she was surprised how much she enjoyed the feel of a small child in her arms. For just a moment she imagined Kelly was hers, hers and Allen's. No, she told herself. She mustn't permit herself to dream about Allen or of having his children. Allen had made it clear he wasn't interested in her and now she knew he was seeing someone else. She had to go on with the old dreams, and let getting an education and forming new friendships be enough.

The children were all in bed and sleeping soundly when the telephone rang again. She knew it was Brad before she said hello. She hesitated for a second, somehow knowing she didn't want to hear what he had to say. His voice sounded hollow and strained.

"Dr. Torgesen just completed a biopsy. The results show Cathy has a malignant tumor in her right breast." He choked on the words then went on. "She wanted me to tell you, but she wants to tell the girls and her mother herself tomorrow."

"Oh no," Holland breathed into the phone. Not Cathy. No, Cathy was too vibrant, too full of life to be harboring a silent killer. Surely someone had made a mistake.

"She's asleep now, but I'll stay the night here at the hospital just to be near her anyway," he went on. "I'll bring her home in the morning." Holland knew the big man's heart must be breaking and she wondered if he should be alone. She ached to offer him comfort, but what could she do?

She hung up the telephone and stared at it for several seconds before reaching for it again. Her eyes went to the number printed in Cathy's careful script on a pad beside the phone.

A woman's voice answered.

"Megan?" Holland suddenly found speech difficult. "Is Allen there?"

"Is this Holland?" Megan sounded hesitant. "Are you all right? You sound as though you're crying." Holland swiped a hand across her cheek and discovered it was wet. She hadn't known she was crying.

"Please, I have to talk to Allen." Her heart whispered that not only did Brad need his friend, but she desperately needed to hear the sound of his voice as well.

"Holland, what's going on?" Allen's voice came on the line full of concern and she found herself reaching for an emotional lifeline, the comfort she knew deep inside only he could give her, and the tears began in earnest.

"Brad . . . Brad needs you," she gasped.

"Has something happened to Brad?" Allen asked in the patient voice adults usually reserve for prying information from small children.

"N-no, not Brad. It's Cathy. She's at the hospital. She's asleep now, but Brad is staying with her. He sounded awful and I don't think he should be alone."

"Has Cathy been in an accident?" Allen was shouting now.

"No, Allen," she sobbed into the phone. "Cathy has cancer. She just found out and her doctor sent her right to the hospital. She's the only friend I've ever had and I'm so afraid she'll die."

"Cancer!" The word exploded from Allen's lips, and in the background Holland was vaguely conscious of the sound of shattering glass.

Holland wiped the tears from her face with her free hand. "Brad's always laughing and joking and he always just seems to be in charge," she began. "Allen, I know he's a good doctor and a good bishop and people always take their problems to him, but I can't help feeling he needs someone to lean on now."

"I'll head right for the hospital. Cottonwood?"

"Yes."

Allen didn't hang up immediately. His voice was soft as a caress when he spoke again. "Are you all right, Holland? Is your aunt with you?"

"I'm fine," she said but her shaking voice nearly betrayed her. "I'm at Brad and Cathy's house with the girls. Cathy asked me to baby-sit while she kept her appointment with her gynecologist this afternoon. I promised Brad I'd stay the night."

"Do you want me to send someone to stay with you?"

"No, I'm fine. Really. Just go to Brad, and if Cathy wakes up and you get to talk to her, tell her I love her."

"All right, but don't hang up. Megan wants to speak with you."

Minutes later Holland hung up after telling Megan the little bit she knew about Cathy's condition and promising to call if she learned anything more. Exhaustion settled like a grotesque weight across her shoulders as she slowly climbed the stairs. She peeked into each of the girls' rooms to assure herself they were all sleeping soundly. In five beds red curls spilled across white pillows reminding Holland how much a part of her friend these little girls were.

"Why God?" she whispered into the night as she made her way to her own room. She didn't remember her own mother, yet she'd always had a feeling of being incomplete without her. Would these little girls grow up the way she had, without a mother? Would Cathy fade from their memories and be lost? A wave of fatigue was her only answer.

Removing her clothes and crawling into bed required a tremendous amount of energy. Dry-eyed she stared at the ceiling and marveled that she could feel so tired, but not be the least bit sleepy.

Her mind persisted in replaying Cathy's words from earlier in the afternoon, then Brad's, and finally Allen's. *"Would you like me to send someone to stay with you?"* Who? Megan, the woman she sensed Allen had once loved? Or perhaps Gwen? The bitterness she recognized shamed her. She wouldn't indulge in self-pity. She had no right to be jealous of any woman where Allen was concerned. She was selfish and childish to consider her own feelings at a time when

Cathy's health and the welfare and comfort of her family were all that really mattered. Leaving the bed she knelt beside it to ask Heavenly Father to bless Cathy and Brad and their little girls.

Allen and Doug moved rapidly down the hospital corridor. The nurse at the desk had frowned when they'd asked for Cathy's room, but when they assured her they wouldn't disturb the sleeping woman, but were only looking for Dr. Williams, she directed them to a small lounge next to Cathy's room.

"Brad?" Allen watched his friend slowly straighten and turn toward them. The three men embraced quickly, then Brad turned his back for a moment and his shoulders shook as he struggled to gain control.

"I suppose Holland told you."

"Yes, she called, but why didn't you? You shouldn't try to face this alone," Allen gently chided.

"How is Cathy? Do you know yet how serious it is?" Doug spoke for the first time.

"She'll have to have a mastectomy. I'm not certain what other treatment will be involved, but she'll probably have to go through both radiation and chemotherapy."

"How is she taking it?" Allen asked.

Brad hung his head and spoke with difficulty. "She won't discuss it with me. I wanted her to schedule the surgery immediately if the tumor was malignant, but she refused. She seems to think that losing a breast will impair our relationship. I tried to assure her that it doesn't matter to me. Saving her life is all that's truly important."

"She'll come around, won't she?" Doug looked startled and Allen remembered his friend's father had died of cancer. "She does understand that delaying treatment is dangerous, doesn't she?"

"I think she understands; she just can't face it yet. Dr. Torgesen says delaying a couple of weeks won't matter and that she'll be emotionally healthier if she has a little time to adjust first and make her own arrangements for the children's care while she's recuperating and to pick a plastic surgeon if she decides she wants one."

"Is there a lot of pain?" Allen couldn't bear to think of tiny Cathy suffering.

"Some." Brad brushed a knuckle against the corner of one eye. "The biopsy is a surgical procedure and she'll be sore for a few days where the incision was made, but the real pain won't begin until she faces treatment. The tumor itself isn't causing any pain." Pressing his lips together, he stared off in the distance for several minutes.

"I'd do anything to save Cathy's life and diminish her pain. That's why I wanted to go right ahead with the surgery while she was already sedated for the biopsy. I thought one surgery would be easier than two and the faster this threat to her life is removed the better."

"Being an obstetrician," Allen spoke thoughtfully, "you must be aware of the importance of body image to your patients. I've had women friends who saw themselves as ugly and misshapen through their pregnancies. You've probably seen a lot more and in more exaggerated terms. Add to that the sense we all have of valuing our bodies. If any of us faced losing part of our bodies, we'd be pretty shaken. If someone told me that I had a choice of losing my life or any piece of my anatomy—an arm, a leg, an ear—I'd resent having to make the choice."

Doug spoke up next and his words were thoughtful, "You know, Megan had a difficult time valuing her femininity. Mentally she blocked out those parts of her body that made her a woman because of her experience growing up. For a woman like Cathy, who seems to have grown up fully enjoying her femininity, it could be a terrible blow to lose what she perceives as a vital identifying feature of her womanhood."

Brad nodded slowly. "You're both right," he said. "Our media-intense society has communicated the message that flat-chested women can't possibly be physically attractive. Then we turn around and tell a woman she's being shallow if she hesitates to lose a breast in the greater cause of saving her life." He paused. "I'm afraid that's where I've failed Cathy. I've made no secret of the fact I find her beautiful and that I delight in every detail of her body, but somehow I've failed to make her understand that although I value 'the package,' it's not the reason I love her.

"She found that miserable lump herself three weeks ago and never said one word to me. She's been worrying herself sick all this time, but I didn't notice. What kind of husband and doctor does that make me?"

* * *

Cathy twisted her fingers together for several minutes without saying anything. Finally in a voice so low Holland barely heard her words, she whispered, "I found a lump in my breast a few weeks ago. It's not very big and at first I thought it was just a swollen milk duct or a zit developing or something like that, but it didn't go away. It didn't hurt and there was no redness either."

"Oh, Cathy." Holland left her chair to kneel beside Cathy's bed and place her arms around her friend's shoulders. Cathy had been home for several hours and this was the first opportunity Holland had had to be alone with her friend. "What does Brad think about it? Is this why he insisted you have a checkup yesterday?"

"I didn't tell him. He wanted me to have a checkup last year, but I never got around to it. This year he made the appointment for me," Cathy admitted.

"Weren't you going to have the lump checked?" Holland gasped.

"I peeked at some of Brad's medical textbooks, but I didn't understand half of what I read, so I went to the library and checked out a couple of books the librarian recommended. She found some current magazine articles, too, so I thought the odds were in my favor that the lump would turn out to be a harmless cyst. Not many women my age get breast cancer, though when they do the survival rate is much lower than for older women. But there's no history of breast cancer in my family, I had my first child when I was only twenty, I nursed all five of my babies, I'm not overweight, and as far as I know I've never been exposed to any kind of nuclear waste or DDT. Broccoli is my favorite vegetable, I don't like eggs, and I've never touched alcohol, so according to every theory I've read about I'm not a candidate for breast cancer. I did everything right and now I feel betrayed. I feel like my own body tricked me. And I'm just so angry!"

"I don't blame you." Holland squeezed Cathy's hands between her own. "But why didn't you tell Brad? Wouldn't it have been easier to face together?"

"It's kind of hard to explain." Cathy withdrew one hand from Holland's. In a gesture reminiscent of her five-year-old daughter she wound a thick red curl around one finger as she spoke. "Brad's a doctor, an obstetrician. Every day he examines women's bodies. Those women are his patients, he's concerned about them, and he takes excellent care of them, but there's nothing personal in the way he touches or looks at them. I'm his wife and I don't want him to see me as another patient."

"You're afraid cancer would change your relationship with Brad?" Holland asked. "I think you are underestimating how much he loves you." She could see how Cathy's husband adored her. How could she possibly believe Brad would care for her any less because of this problem?

"I'm not explaining myself well." Cathy's brow wrinkled as she tried to clarify her feelings. "I know Brad loves me, and he'll still love me no matter what the outcome, but there will be a difference. He'll no longer see me as a lover first. Instead the doctor in him will always think first of my health."

"Is that bad?" Holland had sensed immediately a strain between Cathy and Brad as soon as they walked in the door, and she didn't understand Cathy's point. Why shouldn't Brad think of Cathy's health first at a time like this?

Holland had listened as Cathy had calmly and rationally explained to her daughters that she would be going back to the hospital in a few weeks for an operation. After that, Cathy had spent some time alone with Bobbi before Brad took all of the girls out for lunch and left Holland alone with his wife. Watching Cathy ever since she had come home, Holland had been amazed at Cathy's strength and courage. Only now was she beginning to glimpse the depths of Cathy's fears.

"Brad doesn't understand either," Cathy spoke with an earnestness that frightened Holland. "He thinks I'm worried about how losing a breast will affect our relationship. He feels guilty because he's a doctor and he didn't find the lump for me or recognize that something was troubling me. He wants to protect me, make decisions for me, order whatever will cause me the least pain. How can I tell him he's reacting in terms of himself? Taking care of me, protecting me will make him feel better, but that's not what I need. I need to know I'm still me, that I'm still competent and capable.

"Don't get me wrong, I'm not accusing him of selfishness.

There's never been anything selfish about Brad. I'm the one who is being selfish. I have to be selfish. This is my body. God gave it to me and it's my responsibility to decide what is to be done to it. I'm not a woman who can blindly turn that responsibility over to my doctor or my husband.

"No matter how intelligently and reasonably I look at this situation, my life will change and never be the same again, and I need to mourn for a loss that will be solely mine. I like my body the way it is; I don't want to change it. I like my life and I have plans and dreams for the future I don't want to change. I like to plan and organize, and I can't bear the thought of my body and my future slipping into an area where I have no control."

She was quiet for so long Holland thought she might have gone to sleep. She considered tiptoeing out of the room, but Cathy's voice stopped her.

"Don't go, Holland. There's one more thing I'd like to say to you, but I can't talk about it to Brad yet. I think I'm going to die, and I don't want to. There's so much I still want to do in this life. I want to raise my girls and be there for each of them when they go to the temple that first time. I want to know the men they'll marry and the grandchildren they'll give me. I want to go on a mission with Brad, I want to write poetry, and I want to spend long, lazy weekends at the cabin with just Brad."

"Cathy, don't talk about dying. You have to believe you will get well."

"I want to believe that and I promise you this, I'll fight with every ounce of strength I have, but I'm afraid." She closed her eyes and Holland watched the first tear she'd seen her friend shed slide slowly across her cheek and disappear in the profusion of red curls spread across her white pillow.

chapter eleven

"There!" Cathy sat back on her heels to survey her kitchen floor, obviously relishing the high sheen she'd just applied to the gleaming vinyl.

"Now will you lie down and rest?" Holland asked in exasperation. "Your kitchen is spotless, you've sorted every paper in this house, you've wrapped your children's Christmas presents, and given half your clothes to D.I. You'd think you weren't planning to come back!"

Shadows hovered in Cathy's eyes. "Megan accuses me of being morbid and Brad just gets tight-lipped and refuses to talk about it, but I can't help thinking about dying. I have to face this honestly. Though I don't want to die, I'm not afraid of death. I'm really not. I know life continues beyond this one and during the past two weeks I've questioned whether I'm ready for that other life. I've thought about it a lot and I've thought about the mistakes I've made. I don't think there's been anything too terrible, but there are a lot of things I should have done or that I planned to do someday that I wish I'd given more attention before now."

"Oh Cathy." Holland wrapped her arms around the smaller woman and urged her to her feet. Just two months ago she wouldn't have considered hugging another woman. In that two months Cathy had become the mother and sister and best friend she'd never known before. Cathy's exuberant pride in being a woman had spread to Holland, instilling in her a confidence and a sense of self-worth Holland would thank her for as long as she lived. "I don't know anyone who has less cause to fear what awaits you on the other side than you do," she whispered.

"Do you remember when we talked about your father's death?" Cathy asked, then went on without waiting for an answer. "I told you then that I don't believe death to be something dark and dreadful. I'm sure it's more like a huge family reunion with sunshine and laughter. It's easy for me to picture myself seated beneath a huge shady tree beside Grandma Best. She's busily stitching one of her beautiful quilts while she prepares me to preach the gospel to those who didn't have a chance to receive it here. Did you know I've always wanted to go on a mission? Brad and I started a small account right after we got married to save for the day when we could go on a mission together."

Holland took a deep breath. "If you have to consider death, then go ahead and talk about it. I'll listen," she said. "It's still hard for me to express myself well, but I'm a good listener." Holland smiled to hide her own pain and worry. The possibility that Cathy might die was unthinkable to Holland. She didn't think she could bear one more loss. But no matter how painful she might find talk of death, she couldn't forget that it was Cathy who broke through her reserve and made it possible for her to talk about Hank's death. She still missed her father and she supposed she always would, but the raw burning pain had eased as Cathy had pulled the words of loss and loneliness from her heart. Yes, if Cathy needed to talk, Holland would listen.

"I know Brad thinks that because I want my life in order, my house clean, and even letters written to my daughters just in case I don't make it, that I'm anticipating death. He's afraid I have some kind of premonition that I'm going to die. Or that I fear losing a breast so much that I'd rather be dead than feel mutilated. That's not true. That's just me. I feel most comfortable when I have everything planned and organized."

Holland nodded her agreement with her friend. "Deep down I think Brad knows that. I wish the two of you could sit down and really talk about all of this before your surgery. This isn't like you to be out of sync."

"I know," Cathy sighed. "Brad thinks of me as a happy optimistic kind of person who keeps the background of his life running smoothly and efficiently. My mood swings frighten him as much as my illness. He can be grumpy or totally absorbed in a problem at work or in the ward, but he's not accustomed to me being self-absorbed. He's good at comforting and reassuring troubled patients or ward members, and he's had a lot of experience helping them work through their fears and problems, but my refusal to let him be my doctor or my bishop has left him feeling like he's failed me. I've gone through denial that this is happening to me. I've been angry, I've mourned, and I've been depressed. If I were really one of his patients I think he'd understand that those are all emotions I've had to experience, but with his overloaded sense of responsibility he seems to think that just because I'm his wife, he should be able to instantly make everything all better for me. And he can't."

Holland listened to Cathy's words, and then asked, "Have you considered that he's facing many of the same emotions you are? He's scared and angry, too. Added to that he feels guilty because he's a doctor and he can't make you well."

"How did someone so young become so wise?" Cathy reached for a tissue to wipe her eyes. "Brad keeps telling me that what happens to me happens to him. I think I've underestimated the pain he's experiencing."

"He'll be here in a few minutes to drive you to the hospital. You better go upstairs and change."

Cathy turned toward the stairs, then looked back at Holland. "Don't look so worried, Holland. I sent the younger girls to Brad's sister ahead of time for a reason. I want a few minutes alone with Brad without the children in the car with us. If we're alone in the car and Brad is driving, he won't have any choice but to listen to me. Brad may never fully understand the complex emotions I've been experiencing. Perhaps only another woman can understand what the loss of a breast means. But I need to remember that Brad isn't worrying about me losing a breast, he's worrying about losing me. I want to reassure him I haven't invested nearly fourteen years of my life in our relationship to let it go now. I love him, and I intend to go on loving him forever." She paused before she continued.

"Thank you for listening, Holland. I want you to know I'm going to fight this malignancy with every ounce of physical and emotional strength I possess—and I'm going to win." Her red curls bounced for emphasis and a cheeky grin lit her face before she turned to dash up the stairs.

Sudden tears stung Holland's eyes as she watched her friend climb the stairs. Cathy had started to behave more like the Cathy she knew, and Cathy tended to be at her best when she was fighting for the things she felt strongly about. If Cathy decided she could beat her cancer, there was a strong possibility she would do it. The thought cheered Holland immensely and brought a lump to her throat.

Halfway up the stairs, Cathy paused, and turned to look down at Holland. "Will you promise me one thing?" she asked.

"You know I'll do anything I can," Holland whispered.

"Next time Todd Chandler asks you out, say yes. Promise?" Green eyes sparkled with mischief.

Holland struggled to hide her dismay. She didn't want to go out with Todd. But as she watched the expectant sparkle in Cathy's eyes she knew she couldn't refuse. Slowly she nodded her head.

Perhaps it wouldn't be so bad. Hadn't she already promised herself she'd put her feelings for Allen behind her and get on with her life?

Allen sank lower in his chair, tipped his head back, and tilted the paper cup in his hand to a steeper level so the remaining chunks of ice would run into his mouth. Crunching the ice between his teeth, he surveyed the other occupants of the room. Cathy's parents huddled together on a sofa. Her mother fussed anxiously over her husband and surreptitiously watched the clock. Brad's father, Judge Williams, appeared lost in the sheaf of papers he'd drawn from a bulging briefcase at his side. Several of Brad's and Cathy's brothers and sisters conversed quietly in one corner. Megan sat a few feet away, looking thoroughly sick and miserable.

Doug entered the room and walked toward Megan with a cellophane-wrapped package of crackers in his hand, which he handed to her as he slid into the vacant seat beside her. Putting one arm around her, he whispered something in her ear. She shook her head and Doug placed his lips to her ear a second time to whisper something more. Allen didn't have to hear the words to know that Doug wanted to take Megan home and that Megan refused to go. No, Megan wouldn't allow morning sickness to keep her from Cathy's side.

Although none of them were actually at Cathy's side when it came right down to it. Not even Brad. They all sat in this nothing room with its beige chairs, beige carpet, pale watercolor paintings, and sorry little aluminum Christmas tree, waiting endlessly with their eyes darting to the double-wide door each time a figure paused there.

Allen's heart went out to Brad, a Brad who didn't even look like the man who had been his friend since they were children. He'd never seen his friend before in baggy surgical greens, nor had he ever seen him so alone. Brad, the man with a wife and five daughters and a million friends, sat with his shoulders hunched forward and his clasped hands braced between his knees. A mask dangled from strings loosely tied behind his neck and red-rimmed eyes stared sightlessly at the floor. Something in Brad's demeanor warned Allen he wouldn't welcome even the most concerned intrusion on his self-imposed isolation.

Brad's aloneness touched a memory hidden deep inside Allen and he saw a young girl press a fur-lined glove against a mesh fence in silent entreaty as the plane carrying her father's body disappeared from sight. At the thought of Holland, his own loneliness swept over him in waves. All around him were couples with the exception of Brad, the judge, and himself. The judge had thirty-seven years with his Sally, Brad was intrinsically linked to the woman who lay helpless beyond those doors, but who did he have?

No one. Holland's face filled his mind and for a crazy irrational moment he longed to run a knuckle down her classic cheekbone, watch her lift her stubborn chin, and feel her wrap her arms around his waist. A familiar ache of regret filled his chest. Why did she have to be so young? The ache spread as he acknowledged that she was closer to Jason's age than his own.

Cathy frequently filled him in on Holland's activities, and he would always be grateful to her for the good friend and guide she'd become to the younger woman. He knew Holland's adjustment to living with her aunt had been difficult, but she was doing well in school and enjoying her classes. He also knew some young man, a recently returned missionary, had been calling her frequently. He set his cup down with a thump that echoed across the silent room as he pictured the young man with his Holland. No, she wasn't his Holland and never would be. The sooner he got on with his own plans, the sooner he could put away this strange infatuation with the little waif for whom he'd taken responsibility three months ago. Because if he didn't soon stop seeing her slender shape and hearing her hesitant voice at every turn, he'd lose his mind.

"Allen?" At the sound of Gwen's voice, disappointment sliced through Allen because it wasn't Holland's voice. Slowly he raised his head, refusing to acknowledge the mournful whisper that reminded him, *She isn't Holland.* He didn't want her to be Holland, he silenced the voice. Gwen was a mature, attractive woman, closer to his own age, who shared his goals and hopes for a future centered around a family and the Church.

"Hello, Gwen," he said softly as he smiled into the worried green eyes peering down at him.

"Is Cathy out of surgery yet?"

"No." Allen took her hand and pulled the attractive brunette down beside him. Gwen was sweet to show up at the hospital to wait with him. Her thoughtfulness was just one of the reasons he enjoyed her company. "As soon as the surgery is finished, they'll take her to the recovery room and come get Brad. It should be soon now."

"This is really just the beginning, isn't it?" Gwen spoke thoughtfully.

"I'm afraid so," Allen answered, grimly thinking of the long months of radiation and chemotherapy that were likely to follow.

Out of the corner of his eye he saw Brad straighten and rise to his feet just as Cathy's doctor entered the room. He spoke quietly to Brad, then turned to face the room. "She came through the surgery well. She'll sleep most of the remainder of the day. When she's out of recovery and moved to her room, two or three of you may visit her briefly, but only her husband will be allowed to stay. It would be best if most of you would wait until tomorrow to visit her." He turned away and Brad accompanied him out the door.

Allen followed Brad with his eyes, noting how eagerly his friend hurried to his wife's side. Just a few short hours ago, he, Doug, the judge, and Brad's counselors had gathered around Cathy's bed to give her a priesthood blessing before an orderly arrived to wheel her into surgery. Warmth and love, as Allen had never before experienced, filled the tiny room. Then Brad had accompanied his wife and the orderly down the hall. The look that passed between the two as they bid each other goodbye was seared in Allen's mind.

Neither envy nor jealousy described the ache that brief, intense exchange left in his heart. He was glad the strange off-balance note he'd noticed the past two weeks between the couple was at an end. Brad and Cathy's love for each other had always spilled over to provide an element of joy and stability in his own life. No, what he felt was closer to home sickness, though what or whom he longed for he couldn't say.

He turned, knowing without looking, that Megan was watching him. Their eyes met and he knew she understood. Megan had always seen beneath the facade he showed the rest of the world. At some basic level they were kindred spirits, two refugees from childhoods of endless sadness.

"We'd better go." Doug helped Megan to her feet. "Cathy's parents and the judge will be enough visitors for today."

Megan nodded her agreement with tears glistening in her eyes. Megan and Cathy were close friends and her friend's illness grieved Megan deeply. Allen knew how frustrated Megan felt that her pregnancy prevented her from spending more time helping Cathy and tending her children. He thought of Holland stepping in to do just that and a sense of warmth encompassed him.

"The boys will be home from school soon." Gwen slipped her arm through his. "I need to stop at the bakery on my way home to pick up Jeffrey's cake. Do you want to come with me now or meet me at the house later?"

Allen groaned inwardly. He'd forgotten all about Jeffrey's birthday and his promise to have dinner with Gwen and her boys tonight. Jeffrey and Lance were good kids and he enjoyed spending time with them; at six and four they thrived on the masculine attention he gave them. He couldn't disappoint Jeffrey by not showing up—nor by showing up without a suitable gift. Perhaps he could pick up something for the boy in the hospital gift shop, but first there was something he had to do.

"Go ahead without me," he told Gwen. "I'm just going to call Holland and let her know Cathy's out of surgery. She's staying with the older Williams girls and they'll want to know."

"I'll call her," Megan interrupted. "You go ahead and have fun."

"Thank you," he said, swallowing his disappointment. Allen

mentally rejected the possibility that his reluctance to turn over the task of calling Holland to Megan was actually disappointment. He was simply reluctant to leave the hospital as long as Brad might need him, he told himself.

Snow was falling lightly that evening when he left Gwen's small house, lending a hush to the night. He thought about checking with Brad to see how he and Cathy were holding up. It was still early. His thoughts returned to the woman he'd just left. Gwen hadn't objected to his early departure; in fact, he suspected she welcomed an early night. The boys had worn themselves out with birthday celebrating and were both sleeping soundly now, giving her a rare opportunity to get some rest herself. She was an amazing woman, he thought admiringly. She worked hard all day for him, then was there for her boys when she got home. Her boys were lucky to have her for a mother.

She'd make a good wife, too, he had already decided. The kind of wife he wanted. One who was easy to talk to, considerate of other people, and active in the Church. A woman like Cathy. A picture of Brad and Cathy swam before his eyes and he felt again the impact of the love that vibrated between the two as Brad released Cathy's hand and the surgery doors swung wide. He'd only seen that intensity of feeling once before in his life and that was when Megan picked up the telephone and told Doug she was coming home for good.

Not everyone was destined for that kind of love. Friendship and caring were enough for him. He wasn't sure he was even capable of the kind of relationship he glimpsed between his friends and their wives. He was more of a loner than either Brad or Doug, at least, that was what he told himself.

Through the screen of falling snow he glimpsed an exit ahead and pulled into the outside lane. It would only take a minute to check with Brad.

A blaze of light greeted him as he pulled onto Brad's street. The prospect of major surgery and a week's hospital stay hadn't blunted Cathy's holiday decorating. Every Utah Power stockholder was probably praying for Cathy's recovery. Without her fantastic display of Christmas lights, the company might suffer irreversible financial disaster.

There were no tire tracks in the driveway, which probably meant Brad was still at the hospital. After a short, but vigorous argument with himself, Allen opened the car door and approached the house. While telling himself to get back in the car, go home, and call Brad from there, he leaned one finger against the doorbell.

Several minutes passed in which he had time to reconsider his actions. He shouldn't be here. He knew Holland was staying with the Williams children and he'd promised himself he'd avoid her as much as possible. Slowly he turned around, prepared to return to his car. He was glad she hadn't answered the door. He told himself that the heaviness in his chest was because he hadn't been able to see Brad, no other reason.

A sound behind him caught his ear and he whirled about to see Holland standing in the doorway. A halo of light emphasized the swirling snow forming an island around her, separating her from the darkness of the night. A burning sensation stung the back of his eyes. His arms ached to reach out to her. What was there about this particular woman standing at an open door with light and warmth behind her that beckoned to him, called to his very soul as no other human being ever had before?

"Allen?" she asked tentatively. His eyes took in her disheveled appearance. Her blouse was wrinkled and covered with wet splotches. A red stain darkened one pant leg. Her cheeks were flushed and her hair looked as though she'd run damp fingers through it repeatedly.

He grinned. "You look a little worse for wear."

A crimson flush climbed her neck as she glanced down at herself.

"Kelly tossed her dinner overboard."

"It looks like she tossed her bath overboard, too." Allen's grin broadened until he saw Holland shiver. Abruptly he closed the distance between them. Taking her arm he hustled her back inside and closed the door.

With one hand firmly gripping Holland's shoulder, he meant to send her upstairs to find dry clothes, but as his eyes met hers a feeling of gradually sliding into thick molasses enveloped him. He opened his mouth, but no words came out. What was the matter with him? He had plenty of failings, but being tongue-tied had never been one of them. Wasn't he the guy who'd been warned all his life about his smart mouth?

"Uncle Allen! Uncle Allen!" A chorus of girlish voices broke through his inertia and he rallied in time to scoop two flannel-clad little girls into his arms as they ran down the stairs. Bobbi and Michelle with Kelly between them followed at a slightly slower pace. Bobbi's freckles stood out against her pale cheeks. Allen suspected she was the only one of the girls old enough to begin to understand what had happened to their mother.

"You have snow all over you," Ashley said, eyeing him disapprovingly as he lowered her to the floor.

"Did you see my mama?" Heidi demanded to know.

"Mama!" Kelly echoed and fat tears welled in her eyes.

"Your mama is fine." Holland picked up the baby and crooned against her soft curls. "She wants you to be big girls and go to bed without her tonight."

"I thought the little ones were with Cathy's sister." Allen looked pointedly at the toddler nestled in Holland's arms as he brushed the snow from his shoulders.

"She brought them back earlier this evening, so they could sleep in their own beds. Cathy wants their schedule disrupted as little as possible." He watched her brush her fingers through her hair and sweep it back from her face. She looked tired, but strangely content surrounded by the children.

"Have you been to the hospital?" Bobbi interrupted.

"I left there several hours ago." Allen looked at Bobbi, but his words were directed toward Holland. "Cathy's doctor wouldn't let anyone but Brad and her parents see her tonight. I was on my way back to my apartment and decided to drop in to see how Brad was holding up."

"He called a few minutes ago to say Cathy is doing fine, but he plans to stay with her tonight."

"We were about to say prayers," Ashley spoke up. "Do you want to say prayers with us?"

His eyes met Holland's and he knew she was remembering a prayer beside a broken-down truck on a lonely Alaska road. A sense of shame washed over him for the way he'd let her down that day. At the time he'd dismissed the arrival of the officers as coincidence, but now he suspected the slender young woman in front of him had drawn on a well of faith that he was just now beginning to fathom.

"Sure, I can stay for prayers," he answered Ashley, but again his eyes met Holland's and he felt that strange sensation once more of something sweet and thick and bright surrounding him, drawing him in deeper and deeper. It wasn't a bad feeling.

He let the girls draw him into the family room where he knelt between Heidi and Kelly. Light from a lamp highlighted Holland's hair as she knelt across from him and added a glow to her cheeks. He waited for her to speak. When she remained silent, he slowly glanced around the circle. Six pairs of eyes were on him.

They expected him to pray! He'd prayed frequently during the past few months, but he hadn't prayed aloud before a group since his cub scout days. What could he say that would bring the blessings of comfort and hope to these children? His hands felt damp and a trickle of moisture inched its way down the side of his face. It wasn't melting snow.

He opened his mouth and words came out, slowly, self-consciously. He'd never approached his Heavenly Father with more sincere intent. By slow degrees his self-awareness slipped away and he forgot his own ineptness as he spoke to his Father with gathering confidence. A small hand burrowed its way into his as he pleaded for the children's welfare, for their mother's recovery, for their father's comfort, and for the continuation of the bonds of friendship. With his final words he opened his eyes and looked across the circle at the bowed heads of one woman and five little girls. The picture left his heart with a fullness that whispered the rightness of the moment and he remembered a long-ago little boy who dreamed of family prayer with his own family kneeling around him. Tonight came close, close indeed, his heart whispered.

chapter twelve

"I'm awake. Come on in," Cathy spoke from the mound of pillows on her bed.

"Are you feeling better?" Holland approached Cathy's side where she struggled to hide the shock that assailed her each time she looked at her friend. Gone were the long, red curls. Even Cathy's red-gold eyebrows had disappeared, along with her rosy complexion and generous curves.

"It's been two hours since I last threw up. I think I'm past the worst of it."

"This time," Holland muttered.

"Yes, this time," Cathy's words escaped on a gentle sigh. "Two more. That's all." She sank back against the pillows and closed her eyes. Holland thought she'd drifted back to sleep, but when she turned to leave the room Cathy spoke again.

"Is Kelly asleep?"

"Finally." Holland smiled. "She fights nap time harder each day."

Cathy's eyes filled with tears. "This is so hard on her. She's too young to understand why I don't pick her up any more or why some days I'm too tired to care for her." Her eyes closed again and Holland watched as Cathy's features tightened in a grimace as she fought the pain and nausea. The tension eased slowly as her exhausted body sought refuge in sleep.

A bright shaft of light seeped through the partially closed blinds. Fearing that the blinding slash of sunshine might waken Cathy, Holland stepped to the window. As her hand touched the cord she noticed a splash of color beyond the glass. Early crocuses and a few hardy daffodils heralded spring, placing winter on notice that its days were at an end. The bright spring flowers raised hope in Holland's heart. Surely they were a harbinger of a turning point for Cathy. And a turning point for herself as well. Memories of Hank were warm and pleasant now. The dark grief had dimmed to a nostalgic ache and the solitariness of her existence had been tempered by Cathy's need. If she found her thoughts still straying too frequently to Allen, then she'd work harder. She had no right to mourn what had never been hers. She had other friends now and she'd never be one of those foolish women who forfeit living life to its fullest because she'd been disappointed in love. And if sometimes her woman's heart longed for a home of her own, she allowed herself this one dream, that some day she would have a home, though the dream had dimmed because neither Hank nor Allen would share that home.

Cathy continued to fight valiantly just as she'd promised. The tumor had been large and tiny cancerous cells had spread throughout the breast involving two of the lymph nodes tested. But she'd been home for Christmas and the Williams household had overflowed with love and laughter just as the kitchen had overflowed with casseroles, homemade bread, and Christmas goodies arriving in an endless stream from the kitchens of friends and ward members.

Following Christmas Cathy underwent reconstructive surgery to complete the process begun by a plastic surgeon during her first surgery. Radiation treatments were next, then a few weeks passed to allow Cathy to regain her strength before starting chemotherapy.

Aunt Barbara hadn't been pleased when Holland had packed up and moved in with the Williams family, but Holland was glad she'd come. In the Williams' home she felt wanted and needed. Both Brad's and Cathy's brothers and sisters were busy raising small children and managing their own homes while Cathy's mother was occupied with her husband's increasingly fragile health. Brad had shifted his office hours so he could be home with Cathy during the morning hours while Holland went to school, and after a talk with his stake president, he had been released from his responsibilities as bishop. With the shift in his office hours, most evenings he barely got home in time to put Kelly and Heidi to bed.

Thinking of Brad brought a twinge of sadness to Holland's thoughts. When she'd first met him last fall his large frame carried a few more pounds than he needed; now he was nearly as emaciated as his nausea-torn wife. The long hours at his office, frequent nights spent at the hospital with his patients, coupled with the hours he spent at Cathy's side, were all taking their toll. Just this morning some small sound had awakened Holland a little after four and she'd crept downstairs to investigate. She'd discovered Brad, unshaven and badly in need of a haircut, sitting in front of the fireplace with a blanket-wrapped Cathy in his arms. His rumbling voice whispered soothing words and his big hands carefully stroked her back. Light from the flickering fireplace revealed two shiny trails leading down his cheeks from deeply sunken eyes. Quietly she'd tiptoed back to her room.

The routine was familiar now. Two days of intense illness followed each chemo treatment, then a better day, and a return to more normal activities until the next treatment started the cycle all over again. Each cycle left Cathy a little more tired and required a little more time to recoup.

Wondering if she possessed even a fraction of Cathy's courage, Holland pressed her fingertips to her eyelids and whispered a quiet prayer of gratitude that the ordeal was nearly over. Two more treatments, then recovery could begin. Over and over she wondered how the tiny woman could survive the bouts of nausea and the crippling loss of strength. But Cathy's inner resolve and faith continued to sustain her. As did her friends. Megan and Doug frequently took the girls to their house and Cathy's visiting teachers brought dinner for two nights each time she had a treatment. Neighbors had volunteered to come if one of Brad's patients went into labor while Holland was at school.

Megan had volunteered to take the older girls for the day and with Cathy and Kelly sleeping, the house was quiet. Holland thought this might be a good time to catch up on her homework.

A light tap on the door caught her attention as she left Cathy's room. Before she could reach the door, it opened and Megan and Bobbi walked in.

"We're going to the park so I need my ball. Jason's needs pumped up and he can't find his needle." Bobbi made a dash for her room, the words trailing behind her.

Megan smiled at Holland. "It's time you got out for awhile. Bobbi said you like to play basketball and I'm no good in that department, so I'll stay with Cathy and Kelly while you go to the park with the rest of them."

"But you haven't been well," Holland argued despite the tempting spring sunshine through the open door.

"I'm fine. In fact I'm looking forward to a couple of quiet hours with Cathy. You've been cooped up in this house or at school all winter, Holland. You need a break."

"I have your shoes and sweatshirt." Bobbi thrust them in Holland's hands as she rejoined them. "Let's go."

"But—"

"Go! And enjoy yourself," Megan urged her out the door.

The pale green of budding trees, the rich aroma of freshly turned earth, and the brilliance of spring's first flowers assaulted Holland's senses. It felt good to step into the sun's warmth, and the absence of her bulky winter coat lent an air of freedom. Yes, she'd enjoy a game or two with Bobbi and Doug, then she'd push the younger girls in the swings.

Bobbi held the van door for her as she ducked inside. Holland turned to greet Doug and the words faltered on her lips. Not Doug, but Allen grinned back at her and reminded her to fasten her seat belt.

Holland contemplated jumping out of the van and hurrying back inside the house, but before she could act, the vehicle began to move. She was trapped. Since the night of Cathy's initial surgery when Allen had come to the house, Holland had avoided spending time in Allen's company although there had been no way to avoid him completely. He dropped in frequently to see Brad and Cathy and he was an eager volunteer when either needed an errand done. Each encounter brought fresh pain to Holland's heart. A protective measure of distance could be maintained in the presence of other adults, but instinct warned her the children alone could not provide the buffer she needed to protect her fragile emotions. Too many times she'd interpreted Allen's smiles or little acts of kindness as caring, then been painfully reminded of her folly. Where Allen was concerned it was too easy to hope and dream, allowing her foolish heart to dismiss reality as she succumbed to the excitement that raced through her veins from simply sitting beside him. But he must never know how much she cared, nor glimpse the pain she felt each time someone spoke of him and his office manager as a couple.

"All right!" Jason yelled from the back seat. "Guys against the girls. We'll cream them, won't we, A.J.?"

"I was thinking grown-ups against the kids." Allen laughed and winked at Holland, who felt her heart do a crazy flip-flop.

"I don't want to play basketball," Michelle spoke scornfully and Ashley seconded her sentiments.

"We're going to swing."

"I want to be on Jason's team," Heidi announced her preference.

"You can be the cheerleader." Jason tugged one of her red curls.

When they reached the park, Holland was disappointed to see the playground equipment right next to the basketball court. She'd have no excuse to cry off from playing ball in order to keep an eye on Ashley and Michelle. Allen spread his car blanket on the grass for Heidi, and Jason tossed her his sweater and wallet to watch for him, ensuring that Heidi wouldn't wander into their game.

"Holland!" Her head snapped up and her arms reached for the pass Bobbi shot her. Good girl, she silently applauded Bobbi's definitive division of the players. She dribbled twice, then shot.

"A three-pointer!" Bobbi screamed.

"No way," Jason argued even as he lunged for the rebound. Allen got there first, hooked the ball, and took off down court. Holland smiled triumphantly at the chagrined expression on Allen's face when she blocked his shot.

All four played aggressively and the ball moved rapidly up and down the court. Holland and Bobbi took an early lead, then Allen and Jason caught up, only to fall behind again.

Holland faked to the right, then whirled back to shoot from the left. Jason slammed into her back and she found herself catapulted into Allen's embrace. Time stood still for endless seconds. She was back in a small clearing in the trees where Allen swung her around in a kind of joyful madness. The trees revolved in a dizzy procession, yet the only real movement was deep in the back of Allen's eyes where something that spoke of need and loneliness and longing went straight to her heart. Her hand moved, seemingly of its own volition, to touch the side of his face. He blinked and a wry smile twisted one corner of his mouth. Slowly he set her away from himself.

Holland swallowed against the dryness in her throat as she averted her face, praying Allen hadn't read in her eyes the longing that filled her soul. Frantically she sought for something to say to break the tension that still engulfed the two of them. Her eyes fell on Heidi, huddled in Jason's sweater. The little girl shivered.

"Heidi's cold." The words sounded normal enough. "I think we'd better go." She tossed the ball she still held to Bobbi and ran toward the sweater-draped figure.

The children, including Heidi, all protested the curtailment of their activity even as they moved obediently toward the van. Neither Allen nor Holland had much to say on the ride back to the Williams' house and Holland was grateful for the confusion the children created as they teased each other and filled the van with laughter. Still she exhaled deeply as though releasing pent-up breath when Allen turned the vehicle into the driveway.

"Heidi's asleep," Jason whispered as the sound of the engine died away.

"I'll carry her." Holland reached for the child and turned with her in her arms toward the house.

"Holland." Megan stood in the doorway. "There's a call for you."

"I'll take Heidi." Allen was suddenly beside her, lifting the sleeping child from her arms. A shudder washed through her as Allen's hand brushed against her. Anger replaced the shock and despair that had held her captive since those crazy minutes in the park. It wasn't fair for feelings to be so one-sided. She clamped her lips together, refusing to yield to the anger and bitterness. Once before she'd railed against the unfairness of loving this man who couldn't return her love, and she had brought them both pain and humiliation. This time she would walk away with dignity if it killed her.

"Take your call in the den." Megan smiled as Holland slipped past her. "I'll get the kids settled."

"Hello," she spoke into the mouthpiece a little breathlessly. She didn't care if her caller was a telephone salesman; she welcomed the reprieve from Allen's presence that the call gave her.

"Hi!" Todd Chandler's deep voice responded. "I just got off

work, so I'll be about a half hour late. I'm sorry, but I couldn't leave Professor Atweiler to clean up the lab alone."

Warmth seeped into her heart. She'd forgotten about her date with Todd. His voice slowly returned a sense of normality to her warring emotions. His timing couldn't have been better, she thought gratefully. She needed the voice of a friend. And Todd had proved to be a friend over the past three months, taking her to movies and dinner, chatting with her on the phone when she needed an adult ear, and constantly assuring her with both his words and actions that she was both attractive and intelligent. Her youth and pride needed the admiration that lingered in Todd's voice.

"I'm running late, too, but I'm glad you called." Her voice held more warmth than she intended and she felt a moment's remorse. She'd gone to great lengths to make certain Todd understood their relationship would never go further than friendship. Even now when her heart felt bruised and she needed someone to care, she knew it would be wrong to let him think she'd changed her mind. But perhaps it was not allowing him to change her mind that was wrong.

"I've been playing ball in the park with the kids, so I need a little while to shower and dress." She laughed and his chuckle joined in perfect understanding. He had numerous younger siblings, cousins, nephews, and nieces so he knew all about the physical wear and tear of an afternoon at the park with a gang of children.

"Eight-thirty okay?"

"Eight-thirty sounds great, Todd. I'll see you then."

A ball of ice took up residence in Allen's stomach. The husky warmth in Holland's voice gnawed at his memory. Once she'd laughed with him and her voice had been like warm honey he could almost taste. He hadn't meant to eavesdrop on her conversation, but he hadn't been able to avoid walking past the den and the sound of her laughter had stilled his feet.

He told himself that he was glad she was dating and had made friends her own age, but his heart knew he lied. A madman crawling around inside his head wanted to scream at her not to go. She should be warned not to trust this stranger. He should forbid her to see him—but he had no rights where Holland was concerned.

Once she might have loved him, but he'd abandoned her to strangers when they'd arrived in Salt Lake last September. It had been necessary to ensure her dreams, he reminded himself, though the argument sounded weak in his own ears. Now she avoided him with single-minded determination. She no longer wanted even his friendship, and he had only himself to blame. What had she felt when she'd found herself accidentally in his arms? Revulsion?

He knew without being told, she'd only gone to the park with him today because she thought Doug was the one driving the van. He'd been startled when Megan announced she was switching places with Holland, but he hadn't been able to control the pleasure he'd felt when Holland joined him in the van, and he'd enjoyed watching the way she threw herself into playing ball. Reminding himself she was closer to Jason and Bobbi's age than to his hadn't been at all helpful. Honesty compelled him to admit he hadn't once considered Holland one of the kids while they were at the park. No, his thoughts about Holland were definitely adult, so much so, he questioned whether holding her in his arms had been entirely an accident.

Why was he standing here being fanciful? He had things to do and Holland would be walking through that door any minute. He certainly didn't want her to catch him hanging around the door and discover he'd been eavesdropping on her conversation with her boyfriend like some lovesick fool. He'd resolved his feelings for her long ago. She was a beautiful and unique young woman, one he admired and respected, but she was too young for him and she had dreams to fulfill that were too late for him. A few quick strides carried him to the door.

"Allen?" He paused with his hand on the doorknob and turned slowly to see Cathy standing behind him with one hand braced on the stair rail. In a Mother Hubbard flannel gown and her head covered by a lace-edged, old-fashioned bed cap, she looked pale but determined.

"Should you be out of bed?" He took her arm and indicated his willingness to carry her back to her room.

"I'm all right." She brushed away his concern. "I'm tired of lying in bed, besides I want to talk to you. Come. We can talk on the sun porch." She led the way to a glass-enclosed room overlooking the backyard.

"Here, sit beside me." She patted the padded cushion of the glider and looked up at him with wide, innocent eyes.

Allen eyed her dubiously before sinking to the flowered seat. He knew that look. Cathy was up to something, no doubt something she considered to be for his own good, something he wouldn't like.

Cathy's expressive eyes looked troubled as though she'd just discovered something distressing. "I never took you for a coward," she said softly.

"Coward?" He echoed the word. He registered an element of hurt that his longtime friend thought him such. "I've never considered myself some kind of hero, but I don't believe I'm exactly a coward either."

"Oh, you're not a coward in the conventional sense," she went on to clarify. "I think you'd face any danger for someone else, but you're obviously terrified of your feelings for Holland."

"Afraid of Holland?" He laughed. "Why should I be afraid of her?"

"You're afraid of the kind of commitment loving anyone as real as Holland requires. You're afraid to risk your heart because you stopped believing you deserved love a long time ago."

"No, that isn't true," Allen said. "I'm not afraid of commitment. I plan to marry Gwen. I care about her. That's commitment."

"Gwen is safe, but you don't love her. You're comfortable with her because you think that since she has loved with her whole heart before, if you fail her, she won't be as disappointed as a woman who only dreamed of love might be."

"Wrong." Allen grinned, attempting to treat Cathy's words as a lighthearted jest. "A man my age isn't looking for fireworks and romance. Friendship and dependability are far more important."

"Friendship and dependability are important," she conceded. "So is shared faith. But those things aren't enough. I care deeply about you and have always wanted you to have the kind of happiness Brad and I share. It pains me to see you throw away your chance at real happiness."

"You mean Holland?" It hurt to say her name.

"She loves you as no one has ever loved you before." The words were a whisper coming from behind him. Turning, he faced Cathy. Something in her eyes made him almost believe it was possible.

It's too late. He silently telegraphed his pain to the one person he knew who understood untenable risk. *Holland wants nothing to do with me.*

"I've got to go," he mumbled before walking briskly from the room. He didn't look back to see if they were watching. Carefully he blanked his mind. The only thought he gave to the occupants of the house was a hope that no one heard the van's gears grind as he clumsily searched for reverse.

April crawled into May, and Allen took care to avoid the Williams' home and thus Holland. Time and distance were all he needed to quell the strange attraction he felt in her presence. His business was thriving and he availed himself of every opportunity to accept out-of-town projects. His bank account was growing and he'd soon have a tidy amount he could apply toward a house. He wanted to provide Gwen and her boys with a larger house than the modest bungalow they'd lived in since her husband's death. Unbidden, memories of Holland intruded on his thoughts—of her leaning against the overhead cabinets in Hank's truck wistfully talking about the house she and Hank had planned to buy. Refusing to acknowledge the emptiness he felt inside, he sharply clamped down on the errant whimsy that placed him inside that house-of-many-windows looking out over a sea of lights beside Holland.

He signaled to change lanes, then swerved sharply as a white sports car cut him off. Struggling to contain his temper and ignore the crude gestures of the occupants of the speeding car, he wondered what crazy attack of chivalry had led him to agree to this errand. He should be out photographing tulips or birds or something, not rushing to spend a Saturday afternoon baby-sitting. But he'd never been able to refuse Megan anything and when Cathy had echoed her plea, the only thing he could say was yes.

Megan had called to tell him she'd promised to tend Cathy's children so Holland could study for finals, but she'd had a few twinges that might be labor pains, so would he please fill in for her? A call from Cathy had soon followed to tell him how hard Holland had worked all winter to get good grades in her classes, and it just wouldn't be fair if she didn't get some peace and quiet to study for finals. If it wasn't convenient for him to watch the girls, Cathy had concluded, she and Brad would just postpone their trip to the cabin. After that, how could Allen do anything but agree?

Cathy's long fight was over and the prognosis was good. It would take many more months to regain the full use of her arm, and she'd have to endure a lifetime of frequent checkups along with years of tamoxifin treatment with its array of side effects. Her appetite was beginning to return and her scalp was now covered with a short, dark red stubble, which she hid beneath a wild assortment of hats. She and Brad deserved a quiet weekend alone. And yes, Holland's need to study did concern him. He wanted more than he could ever admit for her to succeed in filling her educational goals.

Cathy had the children ready to go when he reached the house.

"No go! Me want Ha-wand." Kelly plopped her behind firmly on the floor and refused to move.

"Hey, we'll have lots of fun." Allen hunkered down beside her. She ignored his cajoling.

"Ha-wand!" She screamed when he attempted to pick her up. He glanced over her head, half expecting, half hoping, to see Holland, but there was no sign of her.

"Holland has to study. She'll play with you later," Cathy stroked her tiny daughter's curls.

"She'll stop bawling as soon as we get in the car," Bobbi spoke matter-of-factly as she plucked her sister from the floor and balanced her on one hip.

"Is Jason coming?" Heidi spoke hopefully.

"You bet," Allen winked and herded the girls out the door. "We'll pick up Jeff and Lance, too."

"Oh, is Gwen with you?" Cathy asked.

"She'll meet me at Doug and Megan's, and we'll take Doug's van from there."

"Allen." Something in Cathy's voice made him turn to look at her. Moments ago she'd been laughing; now she appeared strangely solemn.

"Yes?"

Several seconds passed before she spoke, then her words came with compelling intensity. "Be careful. It would be so easy to make a serious mistake and I don't want people I care about hurt." Her eyes said more than her words, which told him she wasn't just telling him to drive carefully.

chapter thirteen

"Here! Hold this." Liquid sloshed in Allen's lap as Jeffrey thrust his cup in his general direction.

Allen looked down at his sticky pants where huge red blotches marred the pale blue denim. Grimly he reminded himself Jeffrey was only six years old and probably hadn't dumped the drink on purpose. He'd have to swing by his apartment to change before dinner anyway. Tonight's plans called for a dinner jacket, not faded jeans.

"He pinched me," Ashley said indignantly and Allen swallowed a groan knowing what was coming. Jeffrey and Ashley couldn't be in the same room together without coming to blows. Sitting next to each other in a darkened movie theater was destined for disaster.

"Did not!" Jeffrey denied the accusation.

"Did too!"

"She took my seat."

"You left it."

"I was thirsty!"

"Sh-h. Come sit by me," Gwen coaxed her son.

"I don't ever get to sit where I want to," Jeffrey whined.

A woman four seats in front of them turned around to glare at Allen. "Is there some law that says the least competent people must have the most children?" she asked the woman seated next to her in a scathing tone meant to carry to Allen's ears.

"Okay, let's do it this way," he muttered as he plucked Ashley out of the seat and settled her on his lap. With one hand he tugged Jeffrey onto the now-empty seat. "Now, sit quietly and watch the show." His voice held a note of warning and Jeffrey began to whimper.

Allen glanced down the row and frowned at the empty seats he'd purchased. Ten seats and they were only using six. Bobbi and Jason held Kelly and Heidi, Gwen's younger son was cuddled in her lap, Allen was holding Ashley, and if Jeffrey didn't stop poking Michelle, she'd soon be all over him blacking his eyes. He shook his head. What was the matter with him? Was Someone trying to tell him he wasn't father material? The kids had scrapped and argued from the moment he'd loaded them all in the van. He'd never seen the girls act up like this before, and Gwen's boys, though a little spoiled, were generally pleasant little guys.

Brad wouldn't have had this much trouble. All five girls and another dozen kids from the neighborhood wouldn't faze him. And look at Doug. He hadn't even known about his son for nine years, but as soon as they got together he'd stepped right into the father role, while Allen couldn't take eight kids to a movie without risking World War III.

He placed an arm around Jeffrey to draw him away from Michelle. The boy shrugged away and slid down in his seat to where he could kick the seat in front of him. Allen let him go. It wasn't the first time Jeffrey had subtly rejected him. He thought longingly of the rapport there had always been between Megan's son and himself. He wondered if he and Jeffrey would ever be that close. It would be different after he and Gwen were married, he assured himself.

A sigh of relief escaped his lips the moment the final credits began to roll on the screen. He'd never sat through such a long Disney movie before in his life.

"Okay, let's go." He urged everyone to their feet.

"I want ice cream," Ashley announced.

"Me too!" Michelle chimed in.

"Keem!" Kelly clapped her hands and reached to pat his cheeks. He captured her chubby hands between his and reached forward to kiss her nose.

"Whatever you want, princess." He smiled at the eager toddler.

"We've only been gone two hours," Jason glanced at his watch. "Mom said we should give Holland as much time to study as we can."

A picture of Holland bent over a thick book, her dark hair obscuring her eyes, immediately came to Allen's mind. He didn't know how she'd managed all these months. Without any experience with children or of running a household, she'd stepped right into the role of surrogate mother. She'd gotten good grades in all of her classes, too, according to Cathy. She'd been there for Cathy even while she grappled with her own grief and the myriad of insecurities left to her by her sojourn as a boy.

"You're right. Two hours isn't much time to cram for finals. We'd better go get that ice cream."

"If you don't want to get ice cream, we could just go to a park." Bobbi spoke quietly and Allen suspected she possessed more than a little of her mother's regard for others and was concerned about the cost of ice cream for ten.

"It's okay." He grinned at her and winked. "My pockets can stand it, and when we're through you can help me pick out which flavor we should take to Holland."

"She likes chocolate." Bobbi grinned back and Allen laughed remembering Holland's penchant for chocolate bars. An odd little ache centered in his chest and his laughter faded away as he recalled Holland's look of ecstasy at her first bite of chocolate back in Fairbanks.

"Are you all right?" Gwen spoke quietly, concern in her voice.

"Sure." He gave his head a slight shake as he made an abrupt 2000-mile jump back to his present surroundings. "Bobbi and I were just talking about taking some ice cream back to Holland, and I remembered how much she likes chocolate. You should have seen her," he laughed, enjoying the memory. "We almost missed our connection in Seattle because we went looking for chocolate bars and were at the wrong end of the terminal when our flight was called. I grabbed her arm and yelled to run, but she wouldn't budge until the concessioner handed over her candy bars."

"My stomach hurts." Jeffrey tugged on his mother's arm and she turned her face toward him. Her eyebrows drew together as she surveyed her son's pale face. Suddenly he clamped his hand over his mouth, and Allen sprang into action, grabbed the child's arm and hustled him into the men's room where the boy was immediately violently ill.

Ten minutes later he returned to the lobby with a tearful child in tow. Gwen hugged the boy and smoothed his hair back from his scowling face.

"I think I'd better take him home," she said worriedly.

"Carry me, Mom," he sobbed against her leg and Lance tightened his stranglehold around her neck.

"I'll carry you." Allen swung Jeffrey up.

"No! I want my mom," Jeffrey shouted his protest as he wildly flailed his arms and legs.

"Be a good boy . . ." Gwen began.

"You're too big for your mother to carry." Allen's patience was beginning to wear thin. "Come on, kids. Let's go." He started toward the door.

"What about ice cream?" Ashley's bottom lip protruded in a pout.

"Keem!" Kelly clapped her hands together and Allen swallowed a groan.

"Some other time," he promised.

"Keem! Me want Keem." She lay her head against Bobbi's shoulder and began to cry. Her wrenching sobs tore at Allen's heart, deepening his scowl.

"Jeffy's a baby!" Ashley glared at the little boy and Michelle stuck out her tongue, bringing on a new round of sobs from the boy.

Allen increased his pace. They couldn't reach the van too soon to suit him. A sound behind him had him glancing over his shoulder in time to see Jason steady Bobbi after she nearly tripped over an uneven spot in the sidewalk. He'd forgotten the girl was carrying her little sister. He shouldn't have hurried them quite so much.

"Jason," he said, "Bobbi's arms must be about worn out. Would you please carry Kelly the rest of the way?"

"Okay," Jason agreed cheerfully and Allen felt grateful once more for the boy's cheerful, even temperament. Jason released Heidi's hand since carrying Kelly required two arms, and Heidi began to cry.

By the time they reached the van and the children were all inside, Allen felt ready to explode. He raked a hand through his hair and whispered to Gwen, "I'm sorry. I thought it would be fun to take all of the kids to a movie. Jason told me Holland took his and Bobbi's whole team plus the younger girls to a movie a month or two ago and they all had a great time. I don't know how she did it, but I suspect she earned a Purple Heart—or perhaps an Academy Award."

Gwen didn't laugh as he'd expected. Instead she climbed into the van and reached for her safety belt. Both boys begged to sit on her lap, but she reminded them they had to stay buckled up and turned a deaf ear to their cries. Her head sank back against the headrest and she closed her eyes.

A wave of tenderness passed over him. Gwen worked so hard. Asking her to help him chaperone eight children had been selfish on his part. He'd accepted the responsibility for the girls this afternoon and shouldn't have dragged her into it. He hoped he could make it up to her tonight.

Uneasily he glanced at her boys. If Jeffrey was really ill, she'd cancel their date. Even if he weren't really ill, Allen suspected Jeffrey would probably claim a stomach ache to keep his mother home with him. It wouldn't be the first time. But tonight he had plans he definitely didn't want the boy to upset. Brad's office nurse owed him a favor. Tonight just might be the time he'd have to collect. If Jeffrey claimed a stomachache, no one short of a registered nurse would be a good enough baby-sitter to persuade Gwen to leave him for the evening.

Allen held Gwen's elbow as the maitre d' led them past a series of tables to an alcove near the windows. Far below, the city spread before them like a carpet of stars. Quickly he brushed aside memories of the girl who once dreamed of a "carpet of stars at her feet." Annoyance with his wayward thoughts tightened the corners of his mouth. Thoughts of Holland had no part in his plans for tonight. Deliberately he turned his thoughts to the carefully groomed woman seated across from him. With deliberate thoroughness he admired her gleaming shoulder-length hair, approved her soft, understated makeup, and wondered if the crystal and etched gold pendant at her throat was an heirloom or perhaps a gift from her husband. No matter. It was a lovely piece of jewelry and if it was a memento of her first marriage he really didn't mind.

Thick linen draped the table and a fat candle glowed inside a brandy snifter. His hand strayed to his breast pocket and he smiled with contentment. A beautiful night, a beautiful woman, and soon he would have the family he'd long dreamed of. A shadow briefly marred his contemplation of Gwen's boys. Time hadn't brought them closer; instead the more time they spent together the more they appeared to resent his attention to their mother. He'd have to try harder. It was unrealistic to expect the kind of rapport that had developed so quickly between himself and Megan's son to happen again. He smiled remembering Little League games and Jason's first camera. Surely that closeness would come in time.

Allen reached across the table to touch Gwen's hand. It lacked Megan's slender elegance and long tapering nails, but it felt soft and warm in his. Cradling her hand between his palms, he noted her shorter, yet finely manicured fingernails that didn't hide the strength and capability of her hands. Oddly enough, Gwen's hands were a lot like Holland's, though they lacked the calluses at the base of her fingers and the faint traces of oil he'd become familiar with during their odyssey across Alaska. One corner of his mouth quirked upward at the absurd picture of Gwen with oil on her hands. Nevertheless, like Holland's, Gwen's hands were accustomed to hard work.

Lifting his eyes from their joined hands, he smiled across the table at the lovely woman he expected to soon make his wife. She returned his smile, but there was something hesitant, almost guarded in her eyes. Or had his imagination suddenly run wild?

"Jim Blaze from *Heart of the Country* called this afternoon." Gwen took a sip from her glass before going on. "He said he liked the photo essay you did on the mule deer and that he'd be interested in something like that featuring the desert tortoise."

"That's great, but I didn't bring you here to talk shop." Allen released her hand and reached inside his jacket for a small velvet box. He set it between them and reached once more for her hand.

"Gwen." He cleared his throat of a sudden obstruction. "We've worked together now for nearly eight months and we've been seeing each other almost as long. Our association means a great deal to me. I know you were deeply in love with your husband and I don't wish to take anything from your feelings for him, but I believe you have some feelings for me, too. We're good friends and we share common goals and values, traits I believe are important to a lasting relationship. I'd like to be a father to your boys as well as a husband to you. Will you marry me?"

He reached for the ring box to gently flip the lid open, revealing an elegant square-cut solitaire. When his eyes returned to Gwen, her gaze was not on the ring or even on him, but locked on something behind him. A haunting sadness briefly touched her face and he turned to follow the direction of her eyes.

A young man dressed in elegant evening clothes stood in a nearby archway gently holding Holland in his arms. Her full skirt of glittering amber swirled against his finely cut trousers and as Allen watched he brushed her rich dark hair back from her face and pressed his lips to her cheek.

A fierce vise gripped Allen's chest. For what seemed an eternity he couldn't catch his breath. A kaleidoscope of dreams and memories swirled before him driving his senses out of focus. Briefly he closed his eyes. When he opened them the couple was gone. He fought an urge to go after them. But what could he say or do? He wanted Holland to be happy. He'd deliberately chosen to make no claim on her. She deserved a much better man than himself, a man her own age to share her dreams.

An awareness of his surroundings gradually returned. Once more he heard the soft murmur of other couples, smelled the aroma of well-cooked food, and heard the soft clatter of silver on china. He had no right to feel any emotion for Holland. Gwen was the woman he'd chosen to share his life. He'd asked her to be his wife. His head felt inexplicably weighted down as he raised his focus to meet Gwen's eyes. He waited for her answer. When the minutes ticked by and she said nothing, he softly spoke her name.

"Gwen?"

Lowering her eyes, she looked at her plate. Her fingers played idly with her fork, but no food made its way to her mouth.

"I don't think marriage would be a good idea." She spoke slowly, hesitantly.

Allen recoiled. He hadn't considered she might turn him down. Did that make him some kind of arrogant fool?

"Are you telling me no?" His voice sounded more harsh than he intended.

"Not exactly," she whispered. "I thought . . . I had hoped. . . I've never been sure how you felt about . . ."

"If you're worried about Jeffrey and Lance, you needn't be. I want to be a father to them, and I swear I'll do everything I can to earn their trust and respect. Jeffrey's possessive of you and anxious to preserve his father's memory, but I understand that, and I'm willing to give him time to accept me."

"It's not the boys. They like you and given time I'm sure they'd learn to love you. What you see as anger toward you is really jealousy because your friends' children have a prior claim on you."

"I don't understand," Allen swallowed a lump in his throat. "We have so much in common and we could have a great life together. If it isn't the boys, then is there someone else?" He let the question drift away. How could there be someone else? Gwen worked long hours in his office, went out with him three or four times a week, and spent every spare moment with her sons. There wasn't time in her life for another man—unless her feelings were still so strong for her dead husband she couldn't bear letting another man into her tight family unit.

"Allen." Gwen picked up his hand and squeezed it gently. Her eyes met his and through a shimmer of tears he could see her determination to make him understand. "There isn't someone else in my life, and I do care a great deal about you. For months I've believed I was falling in love with you, but those feelings never fully developed and tonight I finally understand why. You're the one who isn't free. Your proposal held no mention of love though I know you care about me; you're just not in love with me. You're in love with Holland Jesperson, and I strongly suspect she feels the same way about you."

"Holland!" He stared at Gwen in shock and dismay. Yes, he had feelings for Holland, but love . . . ? "No," he blurted out a denial, frantic to silence the whisper inside his heart that questioned whether he was being honest with himself or Gwen. "She's too young, too inexperienced. I want a mature woman and a family now. I'm too old to wait for a schoolgirl to grow up."

"I think she's more mature than you realize." Gwen smiled sadly. "When I saw her walk into the room tonight I finally understood the hints both Megan and Cathy have been giving me from the time we first started going out together. They both saw what I let rosy dreams block from my sight. She loves you, and your reaction to the sight of her in Todd's arms tells me the rest of the story."

Allen snorted. "Cathy's been matchmaking since Holland and I arrived from Alaska. She's always been a romantic. She just can't stand to see any adult in her sphere of influence remain single. She's been shopping for a wife for me for so long she can't stand the thought that I might find someone without her help. I can't believe you'd take her seriously."

"Oh, Allen," Gwen sighed. "Holland's a wonderful girl and she can make you happy in a way I never can. I'd be lying if I didn't admit I'm a little jealous, but I was completely head over heels in love once. I'm not ready to settle for anything less now, and I care too much for you to wish you anything less. I don't understand why you're resisting admitting your feelings for her."

"Girl is the operative word. She's twenty years old and I'm thirty-three, in case you haven't noticed. Do you take me for a cradle snatcher?"

"Cathy told me Holland turned twenty-one several months ago while Cathy was undergoing chemotherapy. No one noticed except Michelle. The child tried to bake her a cake, set a towel on fire, and nearly burned down the kitchen. Fortunately Brad came home, put out the fire, and rushed right out to buy a cake. As luck would have it, the only cake he could find said 'Happy Valentine, Mindy Sue.'" Gwen patted his hand and he rewarded her with a scowl. He didn't want her to see the guilt stabbing his conscience that Holland's birthday had passed with no one noticing.

"Please Gwen, don't end our relationship because of one of Cathy's romantic whims!"

"Oh, I don't plan to end our relationship." Gwen attempted a laugh. "You pay me too well to consider giving up my job—unless you plan to fire me."

He recognized her flippant words as an attempt to lighten the atmosphere between them, but he couldn't summon a smile to acknowledge her attempt. His mind felt numb and at the same time bombarded by a million shards of thought. He felt disappointment, hurt pride, loss, and yes, if he were honest, there was relief, too. True, his heart wasn't broken, but giving up his treasured dream left him feeling empty. A picture of Holland as he'd seen her moments ago in the arms of a strange young man came to his mind and he shook his head to clear away the image. He wasn't in love with Holland. No way. There had to be another explanation for the lump in his throat and the sharp pain gnawing at his belly.

Todd kept his arm firmly around Holland's shoulders as he led her stumbling steps away from the restaurant and helped her into his car. She leaned her head back against the headrest and closed her eyes. Why? Why did she have to see *him* with Gwen tonight? And why had she made such a fool of herself? Todd was fun and they'd both enjoyed themselves at the dance, but the moment they'd walked inside the restaurant her eyes had gone to Allen as though drawn by a magnet. She'd seen their joined hands, the small jeweler's box on the table, and she'd wanted to die.

Instead of merciful oblivion, tears had blinded her eyes and she'd staggered. Only Todd's quick reaction had saved her from falling and making a bigger fool of herself. His arm slipped around her shoulder as he slid in beside her. Carefully he drew her face against his chest. He didn't say anything, only held her as she sobbed. When at last her tears subsided, he handed her a handful of tissues to wipe her streaming cheeks. His ruffled white shirt was damp beneath her cheek and she swiped futilely at the large damp spot there.

Guilt made her want to writhe. She didn't deserve Todd's gentle concern. Selfishly she'd ignored his deepening feelings for her, enjoying his friendship and allowing him to spend his time and money on a relationship that would never go where he wanted it to lead. Or could it? Now that she knew Allen would be marrying Gwen, could she finally put her hopes to rest and give Todd the chance he deserved? Slowly she lifted her face. With his thumb Todd wiped away a lingering tear and gave her a tentative smile. Her lips trembled, but she offered him the best smile she could. Yes, she'd try. Surely it wouldn't be too hard to change liking and friendship into something more.

chapter fourteen

Allen had expected returning to his office would be awkward and his professional relationship with Gwen might be strained, but strangely after only a couple of days, they slipped into their old easy pattern minus the pressure of a personal relationship. He was chagrined to recognize an element of relief in their association and acknowledged that though he still desired a home and family, Gwen hadn't broken his heart. Contrary to his expectations, he felt more like a burden had been removed than that he had been rejected. Still an emptiness crept in where once there had been hope.

Nights in his empty apartment were the hard part. He'd lived alone his entire adult life except for those two weeks he and Holland shared Hank's truck, so it shouldn't bother him to be alone now. But it did bother him. The walls seemed to close in on him and he grieved for the loss of his dream.

At first he thought he grieved for Gwen, but during a long sleepless night, he faced the truth. All he had wanted from Gwen was a pleasant friendship and a trustworthy office manager. He hadn't lost that. What he'd really lost was a chance to live a life like Brad's and Doug's. For that he needed a wife, children, and a house. As the hours dragged their way toward morning, he scrupulously examined his motives, concluding at last that he'd wanted to marry Gwen because of all she represented, not because he had deep feelings for her and her children. In that, he had done her a grave disservice. She deserved a man who wanted her for herself.

Morosely his thoughts turned toward his own failings. Had he lost the opportunity for a home and family because of a defect inside himself? Was he like his father, able to provide material comforts and social position but incapable of truly giving of himself?

He slipped from his bed and sank to his knees. Was a home and family too much to ask for? Was there something in his life so amiss Heavenly Father would deny him the one blessing he truly desired? Slowly he recounted his shortcomings to the Lord and acknowledged the mistakes and errors he'd made. He thought of Enos in the Book of Mormon who prayed all day and into the night and wondered if such was expected of him. If that was what the Lord wanted from him, he would do it, not that he thought the length of the prayer was important, but the commitment and purpose it represented mattered greatly.

When he'd gone to Primary as a child and learned the basic steps of prayer, he'd been taught to express gratitude for the good things in his life before requesting the blessings he desired. Perhaps that was where he'd gone wrong. He'd spent so much time with an awareness of what his life lacked, he'd given little thought to all he already had. Darkness deepened in the early pre-dawn hours as he pondered over those things in his life that held meaning. Perhaps it sounded trite, but he believed he had been blessed with a quickness of mind and body, he'd been given the ability to appreciate beauty, he had the support and respect of good friends, and along with never lacking for the necessities of life, he'd been allowed to enjoy much of the world's material wealth. Those were not blessings to scoff at.

A sense of shame filled his soul. Instead of crying for those blessings he lacked, he should be demonstrating his appreciation for those blessings already in his life. He should be serving in the Church and in the community, where he could be helping those less fortunate than himself. He should be seeking ways to enrich the lives of others. Humbly he asked for forgiveness for his failure to see his blessings and express his gratitude. From now on he would look for ways to serve.

Weariness invaded his body; first, his thoughts, then his words slowed. Even closed, his eyelids felt heavy and he drifted to sleep in an attitude of prayer.

Allen awoke to brilliant sunshine playing across the rug where he lay flat on his back staring up at his bedroom ceiling. He should be stiff and uncomfortable, instead he found himself reveling in a sense of lightness and well-being. Relaxed and happy he watched tiny dust motes dancing in a beam of light. For the first time in his life he felt loved, totally, unconditionally loved. He'd always assumed on some remote level that God loved all his children, but he'd never before experienced this certainty that God loved *him*. Brad had spoken on several occasions of the Savior's love and Allen had suspected his friend knew something more than he did, but still it was a distant concept.

Now he knew. He couldn't say how he knew or what had happened to give him this certainty. But he knew. Quietly, peacefully, in the deepest reaches of his soul he knew his Savior loved him. And just as surely, he knew he could never deny this great love.

An overwhelming need to share this profound knowledge surged through his veins and he quickly rose to his feet. Only those he loved most dearly would understand and share his joy. He thought of Doug and Megan, Brad and Cathy—and Holland. Tears coursed down his cheeks when he thought of Holland. It was all right to admit he loved her. He'd believed himself unlovable, unworthy, that somehow he might taint or contaminate any relationship he prized too dearly. Now he knew the greatest love of all and with that knowledge rose a conviction that God truly did wish for him to have the righteous desires of his heart.

He was still twelve years older than Holland, though that no longer seemed an insurmountable barrier. Her educational goals needn't be an obstacle either. Many married students continued to pursue degrees and he'd be the first to support her decision to do so. Closing his eyes, he sank his teeth into his bottom lip in deep concentration. The obstacles were gone in his mind, but how did she feel? He wondered if she would be able to put aside all the walls he'd built between them. Would she even want to try?

A sudden urgency to see her had him rushing through his shower and dressing at record speed. He paused to gather his keys from his dresser top and an envelope caught his eye. He snatched it up and stuffed it into his pocket. He'd promised Jason he'd develop the pictures the boy had shot at his team's Lagoon Day. He could drop them off on his way to see Holland.

"Are you sure you don't mind?" Holland glanced at the neatly labeled boxes lining one side of the Williams' storage room.

"Positive." Cathy grinned. "You can leave anything you want, including yourself, here as long as you like."

"Oh, Cathy," Holland hugged the smaller woman. "I never knew having a friend could be so wonderful. I'll miss you."

"You'll be too busy to miss me," Cathy laughed. "It's only nine weeks, and you are coming back, aren't you?"

"I'm not sure," Holland admitted as honestly as she could. She didn't want to tell her friend that if this semester abroad didn't work out the way she hoped, she'd be transferring to another school in a different state. She and Todd had both registered for a semester at the Jerusalem Center through BYU. Hopefully she would come to share his feelings during that time and put her infatuation with Allen far behind her. With luck Allen would marry while she was gone and she wouldn't have to face being invited to his wedding nor be included in the activities the three men and their families would share through the summer.

"I've been thinking about getting an apartment close to campus. You don't need my help any longer, and I've intruded on your family long enough."

"You've never been an intrusion. You've been more like our own personal angel. We love you and I owe you big time. Without you, the girls would have had to go to different relatives while I was ill. You made it possible for my family to stay together through a difficult time." Cathy wiped away a tear and Holland hugged her closer.

"Actually your family fulfilled a fantasy for me," Holland spoke around the lump in her own throat. "I used to pretend I had little sisters to share tea parties and play games with. I loved every minute I spent with your daughters. In a strange way it was a second chance for me to grow up, as a girl this time, through them."

"Well, Todd certainly has no trouble seeing you as a girl," Cathy laughed, then suddenly sobered. "What about Allen? Are you really ready to write him off?"

She fiddled with the tape dispenser and debated whether or not she could answer that question. She had never been blind to Cathy's machinations and loved her all the more for her attempts to bring her and Allen together. But it wasn't to be, and she had to tell Cathy something or she'd embarrass them both eventually with her continued matchmaking.

"I read somewhere that a woman never forgets her first love and I've come to believe that's true," she started out carefully. "I won't forget Allen. He'll always have a spot in my heart and when I think back to that time immediately following Hank's death, I'll forever be grateful Allen was there to help me through it. I confused his kindness with my need to hold onto something familiar. I needed someone to love and to love me and I projected him into that role. Reality has a way of catching up to us, and the reality of the situation is that Allen was just an infatuation. He was kind to me when I desperately needed him and careful in the way he attempted to deflect my crush on him, but the time has come for him to get on with his life, and it's time for me to do the same."

"What about Todd? Your relationship with him seems to have changed over the past couple of weeks and your decision to go abroad with him to study seems abrupt." Holland got the distinct impression Cathy didn't approve of her joining Todd's study group. She wasn't going specifically with Todd, she wanted to remind Cathy. It was just that she was enrolled in the same summer program he had enrolled in. Perhaps she should resent Cathy's intrusion into personal aspects of her life, but she didn't because she understood her friend's genuine concern for her.

"I'm not rushing into anything with Todd," Holland said as she smiled a bit too brightly. "I've always wanted to visit the Holy Land and this seems like a good opportunity. It will also give Todd and me a chance to get to know each other better and decide if we want to take our relationship further. We both have career choices to make, too. Todd thinks his mission to Hong Kong and all the traveling I've done will be assets to his career if we marry and he goes into diplomatic service, which is what he thinks he wants to do."

"But, Holland, what do you want to do?" Cathy was interrupted by the ringing doorbell. "Darn!" she muttered under her breath as she moved toward the door. "We aren't through talking," she called over her shoulder to Holland and Holland shook her head. She might have known Cathy still had more to say about both Todd and Allen.

Holland glanced at her watch. It was too early for the cab she'd called. She had almost an hour before she needed to check in at the airport. Cathy had offered to drive her, but Holland hadn't wanted to disturb Kelly's nap. Todd, too, had offered, but she knew his family wanted to accompany him to the airport and between kids and luggage it would be a tight squeeze to get her and her luggage into the Chandler family's station wagon. A cab seemed the best option.

"Allen?!" Cathy's voice from the next room revealed surprise as she answered the door. "I didn't expect to see you. Come on in."

"Hi! I've got great news, so great I had to come tell you in person instead of calling." Holland could hear the happy excitement in Allen's voice and she took a step backward. Her hands clenched into painful fists and she closed her eyes, wishing she could close her ears. She didn't want to hear Allen announce his engagement. When the announcement hadn't come immediately after she'd spotted Allen and Gwen in the restaurant, she'd begun to hope she'd be gone before they made their plans public.

"Is Holland here? She should hear this, too." Holland cringed at the thought of actually facing Allen when he said the words. She felt a surge of anger. He'd ignored her for months, so why did he need to seek her out to announce his engagement?

"Holland?" Cathy called her name and for just a moment she considered not answering. If she slipped out the backdoor, she could disappear until after Allen left. But no. She squared her shoulders. Hank hadn't raised her to be a coward. She'd get through this, she'd even smile and congratulate him. She had her whole life ahead of her and just because that life wouldn't include Allen didn't mean she'd live it alone or without love. She closed her eyes and tried to focus on Todd, but her thoughts betrayed her and it was Allen's face that boldly formed in her mind. Angrily she banished his image and walked through the door, lifting her chin as she went.

She hesitated when Allen's eyes met hers. His hair was tousled and his clothes rumpled, but a glow surrounded him, almost like a light shining just beneath his skin. A camera dangled forgotten from a wide strap around his neck and a grin lit his features while his eyes sparkled with delight. He looked wonderful. Her chin went up another notch.

"Megan had her baby!" The words practically exploded from Allen.

"What!" Cathy squealed and Holland blinked uncomprehending.

"Megan had her baby," Allen repeated. "A little girl with wispy blond hair. Brad said I should tell you she's seven pounds and five ounces, and they're both doing great."

"When . . . ? How did you . . . ? Oh, I've got to see her." Cathy was practically stammering in her excitement.

Allen continued to grin. He looked at his watch and said, "She was born thirty-eight minutes ago. I stopped by their house this morning to drop off some pictures I developed for Jason and found the house in an uproar. Doug was throwing things in the van and yelling he couldn't find his keys. His mom was timing contractions while Megan was panicking because her doctor was delivering another baby and couldn't be reached. Jason was on the cellular phone with the emergency room demanding they page Brad. I found Doug's keys, persuaded Jason to ride with me, and followed them to the hospital where Brad met us at the door.

"Little Mary Catherine arrived six minutes later with Brad's help, two minutes before Megan's doctor finished delivering a little boy in the next room."

"And they're really all right?" Cathy whispered and wiped her eyes. Allen beamed and nodded his head in the affirmative.

"Come on, Holland." Cathy reached for her arm. "I'll call next door and have my neighbor watch the girls. If we hurry we should just have time for a quick peek at the baby before you have to check in at the airport."

"But what about my cab?"

"Oh!" She paused, then brightened, her short curls bobbing. "You go ahead with Allen, and I'll cancel your cab and make arrangements for the girls. He can take you on to the airport after you see the baby. Hurry now! I'll meet you at the hospital."

Cathy left the room at a run, and Holland and Allen stared at each other helplessly.

"Will you come with me?" Allen spoke softly.

"Yes," Holland agreed dumbly, blinded by the glow emanating from his radiant face. Horrified by her easy acquiescence, she attempted to retract her acceptance only to have Allen take her hand. A shiver shuddered up her arm from the spot where his warm fingers touched hers and all she could think was how terribly long it had been since he had voluntarily touched her.

"Uh, you're on your way somewhere?" Allen asked awkwardly as Cathy's words penetrated his euphoria. Of course she was on her way somewhere if she was headed for the airport. For the first time he noticed the bags stacked beside the door.

"I'm registered for the summer semester abroad."

"You're going away?" Aghast he could only gape at her. The feeling had been so strong. He'd been so sure his future included Holland. How could she be leaving?

"Yes, I'm going to Israel for a few months, then when the semester ends some of us may stay in Europe and tour for a few weeks." She sounded so calm, so sure of herself. She didn't appear to have an inkling of the turmoil racing through his heart and mind. There had to be a way to stop her. They needed to talk.

"Holland, please don't—"

"You two go ahead," Cathy called as she reentered the room. "Bonnie will be here in twenty minutes to watch the girls. You'll have to hurry. Here, Allen, take her bags." In seconds Allen found himself stowing Holland's suitcases in the trunk of his car. Perhaps on the way to the hospital he could dissuade her from leaving.

Allen settled himself in the driver's seat and glanced sideways at Holland as he reached for the ignition key. Her face was carefully blank, but he sensed she wasn't overjoyed to be in his car. He couldn't blame her; he'd gone to great lengths to sever their friendship. She'd been just as careful to avoid any contact with him for months now. Once they'd shared a fantastic experience, an interlude out of time; now he feared she hated him. *No, not hate,* he amended. Holland wasn't one to hate, but he suspected she certainly didn't like him much and wished she were anywhere other than here beside him. Was he too late? Had he ignored the promptings of his heart so long he'd lost his chance?

The miles rushed by as he searched his mind for an opening. He had to say just the right thing. He glanced once more at her silent profile and felt one more regret. He'd never photographed her, though he'd longed to from the beginning. He wondered why he'd never once lifted his camera to capture her perfect bone structure, then in a rush he knew. He couldn't capture her image on film. He couldn't view her through the lens of a camera and continue to deny that her image was blazoned on his heart forever. The camera was the medium of his art, and his art was truth. Somewhere deep in his subconscious he'd always known that to photograph her would force him to a level of honesty where he could not deny the depth of his feelings for her.

"I thought you'd had enough traveling." As an opening that was less than brilliant, he mocked his stumbling attempt to start a conversation.

"I might do a lot of traveling someday." Her words were stiff and defensive, and he remembered someone mentioning once that the young man Holland was seeing was interested in a career with the diplomatic corps. He opened his mouth to tell her traveling around the world with Todd Chandler would be a mistake. She had learned to relax and feel comfortable with a few friends, and according to Cathy had even conquered her fear of participating in class, but he knew she still froze into silence in the presence of strangers. No, he wouldn't say anything. Instinct warned it would be a mistake to remind her of her fears—or imply any criticism of Chandler.

Instead he filled the silence with talk of Megan and her new baby. He laughed at the nervous wreck his old friend had sunk to when faced with the reality of the baby's imminent birth. And all the time the miles slipping away were a steady torment reminding him there was no way he could prevent Holland from leaving him.

At the hospital they stepped quietly into Megan's room only to be greeted boisterously by an exuberant Doug. Allen watched as Holland left his side to approach the bed where Megan lay propped against the pillows with a tiny bundle in her arms. No regrets tinged his pleasure in the obvious happiness radiating from Megan's face as she drew back the blanket to allow Holland a closer look. Then she lifted her eyes and as she looked at Allen, something intangible, yet very real passed between the two old friends. She knew. And her eyes told him of both her concern and her approval.

"Would you like to hold her?" Megan turned back to Holland and asked in a near whisper.

Startled Holland backed up a step. "I don't think so. I-I've never held a baby."

Megan's musical laughter filled the room. "You've been holding Kelly for months."

"Kelly isn't a baby. She's—she's bigger, not like . . ." She gestured helplessly toward the tiny newborn.

"It's easy," Jason stepped forward to lift his sister from his mother's arms. "Sit in that chair." He indicated the bedside chair with a nod of his head.

Allen felt a grin spread across his face as Holland complied with the boy's command. Her cheeks paled and her arms revealed a slight tremble as she held them out for the baby. At first she looked terrified, then her nervousness gave way to wonder as she cuddled the child. A look of tenderness and peace stole across her features, and Allen swallowed a sudden lump in his own throat. This is how she would look when she held her own babies for the first time. An ache told him deep in his soul he wanted Holland's babies to be his. Slowly, deliberately his fingers slid along the wide strap around his neck and he lifted the camera to his eye.

Holland didn't speak much on the way to the airport and he noticed more than once the quick glances she gave her watch as though fearful she wouldn't be in time. He'd hugged Megan and reverently touched the baby's cheek without disturbing Holland's careful hold and hoped she would forget she had a plane to catch, but she hadn't forgotten.

When they reached the airport she appeared anxious, even eager to check in and be on her way. It would be futile to ask her to stay. The most he could hope for was that they would part on good terms and he could start over again when she returned. He caught her hand when she reached for her bags.

"I'll carry those." He gripped both large cases, leaving her a matching carry-on bag. For just a moment he regretted it wasn't the cheap athletic bag he'd bought her in Fairbanks.

"You don't need to come inside," Holland argued. "My bags have wheels and I can handle them myself."

"It'll be faster if I take them." Allen smiled at her and she turned her head away. He didn't want to guess why she preferred not to look at him. She wanted him to leave, but he couldn't. This wasn't the kind of traveling she was accustomed to and he couldn't help worrying.

"I assume you have your passport, but do you have an international credit card?" He stopped abruptly, set down her bags, and reached into his pocket for his wallet. He pulled out a small white card. "If you have any trouble, call me." He pressed his business card into her hand. "What about your itinerary? Is there a phone where you can be reached?"

She didn't answer. A flush of color topped her cheeks, her eyes glittered, and her chin assumed the haughty angle he knew so well.

"I don't need a baby-sitter!" she snapped. "You fulfilled your promise to Hank." Bending down, she grasped both suitcases and walked away.

He stared after her in shocked surprise for several seconds, then plunged into the crowd intent on catching up to her. At the top of the escalator he caught a glimpse of her nearing the bottom. By the time he broke free of the escalator, she was halfway across the wide corridor. Jostling his way through the throngs of people, he finally caught up to her in the line before the check-in counter.

"Holland, I didn't mean to offend you." He reached for the heavy bags.

"That's okay, Mr. James." Long arms lifted the bags out of his hands. "Thanks for your help, but my luggage is already checked, so I have plenty of time to help Holland with hers."

Casually Todd Chandler slid Holland's bags onto the conveyer belt, then while they were tagged he dropped one hand to Holland's waist in a proprietary gesture.

Todd Chandler! She was leaving with him!

chapter fifteen

"Hey, Holland. Phone."

Holland set down her pen and sighed. She didn't want to talk to Aunt Barbara tonight. Her aunt meant well, but international telephone calls weren't cheap, and she always said the same thing. She could feel compassion for the older woman who had never had a child and who felt she had been cheated out of the little girl she'd loved as her own. Her aunt couldn't accept that Holland was grown now and though she had returned from her nomadic life with her father, she'd never be the daughter Aunt Barbara wanted her to be. All the pleading and tears in the world wouldn't convince Holland to leave Israel two weeks early to hurry back to her aunt's restrictive care.

As she rose to her feet, she acknowledged as she had so many times before, that she had no desire to alienate her only living relative. She'd talk to her, soothe her fears, and assure her she'd never lose contact with her aunt again. Once more, this time more firmly, she'd explain she would be transferring to BYU this fall and that she planned to live with a friend she'd met here at the Center. She noticed her friend, Janey, across the room with Todd. *Probably arguing again,* she thought wryly as they both paused in their energetic dialogue to watch her cross the room.

She picked up the phone, took a deep breath, and spoke a tentative hello.

"Holland?" She nearly dropped the instrument when a man's rich, warm voice spoke her name. "Holland? Is that you?" The voice repeated anxiously when she failed to respond.

"Yes," she whispered. It was Allen's voice, but it couldn't be. Why would he be calling her from halfway around the world? It wasn't fair that she only had to hear him speak her name and all the old longings came swirling back. He had no right to call her, stirring up old memories, making her doubt her decision.

"There's no easy way to say this . . ." His voice trailed off and Holland registered the pain behind his words. Even from so far away something inside her immediately responded to the slightest nuance in his voice. Something was wrong, terribly wrong.

"Allen, what's going on?" The pitch of her voice rose on a worried note. "Has something happened . . .? Are you all right?" *If anything happened to Allen . . .*

"It's Cathy. I'm sorry to tell you like this." His voice dropped to a hoarse pain-filled whisper. "She died this morning."

"Cathy?" she repeated in a hoarse whisper. "No! It's a mistake. Why are you telling me this? She's getting well. Her doctor said so. Even her hair is beginning to grow back. I-I got a letter from her yesterday and she said she's fine. She couldn't just die." Her words ended on a sob of denial.

"It wasn't the cancer." His voice broke and Holland heard him breathe deeply before going on. "She was making a dress for Heidi's first day of school and ran out of lace. It was only a few blocks to the fabric store, but some drunk going eighty miles an hour ran a light and slammed into her car. She died within minutes after reaching the hospital."

"It's not fair." Holland swiped angrily at the tears coursing down her cheeks. "She lost a breast, then her beautiful hair. She suffered so much pain and nausea day after day, but she never stopped fighting. She did all those exercises every day just so she'd be strong enough to hold Kelly again. But she—she wasn't afraid of dying. She fought so hard because she couldn't bear to be separated from Brad and their little girls. She loved them so much."

"I know. Their love was something rare and beautiful, a love I'm convinced will endure through eternity." He spoke with a solemn sincerity that touched Holland's soul and told her he desired with all his heart to offer her comfort.

"What will Brad do? Worrying about losing her to cancer tore him apart. How can he go through that kind of agony again, this time knowing that she . . ." Holland couldn't finish.

"Right now he's going through the motions, preparing for her funeral, doing what has to be done like some kind of robot. I don't think he can face her loss yet, so he's letting the conventions and formality of her funeral provide a buffer zone," Allen responded.

"When Hank died I tried to make my mind completely empty. I thought if I didn't think about him being gone I wouldn't feel anything. Later I was angry; I felt consumed by rage at him for leaving me and at the construction camp foreman for not getting him medical help in time. In a way I guess I blamed God for a little while, too."

"Oh, honey, the foreman did all he could and blaming God is unfair." In some distant part of her mind she registered the endearment and let it go as the soothing word of comfort she understood it to be.

"I know that now," she responded. "God didn't cause my loss. He helped me through it."

"Megan found out first and broke the news to Doug and me," Allen went on after a brief pause. "We didn't know Cathy was already gone, so the three of us tore over to the hospital in a state of numb shock. When we found out the truth and learned the drunk who killed her was still alive and moaning over a few cracked ribs, I wanted to pound the bum until he didn't have a whole bone left in his body. Doug felt the same way and we probably would have done something stupid if Megan hadn't hustled us out of there."

"The girls? Who is taking care of them?"

"The judge moved his housekeeper over there. She's a good woman and will take excellent care of them." He paused then added, "They miss you. When Brad told the girls about their mother, Kelly said with all the confidence of a three-year-old that if her mama had to go away, her Holland would come."

"I will come." Fresh tears clouded her vision and choked her voice.

"The girls are well taken care of. There's really nothing you can do and you only have two more weeks until you'll be coming home anyway." Allen spoke reasonably.

"I have to be there," she sobbed. A comforting arm encircled her waist and Todd's voice penetrated her grief.

"What's going on?" he whispered quietly.

"Is someone giving you a bad time?" Janey's voice wasn't so subtle.

Holland shook her head helplessly, too overcome to speak coherently. Todd took the phone from her trembling fingers. His mouth moved, but she didn't hear his words. She saw him frown as he appeared to listen. It didn't matter. Nothing mattered. Cathy was dead. Dear, funny, bright chatterbox Cathy was dead, so nothing mattered. No, that wasn't true. Many things mattered, but what mattered most to her right now was that she be there. She had to go home.

Janey and Todd tried to talk her out of leaving, but once they realized they couldn't change her mind they helped her make arrangements and accompanied her to the airport.

When her flight was called Todd gently pulled her into his arms.

"I wish I were going with you," he whispered. "You have to change planes in London and again in New York, and I know you don't like crowds. Just imagine I'm there beside you because, in spirit, I will be."

"I'll be all right," she answered. Inside she wondered if she'd ever be all right again.

"Holland?" He tipped her chin up with two fingers and met her eyes with a measure of longing and sadness in his own. "Can you give me an answer before you leave?"

She wanted to say yes. She'd decided just two days ago that when she and Todd visited the old city on Sunday she'd tell him she'd marry him. Her friendship with him had deepened and it was pleasant to be coddled by him, though lately she'd found herself unpleasantly reminded of Aunt Barbara's penchant for running her life. Todd was so proud of the careful agendas he worked out each week so they could get their studying done and see as much as possible of the fascinating city.

Returning would be easier if she carried with her the protection of Todd's love. A picture of Brad rocking Cathy in his arms before the fireplace rose in her mind and she slowly shook her head. How could she think about marriage and her own happiness when Brad and Cathy would never be together again in this life?

"No, this isn't the time to ask." Todd's voice was low and a shine in his eyes told its own story of emotion trembling near the surface.

"I'll see you in two weeks, then we'll talk." He bent to lightly kiss her lips, then with his arm about her waist walked her to the boarding gate.

"Janey." Holland turned to her friend to give her a quick hug. "Look after Todd for me please."

"I will," she promised with a watery smile.

Numbness settled around her as the plane arced its way across the sky. She pressed her face against the window, but it wasn't the Holy Land slipping away she saw. As if from a great distance she saw Cathy's fiery curls, Cathy's smile, heard her laughter-filled voice, and once more witnessed her struggle to beat the invader that threatened her body, her way of life, and her dreams for the future.

At Heathrow she felt her old fear of strangers close around her as she raced in near panic to find the gate for her flight to New York. She opened her mouth to ask directions and no words came out. Closing her eyes, she tried to follow Todd's advice. Frantically she tried to picture Todd beside her, smoothly taking over, knowing which piece of paper she needed to show. But it was Allen's face she saw. The skin around his eyes crinkled and he laughed.

"What you need is a chocolate bar."

"Chocolate!" She gasped then flushed in embarrassment as the man behind the counter gave her a strange look.

"I mean New York," she stammered, holding up her tickets and passport.

She listened carefully to the instructions he gave her and tried valiantly to shut out the persistent little voice in the back of her head that sounded suspiciously like Allen saying, *I knew you could do it.*

Her flight was delayed two hours and the sun was disappearing into the western sea by the time she was airborne again. Sunset gave way to night and Holland tried to sleep, but sleep wouldn't come. She couldn't concentrate on the book Janey had tucked in her bag, and had no interest in the in-flight movie.

She leaned her head back and closed her eyes, shutting herself into a terrible blackness. Why had Cathy been subjected to all the pain and struggle of fighting cancer, only to lose her life to a drunk driver? Everyone around Cathy had been terrified she would die when they learned she had cancer. People die of cancer every day, but they don't die because they drive to the store to buy a piece of lace to trim a little girl's first school dress.

Anger enveloped Holland, rising like a vicious tide. Cathy deserved to live. She wanted to live and she had fought with every ounce of her strength to survive. She had dreams and plans that included a husband she loved with all her heart and five children she wanted to guide into adulthood. She wanted to serve a mission and write poetry. Cathy had beaten the cancer; she had won. It was a stupid, irresponsible drunk who ended Cathy's life and left her children motherless. He is the one who should be suffering. He should be sent to prison. The greedy distillers who grow rich on the misery they sell to weak, irresponsible alcohol addicts should go to prison, too. Along with the drunks and the distillers, Holland would send to prison all the advertisers who made drinking look glamorous and adult when it was really even more dark and ugly and far more insidious than cancer.

"Are you all right, miss?" A stewardess leaned toward her and Holland became aware that her cheeks were wet and her breath was coming in short, sobbing jerks.

"I-I'm okay," she whispered back and turned away to hide her face.

At JFK she was too tired to worry about strangers. The delay in London had cost her her connecting flight and she had been rescheduled on a later flight with a brief stop in Chicago. Anxiously she checked the time and reset her watch. Without any further delays it would be nine o'clock before she reached Salt Lake. Too late to attend the viewing.

Wearily she walked to a bank of phones and placed a call to Aunt Barbara to inform her of the time change. For just a moment she wished Allen were meeting her flight or even Megan, but they'd be at the viewing when her plane landed, and Aunt Barbara was already expecting her. She'd wanted to call a cab and stay at a hotel, but Todd had called her aunt, insisting she shouldn't be alone.

She succumbed to the demons—anger and despair—all the way to Chicago. Over and over in her mind Holland watched Cathy's struggle with cancer and let her hatred and anger for the drunk who had killed her rage. Finally she opened her bag and pulled out the book Janey had given her and was surprised to see a small New

Testament with the words of Christ highlighted in red. Slowly she began to read the comforting words of the Master.

Holland fell asleep for a few hours on the last leg of her journey and awoke strangely at peace. Memories of Hank, mingled with the long talks she and Cathy had shared, lingered in her mind. The anger was gone and only the sorrow remained.

"Daddy." Her lips formed the word soundlessly and realizing this, Holland gave an ironic smile. She hadn't called Hank "Daddy" for years though she couldn't exactly remember when or why she'd begun calling him by his first name instead of Daddy.

Oh Daddy, she thought, *when you died and I was all alone, Allen kept his promise to you and got me safely to Salt Lake. He was kind to me and helped me start the changes I needed to make. I think you hoped he'd fall in love with me and take care of me, as you had, for the rest of my life. I wanted that, too, but it didn't work out that way, and I now think that was for the best. I really did need to learn who I am and how to stand on my own feet.*

Allen's greatest kindness was Cathy. He brought her into my life when I was alone and confused. They helped me believe I was ready to go on with my life. Cathy assured me you were happy and with Mamma. She was there for me all the times I missed you so much I wanted to die, too. So, Daddy, please find her and if she's feeling lost and alone, love her as she loved me.

Exhausted and bedraggled, Holland finally reached the end of her journey. Aunt Barbara clucked and fussed as she shepherded her to her car and within minutes of reaching her aunt's house, Holland collapsed into a dreamless sleep. She didn't wake until her aunt nudged her softly to tell her it was morning and Todd was calling to make certain she'd arrived safely.

With some reluctance Holland pulled the dark green dress over her head. Her luggage was lost somewhere between London and Salt Lake and most of her other things were stored at the Williams' house. She hadn't wanted to bother the family early this morning to rummage for a dress she could wear to the funeral. She'd never again worn this dress since the night Allen hadn't come to dinner at the Williams' house. It had hung in the back of her closet at Aunt Barbara's for nearly a year.

With both hands she smoothed the rich fabric and thought of that long-ago shopping trip when Cathy had helped her buy the dress. She'd been so naive then, thinking once Allen saw her in the dress, he'd fall in love with her.

"I don't think you should go alone," Aunt Barbara remonstrated as she walked into the room. "I promised your young man I'd keep an eye on you and though I scarcely knew your friend, I'll be glad to sit through the funeral with you. It'll only take a minute for me to change."

"No." She knew her aunt meant well. Todd did too but she had to do this alone, though she felt she wouldn't really be alone. Ever since she awoke on the plane, she'd had the comforting sense that Hank was close by. "After the funeral I'll be going to the cemetery, then over to the Williams' home. I spoke to Brad this morning on the phone and he thinks it will be good for his children and for me to spend a little time together."

"Those poor motherless babies." Barbara wiped her eyes. "I remember when your mother died, you were so grief-stricken. You wouldn't eat and you cried endlessly. I wanted to comfort you. I knew I couldn't take Nancy's place, but I didn't want you to be without any kind of mother. I've had nightmares all these years of Nancy's little girl growing up without a mother's care."

"Hank took care of me," Holland spoke defensively.

"Oh that man! He never should have married Nancy in the first place. She wasn't the kind of woman who could live a gypsy life."

"They loved each other and they lived right here in Bountiful until she died. You can't blame her death on his wandering."

"But he took you away." She dabbed at her eyes. "And now that you're back, you shut me out of your life, you never want me to help you."

"Aunt Barbara." Holland turned and placed her arms around her aunt. "I don't mean to shut you out. I love you and you're all the family I have left. I want us to always be friends."

"Hank was willing to share you with me, but I resented him so much," Barbara admitted, "first for taking Nancy away from me, then taking you. I dismissed his rights as your father and tried to get sole custody of you." The woman's shoulders shook with sobs as she admitted her folly. "I can't blame him for hating me and teaching you not to trust me."

"Hank never hated you. He always understood and he made me promise years ago that if he died or I was alone, I'd go to you. All these years he made certain I had your address committed to memory. I loved you as a child and it's always been a comfort to me to know that even though I was growing up in a man's world, back in Bountiful, Utah, there was a lady who loved me and remembered I was a girl."

"Well." Aunt Barbara stepped back, rubbed her eyes, and stared critically at Holland. "You'll have to forgive an old woman for being weepy and sentimental. That dress reminds me of one your mother used to wear. She used to borrow my jade earrings to go with it." She bustled out of the room and returned a minute later with the earrings and insisted Holland try them on. Three tiny delicate gold chains each weighted with a deep green stone swung free from a larger stone at each ear lobe.

"They're beautiful." She smiled into the mirror at her aunt's reflection.

"She wore this, too." Her aunt slipped a ring on Holland's right hand. "Hank gave it to Nancy when they got engaged. I shouldn't have kept it."

Holland glanced down at her hand to where a ring of small diamonds surrounded a clear, brilliant emerald. A lump rose in her throat and suddenly she remembered the ring on her mother's hand. She didn't have many memories of her mother, which made this gesture all the more dear to her. Raising tear-drenched eyes, she whispered, "Thank you."

"I never was sure it was quite proper to wear jade and emeralds together, but your mother said they matched." The older woman straightened her back and sniffed as though wary Holland might challenge her.

"I do love you." She kissed the papery-thin cheek, snatched up her handbag, and disappeared through the door before further tears could render her incapable of driving.

chapter sixteen

Allen lifted his head as the last softly spoken amen floated in the still summer air. Across the casket, made higher with a rainbow of flowers, he saw her, standing alone. With head still bowed and long dark lashes sweeping the tops of her high cheekbones, Holland stood like a classic marble statue to love and sorrow.

No thick fur hood hid her grief this time. Her hair shone in the brilliant August light and a deep green dress clung softly to her form. No one could mistake her beauty for the raw, gaucheness of emerging masculine adolescence. With a quick pain-laden tug of regret, he wondered if the girl who hot-wired trucks and pretended to be a boy had gone away as completely as Cathy had.

With the other pallbearers Allen stepped forward holding the pale pink rose he'd worn on his lapel through the service and placed it on the casket. Resolutely he stiffened his features, forbidding more tears to fall. Cathy would understand and accept a few tears, but she'd be disappointed if he lost sight of his faith to wallow in grief to the exclusion of accepting the mission she was surely about to begin. His heart lifted when he thought of Cathy marshaling the spirits in heaven, getting them organized to do their work, and scattering her enthusiasm among them with her happy, loving chatter. She'd tell him she had her work to do and that his was to remain Brad's friend.

Cathy had always been a firm supporter of the three men's friendship. When she married Brad, his closest friends became her brothers. He'd miss her sorely and in his heart he knew she'd soon be busy organizing and teaching, but the depth of love she held for her family might hinder her work until she received assurance they were comforted and able to move on with their earthly lives. The only gift left he could give to honor the friend he loved and admired would be to love and support those she loved.

He sought out Brad's tall shape, and something twisted deep inside him at the evidence of ravaging pain in his friend's face. Bobbi stood beside him, staring into space. Ashley and Michelle clung to him on either side. He caught sight of Heidi's tear-stained cheeks as she stood clutching Jason's and Megan's hands. Behind them Cathy's mother stood with Kelly in her arms. What would happen to this family now? Would five young girls grow up alone and confused as Holland had? Would little Kelly retain any memory of the mother she had adored? Even with his tremendous faith, could Brad survive losing his beloved Cathy? Why had God allowed this to happen?

Guiltily Allen started as though he'd received a swift poke in the ribs. He glanced uneasily to his side and was surprised to see Gwen. She patted his arm consolingly and he gave her a small smile, though he knew she hadn't poked him. It was the kind of thing Cathy would have done to remind him she had no patience with people who blamed their problems and shortcomings on God. It was her opinion that most disasters and disappointments in life could be placed quite firmly at the feet of some human rather than God.

Family and friends gathered around the bereft family and Allen stood back. He sensed now was not the time his friend would need him most. It would be later, when most of the people gathered on this grassy slope to bid Cathy farewell and offer Brad their sympathy would be gone and Brad would be alone. Allen knew about loneliness. It came during the black hours of the night, in solitary walks and in vast crowds, and in sudden glimpses of someone else's belonging. He would be there for his friend though it would never be enough.

Once more his eyes sought Holland. He hadn't seen her in the chapel, yet he'd had an uncanny sense that she was close. He'd caught his first glimpse of her as she left the stake center beside Megan while he stood with Doug and the other pallbearers around the hearse. His impulse had been to go to her in spite of the responsibilities of the moment. If he'd been certain of his welcome, there would have been no hesitation; but in his hesitating, she'd been swallowed up in the crowd emerging from the church.

A movement caught his attention and he watched as Kelly launched herself with a squeal from her grandmother's arms to Holland's. The other girls gathered around her and Allen witnessed the first feeble smiles the girls had given in days.

Brad turned to Holland and put his arm around her in a quick embrace, then stood in deep conversation with her for what seemed a long time.

Allen caught his breath in a short gasp of pain. The girls already loved Holland and he could easily picture them accepting her as their mother. Not for a second did he doubt Brad's genuine love for Cathy, and his grief for her loss was deep and terrible, but with time he'd want a wife again and who better than the beautiful woman he already admired, and who loved his children dearly?

"Go to her. She needs you." Startled out of his unhappy thoughts, Allen glanced down at Gwen. He didn't need to ask who she thought needed him. He looked toward Holland and watched as she returned Kelly to her grandmother. For just a moment she and Megan clung together, then broke apart. Megan reached for Doug's solid support, and Holland turned to walk with rapid strides up the hill.

"Brad is surrounded by friends. It's Holland who needs you," Gwen whispered persistently. Allen's eyes followed Holland's disappearing figure, then sought out Brad's tall shape once more. For just a second he imagined he saw Cathy standing next to Brad. She flashed him a saucy grin then bobbed her mop of curls in Holland's direction.

He was practically running when he topped the hill and looked about anxiously. There was no sign of a tall young woman in a hunter green dress. It was as though she had vanished. He should never have allowed grief and a lifetime of insecurity to undermine his faith. He'd waited seven seemingly endless weeks for Holland's return; he couldn't let her leave again without telling her he loved her.

Holland sank onto a low stone bench concealed in a small grove of trees. Someone had placed the bench there in memory of a loved one, knowing there would be times when someone such as she would need a moment's peace in the midst of grief. She unclenched a tightly held fist to stare at a slip of lavender paper. Placing it on the glazed stone beside her, she took her time smoothing the paper with two fingers.

Brad had reminded her of the letters Cathy had written to her children before her cancer surgery. He told her his wife had kept the letters even after her recovery seemed certain, and during the ensuing months she'd added several poems to the box where she kept them. To this one she'd added a personal note to Holland. Tears had glistened in Brad's eyes as he told her that morning he'd slipped one special poem Cathy had written for him into his pocket to lend him strength and some impulse had told him to carry this one with him, too.

The words blurred before her and she had to blink several times before Cathy's artistic script came into focus. Across one corner she read, *Holland, you were the one who encouraged me to join a support group and it was you who urged me to express my emotions on paper. My first poem was a tribute to the women in that group who bravely faced breast cancer themselves and helped me deal with the emotional garbage of my illness. But it was you, my family, a few other choice friends, and my Heavenly Father, who I know loves me, who are my "forever" support group. I love you. God bless you always, Cathy.*

Several minutes passed before she could see clearly to read the poem. The words shimmered on the paper causing Holland to blink several times before the simple words emerged.

The Support Group

Each Thursday night we meet like the bridge club,
But we play a more urgent game. In place
Of neighborhood gossip our conversation is
Filled with medical jargon lately learned.
We swap recipes: what stays down best. When we
Speak of husbands, it's not complaints of quirks,
But how they help us. The cards we play are
Feelings and we don't hide them fanned close to
Our chests, but throw them on the table.
We bring a potluck of problems; we all
Take home the winnings. The prize is hope.

Holland bit back a sob. Cathy had hoped for so much and she'd been good at infecting others with hope. Closing her eyes Holland shut out the small group of people still gathered around the mound of flowers in the distance beyond the sweep of green grass stretching out beneath the glare of a brilliant August sun. She no longer felt the slight sway of the trees around her or heard the buzz of a persistent insect's wings. Cathy had encouraged her to hope and dream, to believe in herself and in her future.

Allen, too, had once encouraged her to hope and to hold onto her dreams. Thinking of Allen brought a twinge of pain to her heart. Even through her grief and the intense emotion of facing her dead friend's family, a part of her had been aware of Allen and of Gwen standing beside him. She'd seen the other woman's loving gesture when she touched his arm. After all this time that small intimacy shouldn't have hurt.

But it did.

The admission came hard, and swift on its heels came guilt and remorse. Weren't the very facts that she still experienced an intense awareness of Allen and that she was jealous of his relationship with Gwen indications of disloyalty to Todd? Or were they signs of disloyalty to herself? That last morning, before Allen's sudden arrival, Cathy had asked her what *she* wanted and she hadn't been able to answer.

Now she knew. Like Cathy, she wanted to be whole and strong within. She wanted to love as Cathy had loved and she wanted to be loved and needed in turn as Cathy had been. She wanted to go on learning, to be able to give her all when all was needed, and to be strong enough to claim her right to needs of her own. Cathy could do that because she had an invincible knowledge of who she was. Being a full vessel, she had much to give.

Holland's hunger for love and security had blinded her, leaving her unable to see in recent months, her gradual decline of hope, the subtle shift away from her hard-won independence. When she faced an end to her hope that Allen would someday love her, she lost faith in herself. Her eagerness to discover herself had faded as she'd allowed Todd to shelter and protect her.

She didn't love Todd, she could admit now, except as a dear friend, and though Allen was lost to her, she wouldn't marry to stave off loneliness. Entering into that kind of marriage would be a mockery of the dreams she'd cherished through all her years with Hank. Todd deserved a woman who would love him as Cathy loved Brad. And she wasn't that woman.

"I deserve that kind of love too," she whispered into the stillness and lifted her chin as though defying anyone to argue. "And if all life brings me is 'a potluck of problems,' I'll still play the game and take home my share of the 'winnings' just as Hank did. Daddy never stopped being his own person and his faith that he would one day be with Mamma again never wavered."

"Are you all right?"

She whirled around so quickly she nearly toppled from the bench. Allen reached forward to steady her and where his fingers gripped her arm she felt a pulsing electrical shock.

"You startled me."

"I'm sorry. I didn't mean to interrupt." He didn't release his hold on her. "I know there is really nothing anyone can say. The loss is too fresh, the pain too sharp to be eased by mere words. You looked so alone, and well, I thought it might help if we shared our grief."

"You lost a friend, too." She stated the simple fact and made no effort to move away from his gentle grip.

"Yes." He didn't elaborate but stood quietly beside her. In the silence her awareness of his presence intensified, bringing her a measure of comfort. She felt his sorrow and sensed more than their shared grief had brought him to her side. Gradually she accepted that concern for her weighed heavily on his mind.

"I really will be fine," Holland sought to assure him.

"I know you will. You're a strong person. When I arrived you were mouthing words I couldn't hear, but when I saw you lift your chin in that determined way you have, I knew you'd worked something out in your mind." He lifted his free hand to brush lightly across her chin as he spoke.

She lowered her eyes, not wanting him to see the confusion his words brought her. She didn't know how to respond. She'd mistaken his caring kindness for something deeper once before. On the stone bench she saw Cathy's note. She reached for it.

"Cathy loved poetry," Holland told Allen as her fingers lovingly smoothed the scrap of paper. "Once she told me that writing the poems that appeared in bits and pieces in her head was one of the things she regretted not accomplishing in her life. During those long months of treatment she began writing to express the emotions that sometimes overwhelmed her . . ." She thrust the paper into Allen's hand with a whispered, "Read this."

Allen sat on the bench, tugged Holland down beside him, and began to read. When he finished he lifted his eyes to some invisible point far in the distance. A wide spectrum of emotions flickered in quick succession across his face. Finally he whispered the concluding line of Cathy's poem.

"The prize is hope." He swallowed before speaking again. "Faith and hope are inseparable and Cathy knew a lot about both. For years each time she saw me she reminded me of Mormon's words when he said, 'How is it that ye can attain unto faith, save ye shall have hope?' She accused me of accepting at face value my father's frequent statement that I'd never amount to anything. She said I spent my life apologizing for being worthless. I had to have real hope for those things I only dreamed about then, and she promised me that faith and fulfillment would come once I accepted that I, too, am a child of God and worthy of those same blessings he offers his other sons. I think when she wrote, 'The prize is hope,' she meant far more than a wish or desire to get well."

Holland agreed. "She encouraged me to believe in myself and she shared her deep faith in God in everything she did. I think she's telling me in this poem that even though I won't get everything I want in life, I should allow myself to grow and use even the bad experiences to increase my faith. We all face adversity in our lives and when we deal with our problems and the problems of those we care about in a positive compassionate manner we become stronger, finer people. I think she truly believed that recovery from physical illness didn't matter nearly as much as the internal growth she made along the way."

"And that's where hope comes in," Allen added thoughtfully. "Hope is the first positive step beyond wishing. It leads to faith, and faith leads to knowledge."

They sat in the intermittent shade provided by the small grove of trees, each lost in thought until most of the mourners had returned to their cars and gone away. The peace and easiness of being together felt right, and long minutes passed before Holland felt anything amiss in her position huddled next to Allen with her hand firmly clasped in his.

Carefully she eased some distance between them and freed her hand.

"Won't Gwen be wondering where you are?" She spoke as nonchalantly as her trembling emotions would allow.

"Gwen has gone home."

"Oh. I see." She moved further away.

"I don't think you do." He reached for her hand and drew her back down beside him. She considered resisting his insistent tug on her hand, but let herself be pulled back to the bench.

"Look at me, Holland," he commanded in a quiet tone. Reluctantly she lifted her gaze to meet his eyes.

"The day you left for Israel I went looking for you because I had some things I wanted to tell you, but in all the confusion of the baby's arrival and the shock of learning you were leaving I didn't have a chance." She tried to pull her fingers free of his clasp, but he wouldn't let her go.

"I suspect you know I asked Gwen to marry me, but I presume you don't know that she turned me down."

"Turned you down?" Holland gasped and forgot her struggle to free her hand.

"Yes, she turned me down for several very good reasons. Sh-h-h, not yet," he wouldn't allow her to interrupt. "First, we don't love each other, and second, she understood better than I did that the only reason I wanted to marry her was to catch up with Doug and Brad. I thought I wanted a lifestyle like theirs, and marriage to a pretty Latter-day Saint woman with two children would provide me with instant home and family. She made me see that my friends' marriages are more than the right time and place; they involve the right person, too. And that brings up the third reason she wouldn't marry me. She pointed out that I have unresolved feelings for you."

"For me?" Holland squeaked. Gwen had turned Allen down! She couldn't take it in. She couldn't believe any woman would reject a chance to be Allen's wife. Compassion for his disappointment mingled with rising joy. Was there still a chance she might win him? Hadn't he said he had feelings for her?

"The night before you left I felt like Jacob of the Old Testament; I felt like I had spent the night wrestling with an angel. When morning came I felt the greatest peace and joy of my life and I can tell you I know God loves me. I wanted to share that understanding with someone, not just anyone. I wanted—in fact, needed— to see you and tell you of my new understanding." He rubbed the pad of his thumb across the back of her hand and watched the emotions play across her face. She remained silent. She had nothing to say. Like the old Holland, thoughts and words failed to merge and form speech.

"Holland, I know you're angry with me and for good cause." Allen's voice took on an element of pleading. "I fell hard for you while we were making our way out of Alaska. I was extremely conscious of your youth and your inexperience. I was afraid of taking advantage of you, but most of all I was terrified of the feelings you aroused in me. I'd been in love before, but only with unattainable dreams. I didn't believe I had any right to feelings as intense as I was experiencing for you. Long ago I learned to protect my heart by not allowing in any really strong emotions, but the old defenses didn't work with you. I thought the only way I could protect myself was to put distance between us."

"I-I'm not angry," she stammered, her thoughts whirling in a jumbled fashion.

"Once Cathy chided me for my cruelty in dumping you alone and scared in the midst of strangers and suggested I was running away from my feelings for you. I made a flippant remark about not being a cradle robber and she reminded me you are far from a child. She was right and I knew it even then. Will you forgive me for my callousness? Will you let me prove to you that I no longer need or wish to protect my heart from what I feel for you? Do you think we might see each other, talk, and get to know each other well enough to see if you might return my feelings?"

Unable to speak, Holland nodded her head.

chapter seventeen

Allen whistled as he took the steps two at a time. Sure of his welcome, he gave the doorbell a couple of quick taps and leaned back to wait. A minute later he pushed the button again. When another wait produced no running footsteps and no girlish voices, he looked around puzzled. Holland's Aunt Barbara had informed him less than an hour ago that Holland's last class of the day had been canceled, so she had gone to the Williams' home. But there didn't appear to be anyone around.

Perhaps she was in the back shooting baskets with Bobbi. In one quick leap he left the porch and hurried around the side of the house. The driveway stood empty. Disappointed, he tried to decide what to do. He'd counted on taking a drive to the Oquirrh foothills with Holland to show her a building lot he'd found. He wanted her to see the magnificent Wasatch range from that lofty western advantage, and then, as the sun set and the stars began to appear and mingle with thousands of twinkling lights on the valley floor, he'd ask her to be his wife.

He quirked one side of his mouth in ironic amusement. Managing a smooth marriage proposal didn't seem to be his forte. He'd only proposed once before in his life and that had been a disaster. Unfortunately Holland had been a witness to that fiasco, which was why he'd determined to skip a candlelight dinner and formal wear. From the moment he'd seen the piece of land, he'd known it was where he wanted to build Holland's dream home. Not only did he anticipate living there and raising a family with Holland, but a vision had crept into his mind of the two of them sitting on a large boulder at one corner of the lot, wearing their blue jeans and talking and dreaming together when he proposed.

Over the past two months they'd done a lot of talking and dreaming together. Holland had decided to stay at the U to be closer to him and she was still commuting from her aunt's home in Bountiful. The chasm between the two women seemed to have been bridged.

It no longer bothered him that she still went to school, and he found himself increasingly proud of her academic achievements. She'd worried needlessly about breaking up with Todd. Her friend Janey had shown every sign of being willing to take on the young man, and he'd appeared perfectly willing to let her.

Now if he could just find Holland. She frequently stopped at the Williams' home to play with the girls and give Brad's housekeeper a break. He hoped she hadn't taken them to a movie or someplace where she'd barely make it back in time for the date they'd planned earlier in the week.

A metallic tapping nearby penetrated his thoughts. Cocking his head he listened for the sound to repeat itself. This time it was louder. Someone was in Brad's garage. Swiftly he moved to the door, eased it open, and peeked inside.

A slow grin spread across his face. Two feet protruded from beneath Brad's ancient Cadillac, but they certainly weren't Brad's big feet. He'd recognize those boy-size lumberjack boots anywhere. It seemed he'd found Holland. He might have known she couldn't resist the old car Brad had bought, well used, when they were seventeen. It held a lot of memories, but it hadn't run for years. He was surprised Brad hadn't junked it a long time ago.

"Holland." He spoke softly but evidently startled her anyway judging by the yell she let out. In moments she pushed her way out from under the car. Seeing him she began a futile attempt to brush herself off.

"Brad said his housekeeper needed a car to run around in for getting groceries and things like that. He was going to look for a secondhand car for her, but I told him I thought I could get this one going." She scrubbed at her hands with a rag that had been dangling from her back pocket seconds ago.

"You missed a spot of grease on your nose." He couldn't help teasing her a little, but he was glad she felt comfortable working on the car. During one of their long talks over dinner she'd confessed she missed working on engines and that if it weren't for her fear of being ridiculed she'd consider majoring in mechanical engineering. Of course, she also wanted to major in English literature. Whether her interest in mechanics became a career or a hobby he didn't care, but he could see some definite advantages in being married to his own mechanic.

Holland swiped at her nose with the rag and Allen laughed. She glared at him and he stepped forward.

"Here let me help you." He took a clean handkerchief from his pocket and rubbed at the grease spot she'd spread across her cheek.

"You'll ruin your handkerchief," she protested.

"I don't care." He could feel a foolish grin spreading across his face. "Wiping your face was just an excuse to hold you anyway." His arms went around her waist and he pulled her a step closer.

"I'm covered with grease." She placed her hands on his chest to push him back. "I don't want to wreck your shirt."

"Too late," he laughed, looking at her hand prints on his pale yellow sports shirt.

"I'm sorry," she apologized. "I'll wash it for you."

"Come here." He pulled her firmly into his arms. "We can discuss who's going to do the laundry later. Right now we have something better to do."

When he finally let her up for air, she had a satisfyingly bemused expression on her face. Until she saw the damage to his shirt.

"What do you mean we can discuss who's going to do the laundry later?" she demanded. "I'll wash your shirt. I'm the one who got grease all over it."

"Not without a lot of cooperation on my part." He couldn't resist making her blush. "But if you want to wash my shirt, I'll let you. In fact I'll be happy to let you do all my laundry, fix my car, and wash my back. And I'll do the cooking."

"What is this, a modern-day proposal?" Holland's eyes sparked with humor and she joined his laughter.

"Almost," he whispered, suddenly very serious. "Go wash your face and change out of your coveralls. There's a place I want you to see."

Not much later they sat side-by-side, their fingers laced together, on the rock, just as Allen had visualized it. He smiled contentedly. This time was right. This woman was right, and she'd just agreed to be his wife. Life with Holland would be full of surprises and he looked forward to them all.

"Could you meet me tomorrow to pick out a ring?" he whispered in her ear.

"I've been thinking," she hedged. "You know I kept some of Hank's gold—not the dust, but quite a few of the small nuggets. Do you think we could have matching bands made from them?"

"I'd like that." He spoke around a sudden lump in his throat. For the first time in his life he felt part of a real family. Holland loved her father and valued his gold nuggets as her greatest treasure. Allen and Holland had found the gold during those emotion-filled days when they'd first fallen in love with each other. Her wish to wear rings made from the gold Hank had left her, as a symbol of his love for her, gave Allen a feeling of continuity to the past and to Holland's parents. It gave him a sense of the future stretching before them.

"It's beautiful here," Holland sighed and snuggled closer. "From here I can pick out the lights of three temples. I can hardly wait until our house sits right here. This is the view I want to see from our bedroom every night before I go to sleep. No matter which temple we decide to be married in, we'll have a nightly reminder that our love is forever."

"We can start looking at house plans right away," Allen suggested.

Holland burrowed deeper into his side. "I think we should start with a fireplace," she murmured.

"Are you cold?" As he asked the question, Allen realized that the fall evening had turned chilly.

"A bit," she acknowledged.

"Come on, let's go home." He urged her to her feet.

"Funny, I feel like I'm already home." Holland sounded reluctant to leave in spite of the cool air around them.

Allen felt it too. His long journey had come to an end. It wasn't the place; it was the woman beside him. Wherever Holland might be would be home for him forever.

ABOUT THE AUTHOR

Jennie Hansen attended Ricks College and graduated from Westminster College in Salt Lake City, Utah. She has been a newspaper reporter, editor, and librarian, and is presently a technical services specialist for the Salt Lake City library system.

Her church service has included teaching in all auxiliaries and serving in stake and ward Primary presidencies. She has also served as a stake public affairs coordinator and ward chorister. Currently she is the education counselor in her ward Relief Society.

Jennie and her husband, Boyd, live in Salt Lake City. They are the parents of four daughters and a son.

Jennie is the author of four best-selling novels, *Run Away Home*, *When Tomorrow Comes*, *Macady*, and *Some Sweet Day*.